The Last
PHONE
BOOTH
— in —
Manhattan

OTHER TITLES BY BETH MERLIN AND
DANIELLE MODAFFERI

Breakup Boot Camp

The Campfire Series

One S'more Summer
S'more to Lose
Love You S'more
Tell Me S'more

The Last
PHONE
BOOTH
— in —
Manhattan

BETH MERLIN **DANIELLE MODAFFERI**

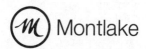

Published by Montlake, Seattle

www.apub.com

Amazon, the Amazon logo, and Montlake are trademarks of Amazon.com, Inc., or its affiliates.

ISBN-13: 9781662516481 (paperback)
ISBN-13: 9781662516474 (digital)

Cover design by Caroline Teagle Johnson
Cover images: © Greens87 / Getty; © Wilqkuku / Shutterstock;
© VasilkovS / Shutterstock; © Hsynff / Shutterstock;
© Anastasiia Veretennikova / Shutterstock

Printed in the United States of America

To all those who dare to take center stage and share their light with the world. May this book inspire you to believe in yourself, chase your passions, and pursue your wildest dreams with all your heart. Break a leg!

No space of regret can make amends for one life's opportunity misused.

—Charles Dickens, A Christmas Carol

Chapter One

I peeked my head out of the bathroom, foamy toothpaste still coating my lips, and scurried in the direction of my ringing phone on the bedside table. Diving across the mattress, I hurried to grab it before it went to voice mail.

"Hi, sweetie!" I panted.

"Hurry and get dressed. I'm sending Leon to pick you up in an hour to come and meet me at the tree for a special little date." Adam's voice was rife with confidence as the noise of the city bustled from behind him and into the receiver.

"Wait, what tree? Like *the tree*? Like the Rockefeller Center Christmas tree? Adam, are you insane? All of that holiday traffic. It's Christmas Eve. It's probably the busiest place on planet Earth right now. Midtown's gonna be a zoo." The plea unraveled from my mouth as more of a rant, and I drew in a long breath once I was finished. "Why can't we just meet closer to the apartment?" I offered by way of a compromise.

I knew Adam had the best intentions planning us an impromptu date, but the thought of navigating the throngs of last-minute shoppers and bumbling gawkers made my anxiety skyrocket. Unease surged through my body at the thought of all those shuffling out-of-towners, the ones who caused pedestrian pileups every time they stopped dead in their tracks to snap a zillionth picture of the tree. I shuddered and burrowed underneath the covers.

Adam scoffed on the other end of the line. "Avery, are you serious? You live in Manhattan. There are crowds everywhere. Every day. C'mon, I promise, it'll be worth it."

"Of course there are crowds in New York, but not like Rockefeller-Center-at-Christmas crowds! Every New Yorker worth their salt knows Midtown is off-limits this time of year," I joked, but I softened my voice, trying to remind myself that Adam's spontaneity and thoughtfulness were just two of the many things I loved about him. "It's cold out, and I say we reschedule whatever sweet idea you planned, and *insteeeead*, you should just come home and get back in bed with me." I punctuated the *me* at the end of my suggestion with a breathy purr, emphasizing my sexy (and hopefully enticing enough) invitation.

"C'mon, don't be naughty, be nice . . . Santa's gonna be checking that list tonight," he teased. "Seriously, though, get dressed. Leon's already on his way to pick you up, and I promise he'll drop you right where you need to be—no crowds to battle, okay?"

I guess spending an afternoon with the love of my life under the twinkling lights of the biggest tree in the greatest city in the entire universe wasn't going to be too shabby. "I'm always nice. You're the one who's naughty." My voice couldn't disguise my grin. I glanced at my phone, the time 12:21 illuminated over a close-up of me and Adam rosy cheek to rosy cheek from his last spontaneous "little date"—a Thanksgiving skiing trip to Vail. "Okay, okay, give me a few minutes to get ready. Love you," I cooed.

"Love you more, kid."

After I took a moment to kick my feet against the bed in defiance—a mock adult-size tantrum that would have been laughable to anyone watching—I sat myself up, remembered I had the most amazing boyfriend in the world who loved to spoil me rotten, and thanked my lucky stars as I scurried my ass to the shower.

Leon, Adam's driver, pulled up alongside Rockefeller Center, where whistle-toting policemen were directing traffic and pedestrians to and fro. Though the sidewalks were as packed as ever, partitions and arches made of winter greenery and fairy lights outlined the square, highlighting the magnificence of the famous tree as its centerpiece.

I rolled down the window to inhale the sweet smell of roasting chestnuts, while a Salvation Army volunteer's silver bell chimed into the air, and I wondered why I had put up such a fight earlier—there was nothing more magical than New York City during the holidays. When I was a young girl growing up in a small Connecticut town, every December my parents would pack up the family car and we'd drive into the city to spend the day looking at the famous Fifth Avenue window displays and graceful ice skaters weaving their figure eights below the glittery tree. Finances were always tight, but somehow Mom and Dad managed to make me feel like we had everything we needed. They created special moments to replace the things we couldn't afford, and those memories became some of my favorites.

The only other time we'd make the trip into Manhattan was on my birthday, when Mom would let me play hooky from school and we'd hop on an early-morning Metro-North train to see a matinee of a Broadway show. We'd stand on the long TKTS line that snaked through the center of Times Square, hoping to score discount tickets, and then wander through the crowded city streets marveling at how much bigger the theaters were compared to our local playhouse.

Mom would even let me stay after to wait by the stage door so the actors could sign the Playbill, which I always proudly added to my collection once I got home. But when Adam started turning my birthday into an all-out extravaganza—usually a surprise trip somewhere exotic or a ten-course private tasting menu at a Michelin-star restaurant—at some point, I guess the tradition of venturing into the city with my mom for a matinee just fell away.

"Hey, Leon, is there any way you can drop me closer to Fifty-Seventh and Fifth? If you leave me here, I'm afraid I'll never find Adam."

As if he hadn't heard me, Leon parked at the sidewalk, hurried to open my door, and offered his hand to help me out of the car.

How on earth am I ever going to—

And suddenly, as I straightened my peacoat and slid on a pair of fluffy earmuffs, turning to look up at the street signs to get my bearings, there was Adam standing in front of the large decorative archway made of crystalline, twinkling, ice-covered branches, highlighted with white lilies and winter sprigs adorned with rustic pine cones. The scene looked like a holiday card, or something from a photo shoot. *Oh! They must be filming a movie?! On Christmas Eve?*

Adam extended his hand to grab for mine as my eyes and brain competed with one another, racing to take it all in. He looked exceptionally handsome in a hand-tailored Tom Ford suit that was the perfect shade of navy against his olive skin and dirty-blond hair. Oh, how I loved that suit on him. He paired it with a long coat, which he left open despite the plummeting temperature. The air was cold, but thankfully there was no wind, just a chilly stillness, the kind that comes before a soft snow.

I gave Adam's hand a squeeze and allowed him to guide me through the archway that led to a mostly wide-open street, the crowds held back behind the partitions. The middle of Rockefeller Center was roped off or blocked by decorative fencing, except for two side entrances guarded by large men in black suits.

As we stepped under the trellis, the notes of "Helpless" from the Broadway production of *Hamilton* floated out through the space, and I couldn't help but hum along. Emerging from behind one of the burly guards at the side entrance and hooked up to a head mic, an actress who looked a lot like Renée Elise Goldsberry (*wait, is that . . .*) was singing out to the crowd. She appeared from the right, while a beautiful young woman who resembled Phillipa Soo, bundled in a faux-fur coat, approached from the left.

I opened my mouth to tell Adam that these actresses looked and sounded just like the original cast members of *Hamilton*, but quickly closed it, certain he wouldn't remember—even though we'd seen it on opening night. He didn't know anything about theater and could pretty much take it or leave it but always got us tickets for the hottest shows in town, knowing how much I enjoyed it.

After the women finished their song, they grabbed hands and left the scene as the music changed to another recognizable tune, "Come What May" from Broadway's hit musical *Moulin Rouge*, which inspired a whole new round of cheers from the crowd. As a flurry of dancers dressed in tight corsets and colorful fluffy feather boas entered from the side opposite where the others had left, I scanned the space for cameras or some kind of indication that maybe 30 Rock was hosting a Christmas Eve spectacular or something? But an ever-growing crowd armed with their phones and GoPros seemed to be the only "cameramen" in sight. I craned my neck to look at Adam's chest for a VIP lanyard or pass, wondering if maybe that would explain our special access, but didn't see him wearing one.

As the actors made it to the center and I could finally get a good eyeful of their faces, my jaw almost hit the asphalt. "Holy crap, is that Aaron Tveit and Karen Olivo?! They were, like, the *actual* leads in the show." I gawked, eyes bulging in Adam's direction to make sure he was understanding the magnitude of this moment, and his eyes met mine with a warm but knowing and mischievous smile.

My brain couldn't keep up with what I was seeing. The twirling and singing were one thing, but this was a star-studded spectacle in the heart of Rockefeller Center?! Adam pulled me by the hand into the middle of the square set in front of the iconic skating rink and golden statues of trumpeting angels. The cheers from the crowd competed with the miked singers who made their way into their places as the music swelled around me. I felt like I was in a movie—no, a Broadway-style alternate universe—and I couldn't catch my breath or stop my mind from spinning like the costumed cast before me.

Wait, is this all for me?

Finally, the closing notes of the medley's section of "Come What May" faded out, and the music shifted to an upbeat throwback I recognized immediately. As a Danny Zuko look-alike gyrated and sang about his *chills multiplyin'*, the rest of the T-Birds and Pink Ladies flanked the lead duo.

"Oh my God, is that Sutton-*freakin'*-Foster?! Am I dead?! Is this a dream? Adam!!" I clasped my hands over my mouth and marveled at the cast of dancers singing around the ever-effervescent Foster playing her very best (winter-clad) Sandra Dee.

How does she look so cute in a blonde bob?! Look at her feet go! Ahhh, jazz hands! Oh my God. Oh my God! Adam wrapped his arms around me and mouthed along to "You're the One That I Want" from *Grease*, complete with the *ooh ooh ooh honeys*.

Somewhere between laughing and awe, I realized what this was, and my laughter quickly caught in my throat. My chest tightened and my giggles shifted to tears of joy as Adam got down, in the middle of Rockefeller Center, illuminated by the extravagant eighty-foot tree, in front of Sutton-*freakin'*-Foster, and asked me the question I'd wanted to hear from him since the moment I'd given him my whole heart six years ago.

The cast and music fell to a hush, and the crowd, astonishingly, followed suit. But Adam was miked and said clearly for what felt like all of New York City to hear, "So, after being rendered 'Helpless' from the moment I first looked into your eyes, 'Come What May,' I know that 'You're the One That I Want,' today and every day for the rest of my life. Avery Jean Lawrence, will you marry me?" He pulled the famously recognizable Tiffany-blue ring box from his coat pocket and popped it open to reveal a ridiculously gorgeous four-carat Asscher-cut stunner tucked inside.

I looked around to take it all in. There was a hum of electricity in the air, and the magic of it all was almost like how I imagined Disney princesses felt when swept off on horseback into the sunsets of their fairy tales. The flashes of cameras twinkled like stars in a galaxy that was made just for me.

Adam glanced up, waiting for my answer with hopeful but assured eyes. My face broke into a wide grin, and I shouted, "YES!" before pulling him up and leaping into his arms. With a wave of his hand, he cued the cast to break out into their final song, "All I Want for Christmas Is You." We kissed in the center of the spectacle, and like the grand finale of a fireworks show, the music swelled and the cast pulled out all the stops, finishing with an *actual* shower of snow flurries, too perfectly timed to even be real. It wasn't, of course. I caught a glimpse of a few well-disguised snow machines tucked behind large topiaries and had to laugh. Adam was always one step ahead, and I was impressed at how he really had thought of everything. The crowd exploded into applause, and the cast came up to quickly congratulate us before hurrying out of the square, the flurry of activity matching the dance of the snowflakes through the brisk air.

Adam took me by the lapels of my winter-white peacoat and kissed me again, almost sweeping me off my feet. The fifty thousand twinkling, multicolored bulbs strung to the famous tree behind us were no match for the thousand-watt smile I was wearing from ear to ear. The moment was positively perfect, and I could hardly believe it was my reality.

I drew back and cooed, "I can't wait to spend the rest of my life with you, Mr. Daulton." And punctuated the sentiment with a sweet kiss to the tip of his nose.

He pulled me in tightly for a hug, wrapping me into his coat against his strong chest, and whispered close to my cheek with a warm breath, "This, my love, is just the beginning."

Chapter Two

When I awoke the next morning curled up next to Adam, who was still sleeping soundly, it all felt like a magical dream. The flash mob. The singing. The perfectly timed shower of silvery snowflakes. (Granted, they were machine made, but still!) It was completely surreal, and I relished the overwhelming and all-consuming sensation of complete happiness. The sun streamed in through a break in the curtains, and I squinted against its light. Soft snow (the real kind) had started falling overnight, and the ground was quickly blanketed in a thin coating of white.

I (silently and spastically) gave a little excited shimmy in celebration, and there was a cramp building in my cheek muscles from smiling so hard for so long. I nuzzled back down into the covers and nestled against Adam. My forever. I glanced over at him and lifted my left hand once again to marvel at the enormous engagement ring now weighing down my finger. And yes, the ring was a stunner, and yes, it probably cost more than most people earn in several lifetimes, but it was so much more than that. This ring was all I needed to know that Adam considered me and our future together his number one priority.

I breathed in slowly, drawing the scent of Adam's intoxicating cologne up through my nostrils in a steady stream of warm air, the fragrance fresh and clean. I laid my head on his chest, listening to his heartbeat, the rhythm steady and soothing. It was like the persistent tick of an old church clock marking time for all to hear. In each beat resounded the echo of the laughter of our future children, the hammering of new construction on our first house, all our days to come. Security. Comfort. Love. Everything I could have ever wished for was curled around me like a cocoon. I stroked a hand up his chest through the soft blond curls that were almost translucent in the morning light. He moaned against my touch and rolled over to tuck me under his arm.

"Good morning, *fiancée*," Adam said, and enfolded me more tightly into his broad chest.

"I love hearing you say that," I said, and lifted my chin to press my lips hard against his. Pushing up, I rolled myself on top of him, his body warm and inviting beneath me.

He reached up and played with the hair at the nape of my neck, drawing me down to him for another kiss. He wrapped his arms around me, and between kisses, I stroked his face and he nibbled at my neck.

Mid-nibble, he eyed the clock and groaned. "Ugh, I didn't realize how late it was. I have an important meeting with some investors who are only in town for the weekend. I told them we could meet today since yesterday we were kinda busy." He smirked at the understatement.

"Seriously?" I pushed off his chest to sit up, my legs still straddling him, and puffed out my bottom lip. "But it's Christmas. How long will you be gone? All day?"

"I'm not sure. I'll try to scoot through it as fast as I can, okay? We can celebrate all the holiday festivities when I get home and *allllllll* day tomorrow. And the day after that, and the day after that . . . I mean, we have forever," he purred in an attempt to assuage the disappointment growing across my face.

But my expression remained unchanged—pouty and frustrated. "I don't understand. You really have to do this now?"

He sighed and hopped out of bed. "Wait here, I'll be right back," he said, darting from the room. Moments later, he returned, pouncing into the plume of sheets. "I wasn't going to give these to you until tonight, but I think I need to pull my ace in the hole now," he teased.

"I planned us a little New Year's Eve getaway across the pond to celebrate our engagement." He flashed two paper tickets like a magician showcasing his latest illusion.

I popped up to my knees. "London?! For New Year's?! Are you serious?" I squealed until I realized that we had made yet another set of plans we'd need to reschedule with my parents, a trend that was unfortunately all too familiar. But they'd understand. I mean, it was London for New Year's!

"*Annnnd*, there's more." He knelt to face me. "We have box seats for New Year's Day to that hit show *Marley Is Dead* playing on the West End. You wanted to see that one, right?"

I pulled my hand away from over my mouth. "But how?! The run has been completely sold out and is rumored to be so for months."

"I called in a few favors," he said with a nonchalant shrug, like it was no big deal that he managed to score tickets to the hottest show in London. *Marley Is Dead* was a modern take on *A Christmas Carol*, featuring a female lead and a revolutionary score. The rumor was that the musical would be making its way to Broadway, but nothing had been announced yet. It was the type of show I used to dream about performing in, but that was before I set my acting career aside to settle into my amazing life with Adam.

"I don't deserve you." I leaned into him and wrapped my arms around his neck.

"Right back at you, kid." Bringing his mouth down to mine, he tightened his grip on my waist and drew me close. My heart pounded against his chest as I melted into the kiss, his hands making their way into my hair and trailing electrical currents along my body. All too quickly, he pulled away, settled one last kiss on my tingling lips, and then climbed out of bed. "I'm going to hop in the shower. The faster I get downtown, the faster I can get home."

My eyes trailed his footsteps, the swirls of flurries in the gray sky behind him flashing into my line of sight, reminding me just how cold it was *out there* and how lucky I was to be staying *in here*. "Want me to make you some coffee before you go?" I offered.

"No, it's okay. Go back to sleep. Enjoy a lazy Christmas morning in bed. I'll grab coffee on my way. We can open all the presents Santa brought when I get home." Adam smirked and disappeared into his walk-in closet to pull out a suit still draped from its hanger. He placed the clothes on a wall hook by the bed.

"My God, there's more?" I called after him. Even after almost six years together, I still couldn't get used to Adam's over-the-top generosity. But Adam felt he worked hard to provide us with a certain lifestyle. He was proud of his success and could never understand why I was still sometimes overwhelmed by that level of extravagance.

I lay there admiring my engagement ring as it winked at me in the morning light. The platinum band spun around my finger with a bit too much ease, and out of an abundance of caution, I slipped it off and into a glass on the nightstand. Better to get it resized than to, God forbid, lose it.

Hearing the ring clink into the glass, Adam turned, his expression sour. "What's wrong? Don't you love it?"

"Of course I love it! Are you crazy? The band's just a little big, and with the cold, I should probably go get it sized so it doesn't fly off into the snow."

"Oh, huh. Well, Marco only works by appointment. I can reach out to him to set something up," Adam offered.

"I'm sure I can take it anywhere in the Diamond District, right? It just needs two of those little balls attached to the bottom part of the band. When we have kids, my fingers might swell like Jimmy Dean sausages, and then I can just have the little ball thingies removed."

"Jimmy Dean sausages? Really?" He laughed. "Either way, I'd prefer if Marco took care of it. That ring cost almost as much as the down payment on this apartment."

"You're joking."

"I never joke about money," he said through a grin and pressed a kiss to my forehead.

I beamed up at him. "Just so you know"—I stuck one index finger in the air and the other to my ear, doing my best Mariah Carey–vocal run impression, and sang the famous chorus from "All I Want for Christmas Is You," my morning voice not quite able to hit those super-octane high notes.

His handsome face lit up. "Very cute." He kissed me one last time, withdrew into the bathroom, and as thick steam from the shower billowed into the bedroom, snapped the door closed behind him.

Chapter Three

After Adam padded off to the bathroom to shower, I checked my phone on my nightstand and cursed myself for once again forgetting to plug it in to charge overnight. After the barrage of engagement selfies with all the celebrity castmates, videos of the spectacle, and texts sent to *everyone* I knew, my phone was deader than dead. I plugged it in, turned it face-down, and rolled onto my side, pulling the covers up over my shoulders and tucking a pillow between my knees.

Curled in a little ball and wrapped in the most luxurious thousand-thread-count linens, my body became heavy with fatigue. Maybe it was all the excitement of yesterday finally hitting me. Or the exertion from the sexy all-nighter I had with Adam, a several-hour-long, post-engagement romp. Either way, I didn't fight the sleepiness that was washing over me and allowed myself to sink into the bed, the scent of crisp snow still fresh in my mind.

Finally, when I was almost lulled back into a hazy, dreamless sleep, a heavy pounding on the front door practically startled me into a heart attack.

"Adam?" I called from underneath the covers but could still hear the water running in the shower. *Frick.*

I debated not getting out of bed and just letting whoever it was knock until they left. I mean, who was knocking at ten thirty on a Christmas morning anyway? Carolers? A lost Amazon delivery guy dropping off a last-minute gift? It was too early for Chinese takeout. I held my breath and waited a few more moments, hoping they'd just go away, but then an even louder pounding practically catapulted me out of the bed. I grabbed my La Perla silk robe (a gift from Adam last Christmas) and hustled through the living room to the front door.

The pounding continued. "Sheesh, okay, okay," I muttered as I picked up my pace and then shouted down the hall, "Hold on, will you?!"

My bare feet slapped the dark hardwood as I hurried to get there before the next firestorm of pounding. I popped up on my toes and looked through the tiny peephole and was even more perplexed by the sight on the other side.

I wrenched the door open just as a large, suited gentleman standing at the threshold raised his hand to knock again.

"Whoa. What is going on?" I asked and wrapped my robe a little more tightly around me to properly cover up all my lady bits.

At the same time, two men in the front, flanked by four uniformed police officers, flashed their badges, the gold of their shields distracting me from actually catching anyone's name. "Ma'am, we're with the Federal Bureau of Investigation and Department of Homeland Security. We are looking for Adam McDaniels."

"Adam McDaniels?" I exhaled a sigh of relief. "No, sorry. An Adam lives here, but his last name isn't McDaniels. You must have the wrong address. Merry Christmas, guys." I moved to close the door when a meaty hand and a shiny-toed shoe stopped it in its tracks.

"Right, sure. Well, so you may know him as Adam Wright, Adam Fields, or Adam"—he looked down at his notepad and then back up again—"Daulton."

My chest tightened as my ears began to ring. *Daulton.* No, this had to be some kind of mistake. Adam had never even gotten so much as a parking ticket.

"Are you . . ." He flipped through the pages of his pad. "Avery Lawrence?"

"Yes," I managed to squeak out, past my throat now drier than the Sahara.

"We have an arrest warrant for Mr. McDaniels, uh, Daulton, and warrants to search and seize property," he said, flashing a series of documents in front of me.

"Hold on, what? Excuse me? No, that's not possible. I don't under—" But before I could even finish my sentence, the officers pushed their way past me at the command of the taller FBI agent.

I'm asleep. That's it. I'm still in a sex-hazed, dream-filled sleep. C'mon, Avery, wake up. Wake up. I pinched my arm, a total cliché, but I was out of options and willing to try just about anything to end the nightmare unraveling in front of me. I scurried ahead of them to the bedroom to at least try to throw on some pants and a shirt as a parade of agents swarmed into our Upper East Side classic six. I managed to hop into a pair of old sweatpants, slip off the La Perla robe, and grab one of Adam's Princeton hoodies, wrenching it over my thin camisole as quickly as humanly possible to give these officers as little of a peep show as I could.

Just then, two agents marched Adam, now dressed, past me through to the living room in handcuffs, a trail of watery footprints leading toward the door. What the hell could he have possibly done to justify an army of agents pulling him from his shower while he still had soap bubbles in his hair? None of this made any sense. Instinctively, I shouted, "You can't take him like that! It's twenty-five degrees outside. He'll freeze to death."

The officers didn't slow but continued to usher Adam through the foyer until he was by the coat closet being helped into his sneakers. I raced to grab a towel out of the linen chest and moved toward him with an outstretched arm, trying to dab away some of the water dripping down his neck onto the floor. Adam kept his back to me as he worked his foot into a shoe.

"Adam? What's going on? Tell them this is all a mistake," I pleaded.

The taller officer raised his voice and forearm to block me from getting any closer. "Ma'am, I need you to stand down. Get back against the wall. Now!" he barked.

"But he'll freeze!" I pushed forward, extending the soft, plush terry toward him again. "Isn't that some form of cruel and unusual punishment? I mean, it's . . . it's Christmas!" I bumped up against the portly agent and thrust the towel in his face, trying desperately to get past him and over to where Adam was shivering.

"Ms. Lawrence, turn around. Arms behind your back." He slapped a pair of cold silver handcuffs on my wrists, the towel falling to the ground between us.

"Wait. *I'm* getting arrested? For what?" I tried to look up over my shoulder at the agent, but was thrust back around and forced up against the wall, the cuffs tightening with the movement. My cheek smushed into the cool plaster, the paint color—Anvil Gray—hitting me with a force almost as heavy as its name.

"Assaulting an officer." The agent's voice remained even and unfeeling.

"I didn't assault you! I waved a towel in your face," I cried. *This can't be happening! He must be joking!* A crushing swell of nausea rocketed through me, and I scanned the foyer for something I could use in case I got sick.

"Ma'am, please don't make me add resisting arrest to your charges. Agent McInerny, please read Ms. Lawrence her rights," the agent ordered.

A young female officer with slicked-back hair and deep-set blue eyes stepped forward to recite my Miranda rights. It was simultaneously exactly how I'd seen it in the movies and the thousand *Law & Order: SVU* marathons I'd logged, and yet, not at all the same. The procedures seemed familiar, but this experience was wholly new and altogether more unsettling than I could have ever imagined.

I swallowed hard, trying to unjumble my thoughts and questions, but in the end, I was so afraid of saying the wrong thing that I said nothing. I prayed that somehow between getting manhandled and Mirandized, Adam would *look* at me. I just needed to see his eyes, his innocent face, a reassuring glance—*something*—to give me a clue as to what the hell was happening and that this had been a colossal mistake.

Throughout the apartment, cabinets were being slammed and drawers emptied, flipped upside down carelessly, items tossed about like junk. The SWAT team was searching every last nook and cranny, rummaging through dressers, pulling down books, files, and prized sports mementos. When they dumped over a box tucked deep in the back of the closet containing some of my old acting memorabilia—tattered scripts, cast photos, trophies from singing competitions—a tight pull in my stomach caught me off guard.

Sprawled out on the floor among the autographed Playbills and ticket stubs was the version of my life I'd given up when I'd chosen Adam six years ago and set aside my dream of an acting career for an entirely different kind of happiness. I'd forgotten that box was even back there. In this mess, it was hard to tell what they were looking for. It would take days to put things back together again.

A young agent I hadn't seen before poked his head into the foyer. "Ms. Lawrence, where's your phone?"

"*My* phone? It's charging next to my bed. Why?"

"Tony, it's by the bed. Bag it up," he called out to a fellow officer.

I looked up at the female agent. "No, wait! They're taking my phone? No, please! My entire proposal's on that phone, my entire life!"

"Once forensics takes a look, you'll get it back. But that could take weeks, possibly even months, if ever," she deadpanned.

After what felt like hours, the lead agent announced they were finished with their search and ready to leave. The female officer tapped me hard on the shoulder and spun me around. "Let's go," she said without the slightest trace of sympathy in her voice.

"My . . . my coat?" I managed to squeak out.

The officer rolled her eyes and snagged the coat that hung on the closest hook, unfazed by whether it was even mine or Adam's. She half-heartedly draped it over my shoulders, not bothering to undo the handcuffs to allow my arms to slide in properly, and gave me a little shove out the door.

I followed her into the hallway just as one of our neighbors, Mrs. Randall, stepped out of her apartment clutching her bratwurst-shaped corgi, Queen Elizabeth. *Wonderful.* During our co-op board interview, Mrs. Randall had made no secret of the fact she thought Adam and I were too young and our money too new for the prestigious apartment building. She'd grilled us on everything from our W-2s to our hobbies, trying to find any reason to deny us entry. In the end, Adam won over the rest of the board, and despite her "no" vote, our application went through.

I could only imagine what she was thinking as she watched us both get hauled out of here in handcuffs. Was she horrified? Vindicated? At this point, how Mrs. Randall felt about me was probably the least of my worries. I closed my eyes, silently counting the number of chimes until the elevator arrived on our floor, but opened them when I felt a small, tubby body brush up against my leg. Queen Elizabeth had jumped out of Mrs. Randall's arms and was now curled up at my feet.

A few weeks ago, Queen Elizabeth somehow escaped from Mrs. Randall's apartment. I found her alone in the hallway, scared and cowering in a corner. I took her in and gave her water and food and let her sleep in my lap all afternoon, returning her when Mrs. Randall finally came home. It seemed Queen Elizabeth hadn't forgotten about my kind gesture, even if Mrs. Randall had.

One . . . two . . . three . . . and then finally, after what felt like an eternity, the elevator arrived at the ninth floor. The doors parted, and Queen Elizabeth reluctantly slid off my shoes and returned to her owner. The female agent and I stepped inside and went down to the lobby, where another dozen detectives and officers were milling about.

Seeing the sheer size of the police presence, I knew this *had* to be a mistake, all a big mistake. *I mean, what do they think Adam is guilty of? Masterminding a presidential assassination or something?* They must have confused him with someone else. That was it. A simple mix-up. Once we got to the police station, they'd realize their error, and we'd be home sitting in front of the Christmas tree unwrapping gifts and sipping on eggnog in no time.

Moments later, the stout agent led Adam out of the second elevator bank. I searched his face for the same wild panic I was experiencing at the sheer absurdity of what was happening around us. But instead, he looked extraordinarily composed, calm, almost resigned . . .

My heart sank lower than I'd ever thought possible, practically to my knees, as an overwhelming sense of dread refilled the now empty space. *Oh my God*, maybe this wasn't a mistake after all?!

"Adam! Adam! Please, just tell me what's happening? Please, baby, just look at me."

He kept his back turned, shook his head—his hair still dripping—and walked toward the sidewalk, a flicker of light winking off the handcuffs clasped behind him as he slid into the back seat of an unmarked police car without even a glance in my direction.

Chapter Four

Apparently, Christmas cheer was not in high supply at the Metropolitan Correctional Center, and many hours (not to mention a full, and I do mean *full*, body search) later, I finally stepped outside the prison walls, the steel gates snapping closed behind me with a loud buzz. I shielded my eyes against the bright glare of the late-afternoon sun setting over Lower Manhattan.

Humiliation washed over me as I relived the last few hours: the sharp click of the camera as it flashed for my mug shot; the guard who forced my trembling hands down onto the fingerprint card; me begging for my one phone call to a lawyer and any information on where they were holding Adam and what he could have possibly done wrong; the feeling of my body unclenching when the door to my cell finally buzzed open and I was told I was getting released on my own recognizance.

I didn't know all the details of Adam's supposed crimes yet, but my lawyer was able to find out that Adam had been named in an elaborate fraud scheme that, in her words, almost put Madoff to shame. Logic and reason were both silenced by the running commentary now looping in my brain.

One voice was calm and soothing, saying all the right things to convince me that this had to be a simple misunderstanding. I mean, this was Adam we were talking about! But the other voice, the one that seemed louder, eliciting a heartier pang of guilt, was viciously repeating over and over the old adage that when something was too good to be true, it probably was. And Adam *was* too good. He'd always been.

My heart and my head were now locked in a fierce battle, the Adam I'd loved for six years and thought I knew better than anyone versus the stranger I saw being led from the elevator, the one who wouldn't even look at me as he was pulled from our apartment.

My eyes welled up, stinging as the cold air bit into the moisture on my lashes, and my body grew heavy with exhaustion. The only thought I could manage to squeak in between all the warring voices in my head was getting the hell home.

I tightened my coat around myself, grateful the officer allowed me one at all in the flurry of activity as she shoved me out our apartment door. The thick wool was providing at least a bit of a barrier against the frigid chill now causing my eyes to water like a leaky faucet. I swiped my finger under my lid to catch the tears before they fell but had completely forgotten I still had black ink all over my hands from being fingerprinted.

I caught a glimpse of my reflection in the tinted glass of the prison's security booth as I passed. My unwashed, bedraggled mop of hair was tied up by a scrunchie holding on for dear life, and now my eyes, thanks to the smudges of ink, looked like I'd gone a few rounds with Muhammad Ali. If it wasn't so damn tragic, it would have been downright hilarious.

I walked out to the curb to survey the mostly empty street, searching desperately for the car my lawyer had arranged to meet me. But the loading lane remained empty, my car nowhere in sight. Whether the temperature was really dropping or I was just finally descending into Dante's icy ninth circle of hell, I wasn't exactly sure, but all I knew was that with each passing minute I was feeling less and less of my feet and working harder and harder to try to turtle myself deeper into my coat. Peeping over the lapels, I scanned the road for a cab instead. But who was I kidding: it was Christmas Day in New York City, and I was in no-man's-land outside the federal prison. I'd never get a ride without specifically calling for one, and I knew it.

Focused on the full length of the avenue in front of me, I scoured each lane and every intersection as far as I could see for a familiar flash of a yellow cab light, but things were hopelessly desolate. I had decided to try to peer down the next block when I almost tripped over a pair of bare feet peeking out from beneath a threadbare throw and a layer of newspaper. *Bare feet? In this weather?* Curled in a ball on a subway steam grate was an older woman with a dirt-streaked face and rags for clothes. In spite of the clouds of hot, chemical-scented air emitting from the underground subway tunnels that she used to keep warm, she was trembling on the frost-covered sidewalk.

"Oh! So sorry, 'scuse me," I said, managing to step over her just in time. The woman barely acknowledged the stir.

I glanced back over my shoulder at her and then up to the street, trying to figure out my next move. And finally, like a shiny beacon of hope, I spotted a taxi with its light on turning the corner in my direction. I jumped out into the street, waving my arms frantically. The car pulled over as the driver lowered his window.

"Where to?" the driver asked.

"Upper East Side?"

"No, sorry, hon. West Side stops only."

I grabbed the door handle. "Okay, that's fine. If you can drop me off as high on the West Side as you can, I'll figure out how to get crosstown."

The driver eyed me up and down suspiciously, his gaze lingering on my empty hands and disheveled appearance. "Lady, you got any money?"

Shit. "Well, not on me *exactly*, but I can get you however much you need once I get home. Plus a very generous tip, I promise. *Orrr* wait, Apple Pay? Or you can give me your Venmo or Zelle." I reached into my pocket, grabbing for my phone to access a payment app, when my stomach plummeted like a broken elevator falling through an empty shaft.

I fumbled around in every pocket only to turn up a butterscotch candy I was sure had been rolling around in my coat since *last* Christmas. I didn't have my phone. The agents had confiscated it as evidence. *Dammit.*

I sweetened my voice and purred, "C'mon, sir, where's your holiday spirit? Whatever happened to helpin' out a fellow man in need? A bit of charity and goodwill for Christmas?"

Between noticing the look of panic on my face at turning up no phone and the unappealing offer of my old, crusty butterscotch, the cabbie peeled away quicker than you could say "Bah humbug!" leaving me coughing in a cloud of the taxi's exhaust fumes.

"Well, Merry freakin' Christmas to you too, pal!" I shouted into the rapidly approaching darkness of the December night.

I stepped back onto the sidewalk and could see the homeless woman was now sitting upright, her whole body shaking from the cold. She reached into a tattered paper bag and pulled out a dirty sheet, doing her best to wrap herself in it for warmth.

I decided I should head back in the direction of the prison, hoping to seek some assistance there, but I was frozen in my spot—this time more figuratively than literally, even though I was still freezing my ever-lovin' ass off. I couldn't seem to put one foot in front of the other, the reality of my hypocrisy ringing loud and clear if I were to walk away and leave this woman out here to possibly die of exposure.

An overwhelming sense of compassion radiated through me, and though, to quote my favorite children's book, today had been a "terrible, horrible, no good, very bad day," looking at this woman now shifted everything into crystal-clear perspective. Without another thought, I slipped my wool coat from my arms.

I knelt down beside her and extended the coat in her direction. "Here, it isn't much, but it's truly all I have on me. Please take this."

Her eyes lit up in astonishment, and she gratefully took the jacket from my hands. "God bless you" was all she could manage through her tears.

"And you. Merry Christmas," I said, pulling the hood of Adam's Princeton sweatshirt up onto my head to cover my numb ears. I stood back up to search the street again for a subway entrance nearby. Coming up empty, I quickly made a U-turn and strode back in the direction of the jail.

Shivering myself now, the hoodie doing very little to shield me from the falling temperatures as the sun lowered between the skyscrapers of the city, I hurried back to the gate to see an older woman reading the newspaper inside the security booth. As I lifted my hand to knock on the window, she flipped to another page and muttered, "Boy oh boy, what has this world come to? So much for honoring Christmas in your heart." With brittle fingers balled into a fist, I rapped on the glass, clearly interrupting her thought. She lifted her eyebrows in my direction, put down the paper, and shook her head.

"So sorry to bother you, but I was just released from here a few minutes ago, and my lawyer said she arranged a ride for me, but it doesn't seem to be here, and I can't manage to hail a cab. Even if I could, I don't have money on me to pay for it. Would you be able to call one for me and explain the situation? I can get them the money as soon as I get home, I promise." I wrapped my arms around myself as the wind picked up, the bitter cold cutting straight through me like an ice pick.

The woman's expression remained as blank and cold as the gray expanse of the horizon, the thin line of her mouth tight as if she heard this same request a hundred times a day. "No, sorry, hon. Against the rules."

"Against the rules? Against the rules?! Lady, do you know what kind of roller coaster I've been riding for the past twenty-four hours?"

She shrugged like she couldn't care less, but I continued anyway. "Just yesterday, Sutton-*freakin'*-Foster proposed to me, well, *she* didn't propose, she sang a song while my fiancé proposed, but still, she was there, *the* Sutton Foster. And there were confetti cannons and jazz hands, and my whole damn life right . . . right in front of me." My voice constricted as I fought hard against the tears threatening in the base of my throat, knowing now it could all be one big lie.

Rightfully assuming this would not be a short rant, the guard abandoned her newspaper and feigned interest by absentmindedly nodding along with my story.

"Then, smack in the middle of Rockefeller Center in front of tourists and commuters and I don't know . . . God himself . . . herself? Whatever, Adam got down on one knee and pulled out the big, iconic blue Tiffany box. You know the one, right?" I asked.

At the mention of "the box," her eyes grew wide, and now fully invested in my story, she enthusiastically nodded as an invitation for me to go on.

"Exactly." I continued, "And I'm sure you can guess what happened next?"

"He asked you to marry him?" she said, leaning closer in anticipation of my answer.

I echoed her words, only louder and with exuberant hand-waving, "He asked me to marry him as a full-scale Broadway chorus sang 'All I Want for Christmas Is You.'"

"Damn, that's beautiful," the guard gushed, her fist rigid in front of her mouth like she was holding back a little whimper.

"Right? And I felt like the luckiest girl in the world, that is, until the FBI and Homeland Security practically kicked my door down this morning with an arrest warrant for an Adam McDaniels, which was pretty surprising considering the man I've been living with this whole time has been going by the name Adam Daulton!"

"Here, honey, you have a bat in the cave," the guard said. She shoved a box of Kleenex toward me, allowing the thin paper to peep through the small window. I snagged a few tissues from the package, pulling one aside for the current bat situation and shoving the rest into my pocket either for finger warmth or a future runny nose. The guard retracted the box after I'd taken a handful, and noticing her shirt had ridden up as she maneuvered to give me the tissues, she quickly yanked down the bottom hem and proudly straightened out the shiny silver-bell broach pinned to her lapel.

"Oh, thank you," I said, pausing for only a moment to blow my nose, barely missing a beat before continuing. "Then *I* got arrested for assaulting an officer when really all I did was wave a towel in his face."

The guard pursed her lips at me disapprovingly and *tsked, tsked* like a disappointed parent chiding a toddler.

"I know, I know . . . not my finest hour. But then I was brought here and booked," I said, holding up my ink-stained fingers.

"Phew, that's *some* story," she said, shaking her head in amazement.

"The thing that kills me is that I truly can't make sense of any of it. I mean, this is Adam we're talking about . . . *my* Adam. How in the span of only a few hours did my whole world completely and epically implode?"

My chest constricted as I struggled to hold my hurt and confusion at bay, worried that once I opened the emotional floodgates, I wouldn't know how to close them up again.

The guard, with her chin resting firmly in her palm, sparkly ornament earrings dangling from her lobes, asked, "Honey, did you ever stop to think that when things seem to be falling apart, they may actually be falling into place?"

The guard's fortune-cookie wisdom was doing little to assuage my desperation, and instead, my devastating thoughts continued to compete with one another for top billing. A flush of heat flooded up my neck until I nearly burst. "What . . . am I going . . . to do?" The sobs were now coming fast and furious.

"I can't help you with any of"—she waved her finger around in the air—"*that*, but, here. I can give you this." The woman shifted in her seat, the wheels squeaking under her weight, and she pulled an off-white business card from her shirt's breast pocket and slid it under the tempered glass. "Walk up three and a half blocks toward the river, then turn right. There's a phone booth on that corner. Right next to a bodega. Actually, they say it's the very last phone booth in New York City. Lucky you."

I patted my wet eyes with my sweatshirt sleeve and said, "Yeah, lucky me."

The guard continued, "Call that number on the card. You won't need any change. It's toll-free." She tapped the counter with her index finger to emphasize her point. "It'll get you where you need to go."

I took the card and scanned it, noting the scrawled number and no other information on it. "Should I ask for someone in particular? Is this the number of like a cab company or something? I told you I don't have any money on me," I repeated through chattering teeth.

Almost as if she hadn't heard my question, the guard simply reached for her newspaper with renewed interest and said, "Good luck, honey. Sounds like you got a lot of ghosts to revisit. And remember, no space of regret can make amends for one life's opportunity misused."

"Ghosts? Wait, what? What does that even mean?" But the woman had already turned her back to me and resumed reading her newspaper. I took a deep breath, the cold air burning my nostrils and clearing my brain with each long pull.

Get it together, Avery.

So, Adam was probably a felon. I didn't have my phone or a coat. It was like twenty-five degrees outside. My hands and face were covered in booking ink, and I looked like a beaten-up raccoon. I was out of options and needed to get home. If this ridiculous quest turned out to be just as fruitless as my other attempts had been at getting a ride home, I decided I would head to the nearest subway station and take my chances at jumping the turnstile.

But in the meantime, tucking the card with the toll-free number into the sweatshirt's front pocket, I tightened the drawstring of my hoodie to cinch my face into a tight O, lowered my head against the wind, and took off in the direction of the Hudson River to find the very last phone booth in Manhattan.

Chapter Five

A sad string of blinking colored Christmas lights was haphazardly scalloped along the top of the dilapidated phone booth, the cord disappearing somewhere down its rusty hinge and into the ground. I used my sleeve to try to pry open the door without touching its handle, but after fumbling with it due to cold fingers and frictionless fabric, I surrendered, grabbing for it barehanded and slamming my body weight forward to force the folding door in like an accordion. I tumbled inside, clearly having never actually used one of these things before. A phone booth? A relic. I couldn't even remember the last time I saw one of these things around the city within the last decade. Two? I mean, people don't even carry quarters around anymore, or any change for that matter.

Finally steadying myself after bouncing around the interior like a Ping-Pong ball, I checked to see how many people caught the embarrassing spectacle, but as usual, the city bustled around me without even the slightest display of interest.

I let out a sigh of relief and turned back to the phone. In spite of the fact that my skin crawled at the thought of all of the germs undoubtedly embedded into the receiver after years of use, I picked it up, reached into my pocket past my pile of tissues for the card the guard had given me, and pulled it into my line of sight. Drawing in a deep breath, I begrudgingly punched in the numbers with a rigid finger and waited.

The phone rang twice before an audible click registered on the line, followed by another pause of silence. I was sure the call had disconnected when all of a sudden, the quiet was interrupted.

"Good evening," said a friendly but clear voice, "the address you are searching for is located at 1843 Worth Street, New York, New York. And remember, no space of regret can make amends for one life's opportunities misused. Goodbye."

The line went dead.

Wait, what? I had barely caught what she said and started to repeat aloud what I could remember of the address in an effort to not let it slip from my memory. But as hard as I tried to reiterate the information, I began mixing up the numbers. I picked up the receiver and punched in the number again, hoping it would reconnect me with the same operator and repeat the message. Thankfully, it did, and I listened to it a few times until it stuck. Though I had the address now firmly solidified in my brain, I hung up the phone more confused than ever.

The only thing I could think was that this was the address of a nearby cab company or taxi stand? It was a strange way to go about arranging a ride, but I was in no position to be particularly choosy or overly analytical. Cold, sore, and looking like a wild animal from a Nat Geo special, I just needed to get home and for this to all have been a horrible, god-awful, dumpster fire of a hellish nightmare that I would awaken from à la Dorothy back in Kansas after her foray to Oz.

I looked up at the signs marking the cross streets and then repeated the mystery address again and again to myself, sounding a lot like Dory from *Finding Nemo. 1843 Worth Street, New York, New York. 1843 Worth Street, New York, New York.* Okay, just a few more blocks from here. My hair slipped out from my loosening hood, and the wind cemented the strands to the moisture on my chapped cheeks. I batted at them with my forearm and blew a raspberry, desperately trying to get the pieces out of my mouth and wrangle them back under the drawstring. Dear God, I must have been a sight.

After what felt like an eternity, I finally turned the corner onto the wide cobblestones of Worth Street, counting down the building numbers until I reached 1843. I peered up at the residential loft building converted from an industrial warehouse. This was *clearly* not a cab company. Panic and arctic wind sliced through me, and my eyes darted around for some sort of an idea of what to do or a sign from the universe on some way to get me the hell home.

Suddenly, I noticed a perfectly timed Uber Eats deliveryman exiting the building, and I rushed up the short flight of steps to catch the handle just before the door snapped shut. I slithered past him and into a small but cozy lobby, hoping to thaw out while I gained my bearings. Maybe the cab company was on a side street? Or through the alleyway behind this building? Someone who lived here would certainly know.

I scanned the apartment doors on the first floor for a few minutes, hoping to see someone coming either in or out for their Christmas Day dinner, but shockingly, all things were quiet in the building. I'd have to knock on one of these doors, but honestly, if I saw me out in the hallway looking like the disheveled mess I was, I wouldn't be much inclined to answer either. I untied the drawstring bowed underneath my chin and yanked the hood down from my head, hoping it would make me appear less suspicious, but aware that, without a brush, the scrunchie that had been barely making do before was certainly on its last leg now.

Huffing out a sigh of defeat, I started with the first apartment. I rapped three times on the solid metal door and was surprised when a leggy blonde in a stunning red dress greeted me. Her face could not disguise the look of pure horror at my appearance, but despite her obvious pity, she stepped forward anyway.

"Can I help you?" she asked, and a sympathetic look washed over her.

"Hi, I'm so sorry to bother you, especially on Christmas. You look beautiful, by the way. That's a Valentino, isn't it? Never mind. I'm looking for a cab company and this was the address I was given. Do you know of one nearby?" I gestured with the business card in my hand, the one the guard had given me, as some kind of proof of legitimacy, even though all that was written on it was the hand-scrawled phone number.

"Cab company? Here? I don't think so, but hold on a sec." She twisted her body away from me and called into the hallway. "Hey, G, you know of a cab company around here?" She turned back to face me with arms crossed over her chest. "Sorry, I don't live in Tribeca."

A beat later, a male voice called back, "What's that?"

"There's a woman at your front door in *desperate* need of . . . a cab?" Her voice went up on the word *cab*, but I'm sure she was thinking I was even more in need of a hair brush or a psych evaluation.

"How is it that at thirty-two years old and after all the events I've attended over the years, I still cannot tie a tie," the man muttered, head down, as he approached the front doorway fumbling with the knot at the base of his neck. "There, I got it." Just then, he lifted his head up to look at me standing in the doorway.

"Avery?" he said, wide-eyed and dumbstruck, unable to conceal his state of shock, "is that you?"

Suddenly it felt as if all the air in the hallway—and possibly all the air on Earth—had been sucked out of the atmosphere and released into oblivion, leaving me breathless and dizzy. "I—wha—Gabe? How?"

His boyish good looks hadn't changed one bit since the last time I saw him, which happened to be our epic breakup almost seven years ago. Only now they were just more pronounced, mature, and *sexy*. His broad chest filled out his suit, and his arms were most impressive against the taut fabric that covered them. But more than anything, I couldn't take my eyes off his, remembering that the last time I looked into them was the day he'd broken my heart and changed my life forever. My tongue suddenly felt too large for my mouth, and I struggled to swallow as I continued to blink at what I could only imagine was an exhaustion-induced mirage.

The blonde interjected, stirring me back to planet Earth. "Wait, you know each other?" she asked, wagging a finger between the two of us.

"We do. We did. In a past life," I said in an almost whisper. "So sorry to have . . . I just . . . I'll find a cab outside somehow. Merry Christmas," I barked over my shoulder as I bolted from the building and out to the lamplit street.

◆ ◆ ◆

I stumbled about in a haze of my own panic-retreat, my body temperature surged, and I no longer felt the bitter sting of the cold. *Gabe? How?! I mean, what were the odds of finding myself on my ex-boyfriend's doorstep?* None of it made any sense.

Gabe was the very first person I met at college. Fresh off the train from Woodbury, Connecticut, I was greener than green. After saving every cent I made working at our local pizzeria to pay for voice lessons and acting classes, I managed to get accepted into NYU Tisch School of the Arts for musical theater, and it was a dream come true. But if New York City was the city that never slept, then Woodbury was the small town that liked a good catnap, and for the first few uncomfortable weeks blundering about like a fish out of water, I wasn't sure I could successfully navigate a new life in the Big Apple—that is, until I met Gabe and his sister, Marisol, who quickly became my closest friend.

Raised by a single mother on the Lower East Side, Gabe *was* New York through and through—from his unwavering devotion to the Yankees to his uncanny ability to pick out the best food cart on any city block. Between meeting him and Marisol, it was like having my own personal Manhattan tour guides, only better. Gabe explained that the city was essentially one big grid, with the avenues running horizontally and the streets vertically, and educated me on which subway exits got you closest to class. Marisol was the one who let me in on the secret—that most of the plays I was assigned to read in History of Theater 101 could be bought at The Strand, a local indie bookstore, for a fraction of the cost they were sold for at the NYU one.

When I met Gabe, he was a junior and prelaw, with the singular goal of making a difference in the world, whatever it took. He could be intense and brooding, but he was also steadfast in his convictions, not to mention undeniably gorgeous. His drive to "do good" was infectious, and it wasn't long before I joined the long line of freshman girls in love with him. We dated all through college, and I was positive I'd found "the one"—that is, until it all spectacularly fell apart. Almost a year later, I started dating Adam, cutting ties with Gabe and Marisol completely in order to dive headfirst into my new life.

In big moments over the past seven years, I couldn't help but find myself reminiscing about Gabe and our relationship, and then about Marisol and what she'd think. It became the strange metric by which I evaluated all my choices. How would Gabe feel about this decision or that one? How would Marisol have done such and such? And every single time, I came to the same conclusion—Adam was my future, and Gabe and Marisol were my past.

Well, until tonight when I randomly showed up at his front door. *But why?*

No, I couldn't worry about any of that now. It was *still* twenty-five degrees outside, and I was *still* only in a hoodie freezing my ass off. Now, I just needed to get home. I power-walked, more like *power-stalked*, back in the direction of the security guard's booth, ready to give that lady a piece of my mind. What kind of sick game was she playing? I mean, who sends a defenseless woman who just stepped fresh out of jail, still in her pajamas, on a goose chase around town for shits and giggles?! A sadist, that's who. A sadist who was going to have to schedule immediate surgery to remove my foot from her ass.

When I made it back to the prison in what felt like record time, I marched right up to the security booth, annoyed to see someone new at the guard post. I banged on the window anyway, startling the man from his coffee, causing him to toss the hot liquid sky-high.

"Dammit!" he swore. He swung around to look at me and then quickly softened at the sight of my bedraggled and desperate appearance. He sighed and asked, "Is there something you need?"

"Yes, sir, there is. I need to talk to the woman who was here on duty before you. Finger-waved hair. Um . . . maybe in her fifties? Fuller figured. A silver-bell broach on her lapel. I need to speak with her *pronto*."

"Ma'am," he said as he continued to mop up puddles of coffee with some ineffectively thin paper towels, "I've been on duty all night. And I relieved a man named Ernie who is about five-two, weighs about a buck-ten soaking wet, and is bald. So, I'm not quite sure who you're talkin' about."

"No, the woman, who was here, I don't know, like an hour and a half ago. She was reading a newspaper. Sitting exactly where you are now."

The man narrowed his eyes at me and took in my whole appearance. He gave an impatient huff, like answering nonsensical questions from annoying strangers was just another perk of manning a street booth outside the prison in the jungle that was Manhattan. "My shift started three hours ago. I've been right here, in this exact seat, from the moment I clocked in."

"I don't understand. I was released from *this* prison, didn't have a ride, and she said it was against policy for her to call me a taxi. So instead, she handed me a business card and sent me on a wild-goose chase."

"Look, young lady, I don't know who you spoke to, but I can call you a cab right now, it ain't against any policy we have, and I've worked here for more than thirty years."

This didn't make any sense. I couldn't have dreamed it or made it up. I had, no *have*, the card she gave me. I called the number. I ended up at Gabe's front door. That all really happened. So what the ever-loving hell was going on?!

I pushed in closer to the window, practically fogging it with my breath as I continued, "Are you sure you can't think of anyone that fits the description I gave you? I need to know who it was I spoke with."

He just shook his head and shrugged, reaching for the phone. "So, do you need help getting home or not?"

I held up my ink-stained hands as the emotion and frustration welled deep in my chest. Tears were springing to my eyes and the guard's posture softened as I explained, "Yes, I do . . . but I don't have any money on me."

The old man set his lips into a sympathetic half-moon and reached into his back pocket for a tattered brown leather wallet, from which he drew a familiar yellow MetroCard with blue writing and slid it through the slot in the tempered glass window.

"I don't think it has all that much on it, to be honest, but should be enough for one ride," he offered. "Merry Christmas. Now get yourself home safe, ya hear?" He smiled as he returned his wallet to his back pocket, resituated himself on his seat, and resumed sipping his coffee.

I clutched the card firmly against my chest and looked back at the prison gate, the one I'd emerged from only a couple of hours earlier. I exhaled, confusion and fatigue hitting with the force of a one-two punch from a prizefighter, and nodded. "Thank you, sir, and Merry Christmas to you too."

Chapter Six

After sleeping for eighteen hours straight, and then spending almost another week in bed both out of sheer exhaustion and not wanting to face reality beyond my duvet, I found myself being led through the tight maze of hallways and cubicles of my defense lawyer's firm, Webber, Wyse & Associates.

My father used to say rock bottom will teach you the lessons the mountaintops never could. Throughout my whole relationship with Adam, I was Maria-freakin'–von Trapp twirling through the highest peaks of the Swiss Alps. And now, here I was, alone in my *defense attorney's* office in the deepest trench of the valley, the lessons almost burying me alive. As tempting as it was to pull a Scarlett O'Hara and punt every single one of my problems to tomorrow (which I actually *tried* to do for the past week while I wallowed in bed), unfortunately, that just wasn't an option anymore.

"Can I get you anything, Ms. Lawrence? Coffee? Tea? Water?" a smartly dressed assistant asked.

A pile of Xanax? "No, thank you. I'm fine."

"Mrs. Webber should be joining you shortly," he said, closing the door softly behind him.

I nodded and crossed the room to the window. It was a cold but clear day, and you could see straight across the river to Jersey City.

"If you arch your neck a little bit to the right, you can see the Statue of Liberty," said a voice from the doorway. I pivoted sideways as directed and looked out to the famous New York monument in all her spectacular glory.

Mrs. Webber set a coffee and stack of papers down on a large mahogany desk. "I waited close to fifteen years for a partner to retire and this office to open up. I jumped on it the first chance I got."

"I can certainly see why," I said, taking a seat across from her, noting that we were more than thirty stories high—just perfect if I felt the need to leap out the window to dodge this endless nightmare.

"I'm glad you called me. It took a few days to sort through the charges, but I cashed in a few favors and think I have the whole of it now that the indictments against Adam have been filed. The holidays caused a bit of a backlog."

I hesitated, not certain I wanted to hear the answer, but in spite of myself asked, "And the charges against me?"

"I'll get to those, but let's start with Mr. McDaniels, a.k.a. Mr. Daulton, a.k.a. Mr. Wright, a.k.a. Mr. Fields . . ."

My head was spinning, but all I could think of was the unbelievably annoying Lou Bega song "Mambo No. 5" . . . *A little bit of Daulton in my life, a little McDaniels by my side, a little bit of Fields in his prime, a little bit of Adam serving time.*

"Is this for real? Just how many aliases does he have?" I asked, trying to wrap my head around which one of his many faux personas I'd fallen in love with.

"Just one more, Mr. Oldham. He's been using different names and different social security numbers as a means to secure loans." She looked up from the stack and sighed. "For simplicity's sake, I'll just refer to him as Adam. It seems Adam's been charged with several federal crimes. One count of conspiracy, two counts of mail fraud, four counts of wire fraud, four counts of money laundering, and several violations of the Senior

Citizens Against Marketing Scams Act of 1994, all of which carry fairly hefty federal sentencing guidelines."

Somewhere after the words *money laundering* I lost count of the charges. I closed my eyes and uttered, "Can you just give it to me straight? In layman's terms, please?"

She sighed and allowed her face to show more sympathy than I'd ever seen between lawyers and their clients on TV. "Your fiancé was part of a very sophisticated ring of scammers that operated multistate telemarketing and in-person sales teams who knowingly and intentionally sold their victims, mostly close-to-retirement small business owners, nonexistent internet marketing services."

I opened my eyes, and the room was spinning. Even though my stomach was empty, bile was threatening to rise up from its pit. "Adam did those things? *Really* did those things?"

While the web of lies had started to unravel with that knock on Christmas morning, I had been holding on to a small but unlikely hope he might actually somehow maybe possibly be innocent. That this had all been a mix-up of epic proportions. But as Mrs. Webber rattled off Adam's charges in very real terms, my shaky resolve completely crumbled, and I knew for certain he wasn't the Prince Charming he'd made himself out to be. Adam was the villain of the story, and he'd conned me right along with everyone else.

"I think I'm going to be sick," I cried.

Mrs. Webber rushed around from behind her desk, clutching a trash can. "There, there," she said, "let me get you some water."

She walked over to a mini fridge, pulled out a bottle, and handed it to me. I took a few shallow sips to make sure nothing would come back up and set it down on the desk.

"What happens now?" I choked out.

"Adam was arraigned this morning and remanded without bail, most likely because they deem him a flight risk. The fact that he was operating under so many aliases means he knows how to work the system. He was appointed a federal public defender, so I'm not sure what strategy they have going forward. It's all still very hush-hush."

"A public defender? But he has dozens of attorneys on retainer for his businesses. Surely one of them would be better than a public defender."

"Ms. Lawrence . . ."

"Please, call me Avery. You and my mom have been friends since you were in Girl Scouts together." I slapped my hand to my forehead. "Oh my God, Mom and Dad, you can't tell them about any of this. I've been dodging their calls all week, shooting them vague texts about being busy. You have to understand, my parents loved Adam like a son, and this is going to kill them. I'll have to figure out a way to break the news."

"Of course. Now, Avery, about the public defender, I don't know how to put this delicately, but"—she leaned forward, her expression full of compassion—"Adam is completely insolvent."

"Insolvent?" I repeated back to her.

"Broke. Bankrupt. He doesn't have a cent to his name," she said, shaking her head.

No, that didn't make any sense at all. "What are you talking about? Our apartment? Our Hamptons house? Our cars? Accounts?"

"All of it's been leveraged to the hilt. You see, Adam's been running this scam for a long time now. As soon as complaints start to pile up against one call center, he closes shop and opens a new one, leveraging his assets until the new business becomes profitable. It's how he's been able to run the game as long as he has. But you can't outrun the feds forever. He owes millions on leases and unpaid salaries. Anything in his name *or names* will go to pay his debts, and then of course his victims. All his assets are frozen. Bank accounts, credit cards, anything liquid."

My stomach dropped like an anchor off a cliff, and my eyes instinctively flashed down to my ring. The night I got home from jail, I'd slid it out of the cup on the nightstand and slipped it back on, wrapping a Band-Aid around its base to keep the band from falling off. It was like having a piece of Adam with me, and I clung to it like I did the hope that this had all been a mistake. "What about . . . ?"

"The law's very clear that an engagement ring is viewed as a gift. Had it been found among Adam's possessions, it would have been included as an asset and used to dispense one of his debts. But, since he proposed, it's yours to keep."

She folded her arms into her lap and said, "I'm guessing that because of the holidays, you haven't been issued an eviction notice as of yet, but come January 2, when offices reopen, you'll be given thirty days before the feds seize the New York City apartment, the Hamptons house, and everything and anything of value inside of both."

"Thirty days? One month to pack up my whole life?" The office suddenly swelled with heat, and I pinched at the collar of my sweater and rapidly plumed it like a makeshift fan in the hope it would create enough of a breeze for me to not pass out.

Mrs. Webber cleared her throat as she rose from her chair and moved across the room to a bar cart situated by an impressive book-shelf. Despite the fact it was only 11:00 a.m., she poured a nondescript amber-colored spirit from a fancy crystal bottle, the trickle of the liquid splashing into the tumbler the only noise in the room aside from the gentle hum of the central heat.

Grabbing a coaster, she set both on her desk, nudging them gently in my direction. "I know this is a lot to digest, Avery, but I have to ask, do you have any money in your name alone? A place to go?"

Before I could stop myself, I threw the glass back, all down the hatch in one gulp, the aromatic scotch hitting my nose and throat like a scorpion's sting. The burning sensation forced me to cough uncontrollably, tears springing to my eyes until I could catch my breath. Mrs. Webber's eyebrows popped up into her hairline and her mouth into a round O of surprise.

She drew the glass away from me and set it back on the bar cart as I answered. "Before I met Adam, I was barely making ends meet as an actress. We traveled so much, and then Adam got me involved with different charities, and . . . I . . ." I let out a breath I didn't even know I was holding and admitted the embarrassing truth of my situation. "No, I don't have much money of my own. Not anymore."

Mrs. Webber pressed her lips together and nodded as she made her way back around her desk and took a seat. "That ring might just be your saving grace then. Now"—she pulled a thin file from a pile on her desk—"let's talk about the charges against you." She used her pointer finger to skim down the long yellow sheet she shimmied out. She arched her right eyebrow. "Assaulting an officer?"

"I waved a towel in his face," I explained, ashamed by the behavior.

"A charge for assault on an officer is a class C felony. The maximum penalties include up to five thousand dollars in fines and up to five years' jail time."

"I could go back to jail?!"

She held up her hand. "Your record's clean. The DA's willing to drop the charges assuming you're willing to cooperate in the case should they need you to. Let's be real, you're not the fish they're after."

"Is Adam the fish?" I asked, even though I already knew the answer.

She slammed my folder shut. "Adam's the whole damn whale."

I nodded, pushed up from my chair, and grabbed my coat off the back of it. "Thank you. For everything. I'm not sure how I'm going to pay you for your time, but I'll figure something out."

"Of course. I'll contact you as soon as I hear from the DA."

"And Mom?"

She held three fingers up in the air. "I won't say a thing, Girl Scout's honor. I can't anyway, attorney-client privilege," she said with a wink before softening her eyes. "I know none of this is easy. I'm sure you feel like you got hit with a wrecking ball."

"If I'm being honest, the only thing I feel right now is numb."

Chapter Seven

I left Mrs. Webber's office in a daze and walked aimlessly, passing block after block, neighborhood after neighborhood, and before I knew it, found myself shuffling through the crowds in Midtown. I looked down at my hand, the four-carat Asscher-cut diamond glistening in the bright sunlight, and realized I wasn't too far from the Diamond District.

I turned up Forty-Seventh Street and walked toward Sixth Avenue, ducking into the first shop I passed. A saleswoman buzzed me into the store and held up her hand, letting me know she was just about finished helping another customer. I nodded and leaned over the glass case displaying sparkling wedding bands inside.

"The third one from the left would look spectacular next to your engagement ring," the saleswoman said as she approached. "Do you want to try it on?" Before I could even answer, she'd already unlocked the case and set the tray down on the counter in front of me. "Go ahead," she urged.

I slid the wedding band on my finger and held up my hand to admire the pair of rings under the light, side by side. What was I doing? *Wake up, Avery. You aren't getting married, not anymore.*

"Perfection, no?" she said.

I swallowed past the lump that had risen up in my throat and handed the wedding band back to her. "It's very beautiful."

"And I can give you a great deal on it if you're willing to take the floor sample. We'll polish it up like new. You'd never know the difference, but it'll save you thousands," she said in a hushed tone.

"I'm not shopping for a wedding band today."

"Sorry, I just assumed. Well, we have some beautiful pendants and some lovely holiday sets marked down. If you can pay all cash, I can take twenty percent off."

"Actually, I was wondering if someone could appraise something for me?"

"My father does the official insurance appraisals, and I'm afraid he's not in today."

"I don't need an official appraisal. I just wanted to get a general sense of my engagement ring's value."

The saleswoman narrowed her gaze. "Sure, I can give you a ballpark idea."

I twisted the ring off my finger, quickly peeled off the Band-Aid, and placed it down in the black velvet box on the display counter. The saleswoman pinched it between her fingers and held the band out in front of her. She lifted the loupe dangling from a gold chain around her neck to her eye and brought the diamond closer for inspection, twisting it in all different directions under the ceiling lights.

"Hmm." She sighed.

"What is it?"

The saleswoman motioned to another salesperson working the floor. "Michael, can you come take a look at this?" Michael set down a stack of invoices he'd been organizing and joined us. "This customer's asking for a ballpark appraisal of her engagement ring," she said, passing him the loupe.

He lifted up the ring and held it close to the magnifying lens. "Fugazi!" he cried, setting both items down on the counter.

I looked over at them both. "Sorry fu . . . what?"

"Fugazi. Fake. Your stone's a fake," Michael said matter-of-factly.

43

My stomach bottomed out. "My ring's a fake?"

The saleswoman stepped forward. "The band's genuine platinum, and the two baguettes are real, about a half carat each and of nice quality, but the center stone's a CZ, a cubic zirconia."

"A fugazi!" Michael shouted, his volume garnering a curious glance from a young couple on the other side of the store.

I leaned in close, hoping to God he would lower his voice and pleaded, "No, that can't be right. Look again."

"Honey, I can look till the cows come home and that stone will still be fake with a capital *F*." The saleswoman leaned over the counter. "If you ask me, you just dodged a bullet there. A man who'd propose with a fugazi has a whole closet full of skeletons, am I right?"

Closet? More like a whole Upper East Side classic six!

She pulled out a small calculator from her back pocket and quickly punched at a few of the keys as she spoke. "If you want to be rid of the ring, though, I can offer you 6K in cash right now."

Did she say sixty?! That's it?!

"I'm sorry, sixty thousand?! That's all the ring's worth?" I asked, recalling Adam's comment about how the ring had cost more than the down payment for our apartment.

The saleswoman laughed. "Sixty?! Oh lord no, honey, I said six-*k* not six-*ty*. And that's only because it's the holidays and I'm feeling a bit generous. If you took it to those crooks down the street, they wouldn't give you more than five. So, what do you say?"

I hugged my left hand close to my heart and was dizzy with a mixture of hurt and hopelessness. I did some quick math in my head. Moving? First and last month's rent on a new apartment? My one credit card? Food? I hadn't even left the store and the money was already spent.

I couldn't believe I'd allowed myself to be blinded by a fugazi—a very shiny, dazzling, expensive *fake*—and I wasn't just talking about the diamond now.

"In light of this new, um, information, I guess I'm not quite sure what I want to do with it just yet."

"Suit yourself," the saleswoman said, "but when you dump the bum, come back. We'll take the baguettes and turn them into a killer pair of earrings."

I slapped my hand over my mouth and scanned the street outside the jewelry store, looking for the nearest trash can. Fighting my way through the window-shopping crowds up and down Fifth Avenue, I made it to the bin just in time. After throwing up the water and scotch from earlier, I dry-heaved a few more times until my stomach was empty.

I had nothing. Nothing left inside me. Nothing at all. No apartment. No money. No security. No Adam. In thirty days, I'd be homeless.

Staying with my parents in Connecticut wasn't an option, not really. Their small antiques shop hadn't turned a profit in the last several years, and being so close to retirement age, they were getting ready to sell and buy that RV they'd always dreamed of and head down to Destin, Florida, a bucket-list item Mom had been blabbing on about for the entirety of my life. I couldn't burden them with this.

No, this was my problem to solve. I got myself into it, and I needed to figure out a way to get myself the hell out. The question was how? I slid down the side of the trash can and put my head between my legs, hoping to slow my heartbeat back to a normal rhythm. A woman pushing a stroller stopped in her tracks to check on me.

"Are you okay? Do you need some help?" she asked.

I looked up. "I'm fine. Just a little nauseous."

"Here," she said, handing me some wet wipes from inside her diaper bag. "You have a little something on your . . ." She motioned to her own chin.

I graciously took them and dabbed at my mouth, balling the towelettes in my hand when I was finished. "Thank you," I managed. "That was very kind of you to stop to check on me. I think I'll be okay now." I looked from her to her round-faced toddler bundled to the hilt, only his bright-blue eyes and rosy cheeks visible from under his hat and scarf. He cooed at me and waved excitedly, and amazingly, it brought a smile to my face.

The woman glanced up and down the street, her expression more serious. "If you're sure you're all right, you might want to relocate when you're feeling up to it. These streets are going to be wild soon. I mean, even crazier than they are now."

I pushed up from the ground using the garbage can to steady myself and patted my wet lashes with the balled-up wipes. "Why, what's happening?"

She looked at me like I was from a different planet. "New Year's Eve? Times Square? It's just a few blocks from here."

New Year's Eve? Tonight? How had I not realized? It was just Christmas, wasn't it? Had it really been a whole week since my world fell apart?

"Right. Yes. Of course. New Year's Eve," I confirmed.

The woman narrowed her eyes. "Are you sure you're really okay?"

"I am or at least, I will be, I hope."

She looked at me skeptically, but said, "Okay, well good luck then." Her voice changed to a singsong tone and she said, "Wyatt, tell the lady 'Happy New Year.'"

Wyatt babbled something that sounded like, "Habab Nef Yah," and waved enthusiastically as she pushed the stroller back into the steady stream of people.

Nowhere to go and no one to celebrate with, against my better judgment, I meandered in the direction of Times Square and the New Year's Eve ball, weaving aimlessly between the blue barricades that lined the city streets and the masses of celebrants. Around me thousands of strangers were ready to pop champagne and ring in the new year with wishes for a fresh start and renewed hope.

The square hummed with an energy of collective excitement in anticipation of the ball dropping, marking the closing of one chapter and the start of a whole new story. And though I tried my damnedest to figure out what my own story might be, I was coming up empty.

A couple toasting with a magnum of Veuve Clicquot bumped up against me in the crowd, the champagne bouncing out of their plastic flutes and splattering all over my coat, pants, and shoes.

The very intoxicated woman covered the top of her glass with her hand and said, "Your suede boots! I am so sorry!"

"Maybe take it easy with the bubbly, Laur?" the man joked to his girlfriend before turning to me. "My apologies, we probably should've packed more than just a liquid dinner."

"Don't worry about it. It's fine," I said, wiping the drips off my jacket.

"Hey, would you mind weighing in on something for us?" he asked.

"Me?"

"We've been talking about New Year's resolutions, and my girl-friend thinks giving up watching reality TV's a good one, but I think that's more like something you give up for Lent. New Year's resolutions should be more significant than that, right?"

"That *is* significant. I love *Love Island*," the woman slurred.

The man rolled his eyes at her. "If you don't mind sharing, what's yours?" he asked me.

"My New Year's resolution?"

A week ago, my future looked so different, full of promises of for-ever. But standing here in the middle of Times Square with a mil-lion strangers under the bright lights of Broadway—the ones I once believed myself to be destined for but had all but abandoned—I had never felt more alone. Like Dorothy, swirling around me was a Kansas-style twister, and in the whirling cyclone I could see the faint flashes of the girl who came to New York City with a singular goal, to make it on the Great White Way. Then came the flood of memories of the acting workshops at Tisch that once invigorated my creative soul and drove me forward with every challenge. That is until the epic failure of my senior showcase and a wasteland of fruitless auditions robbed me of my confidence.

Each rejection and failure was the hacking of an axe, one chop at a time against the trunk of a mighty oak. After enough blows, that sucker *will* come crashing down—*did* come crashing down—and it was just easier to be whisked away by Adam into a life that didn't feel so punishing and insurmountable. He helped build my confidence back up in a whole different way, and I told myself I no longer needed the stage. But that was a lie too. Like the engagement ring—the one that winked up at me from the Tiffany-blue box—I could see now my life was nothing more than a cheap imitation of what it could have been.

Amid the storm of questions and missed opportunities, I stood in the center, the eye of the hurricane, until my vision refocused on the sea of strangers around me, all out in droves to celebrate the promise of new beginnings as I questioned the loss of so many things: my home, my relationship, my career, but most of all, myself.

How was I supposed to think about resolutions for a happy future with so much unresolved in my past and present? In the twinkling glow of the New Year's Eve ball, one thing became painfully clear: I would never be able to move forward, not until I got some answers. And I knew that quest for understanding would have to start with Adam.

"My New Year's resolution?" I repeated, scanning Times Square and taking in the colorful, well-lit Broadway billboards. "To confront the Wizard head-on and make my way back home again."

Chapter Eight

I approached the prison's visitors' gate weighed down by an arresting anxiety that made it feel like my skin was trying to jump off my body, and extended my shaking hand to offer the guard an ID. Two weeks after New Year's, Adam's public defender finally sent word she'd cleared my visit. After learning she typically juggled over seventy cases and defendants at any given time, I wasn't convinced she'd actually done it. Relief washed over me when the guard handed me back my license, checked my name off the list, and nodded me into the building. Once inside, I was directed to empty my pockets and step through a metal detector. After two steps forward, the machine let out a loud and resounding *beeeeeeep*. I reached into my pants and turned the pockets inside out. Empty.

"It's probably the underwire in your bra," the female guard said. "Come this way."

I stepped to the side of the line while she waved the metal detecting wand across my body. It chirped a few times as she passed it over my shoulders and chest. She patted both sides with the back of her hand and, once satisfied I wasn't trying to smuggle in a phone or weapon, ushered me into the visiting area lined with crumbling walls and rows of old vending machines.

I made my way over to a cold orange plastic chair like one you'd see in an elementary school cafeteria, as far from the other visitors as I could, and rested my forehead in my hands, second-guessing my decision to come at all. Actions spoke louder than words, didn't they? And I should have known everything I needed to know based on his very, very, *verrrrrry* long list of criminal charges. But, what was still missing for me was the why. Why had he done it? How far back did his misdeeds go? How long had I been blind to his lies? And was any of what we had together even real? Those were the questions that kept me up at night, haunting me like a veiled apparition. They were the questions that forced me to come.

In the far corner of the room, there was a small wilting Christmas tree left over from the holidays. It still had a few handfuls of glittery tinsel sprinkled over the top of it and was sitting underneath a wall of ornate service plaques commemorating honorable service to the prison over the years. I scanned the images, coming to an abrupt halt on the third one from the left.

I walked over to get a closer look, and there staring down at me was the guard who directed me to the phone booth on Christmas Day. Same finger-waved hair. Same round-faced grin, and the name *Mabel Jacobs* and the years *1908–1969* etched below her photograph. *No, that couldn't be.* Mabel Jacobs had been dead for more than fifty years, but the guard I spoke to that day was very much alive—and apparently dispensing terrible advice to strangers. Maybe they just shared an uncanny resemblance to one another? Or were they possibly related?

As much as I tried to put the odd coincidence out of my mind, my thoughts kept returning to Mabel and the last phone booth. The strange directions she offered that took me to Gabe and not a taxi stand. The fact that the guard had disappeared when I went back to find her. None of it made any sense, and my wheels were spinning out of control. Before I knew it, almost an hour later and still lost in thought, a sharp poke to my right shoulder startled me back to the moment. "Hey, you Avery Lawrence?" a guard barked.

I glanced at the clock, noticing how long I'd been waiting, and sprang upright. "Yes, I'm she . . . her. I'm Avery Lawrence."

"Follow me," he ordered.

I trailed the guard down a dark hallway with weak fluorescent lights overhead that flickered as we walked. It was cold and damp, and I clenched my jaw to stop my teeth from chattering.

"Who are you here to see?" the guard asked.

"Adam Daulton, I mean Adam McDaniels," I answered, still not used to saying his real name.

"Real Scrooge, that one. My aunt Belle lost about 10K out of her retirement savings in one of his telemarketing schemes, greedy bastard," he said and directed me to a table with thick plexiglass partitions. I spotted Adam, who looked small and spindly next to the hulking security guard whose uniform hugged him so tightly in the middle that the buttons seemed to be holding on for dear life.

The orange of Adam's jumpsuit stood out against the whiteness of the walls and the light blue of the officer's uniform, like something that didn't belong, didn't quite fit into the landscape. Adam kept his head lowered as he approached, and I wasn't even sure if he knew it was me who was here to visit. On impulse, I lurched forward to go to him, but then reason and the thick plastic that separated us kept me rooted in place. He sat down, the partition firmly between our chairs, and took the moment of silence as an invitation to speak. "Avery, you look so beautiful."

That was certainly not the first thing I thought he'd say. It was a punch to the gut, and my stomach twisted with its force. My eyes lifted to his, tears pooling at the rims and threatening to fall. The tightness in my chest was a boa constrictor around my lungs hoping to squeeze out all signs of life.

Adam looked almost swallowed whole by the state-issued jumpsuit, a far departure from his custom-tailored Tom Ford suits. I was so used to his calm, cool, and in-control demeanor that seeing him like this completely threw me for a loop. It felt like an eternity before I finally found my voice. "Who even are you? What's your name? Your *real* name?"

It was Adam's turn to fall silent and lower his eyes. Thick waves of shame radiated off him, and all he could do was shake his head. "Please, Avery, listen to me. This has all been a misunderstanding. I swear to God, I didn't do what they're saying I did. I can show you, if I could just get in touch with—"

"Stop lying, Adam McDaniels, or whoever the hell you're choosing to be today." My trembling voice came out louder than expected. "I know about the innocent and vulnerable people you defrauded. And now I know I was one of them. One of the hundreds of people you duped with your smooth words and charming smile."

I slammed the back of my left hand against the glass, the ring clinking as it hit. "I had this appraised. And do you know what they told me?" I stared him down, the force of my words concealing the warble of hurt and devastation at the sheer depth of his deceptions. "I have a feeling you do?" He lifted his face to look at me, and my insides turned cold. I'd been ready to collapse under the weight of his remorse, but having him sit there and attempt to lie made me acutely aware of how comfortable he'd become with the entire practice. Like it was second nature.

He sat up straighter and leaned forward, his eyes, his posture, and his long face begging for compassion. "Avery, please, you have to understand, that stone was a placeholder. The baguettes are real, the band is real, but the diamond . . ." He went to muss his hair and seemed surprised when the other hand came up too, bound together by the weighty handcuffs. "The diamond *had been* real. I had one picked out and everything. And at the last minute, I . . . I needed the capital to fund . . . well, to help continue the business. But I swear, I had every intention of replacing the stone with the diamond I'd first chosen just as soon as the new venture was off the ground and on its feet. You have to believe me," Adam pleaded, his face moving so close to the partition that with every iteration, his breath fogged up the plexiglass a bit more.

"Do I, Adam? Do I have to believe you? How could I? It's not about the diamond or the ring. I don't care about any of that. It's about what that ring represented. But no, every single thing you've ever said to me has been a lie or a version of the truth, always more gray than black-and-white. I just don't understand how I could have been so wrong. Don't you see? I chose you. Instead of . . ."

Adam shifted his weight uncomfortably in his seat, and his brows furrowed as he glared at me. "Don't put that on me. You chose to give up whatever dregs were left of your acting dream. I never asked you to. I offered you a reprieve from your life, and you accepted it with open arms and never looked back."

When I finally agreed to go on a date with Adam almost a year after my breakup with Gabe, I was barely scraping by, auditioning by day and waitressing at night . . . and the fact he had money did make things easier. But it wasn't the reason I fell in love with him. I'd never met anyone like Adam before, so persistent, self-assured, and effervescent. He was charming and most of all, he was fun. He looked at life through rose-colored glasses, and when I was with him I did too. I'll admit my confidence in my acting career had taken so many hits back then it was nice to step away for a while, but I never planned to stay away forever.

With each failed callback and the fading hope this dream would ever really come to fruition, I convinced myself I could find a different source of happiness and fulfillment and decided to go all in with Adam. And sure, maybe there had been some red flags I'd dismissed over the years. Things that didn't quite make sense about our life. But I'd chalked it up to simply not understanding what it was that he did for a living, even though he'd explained it vaguely to me a dozen times. And was it worth rocking the boat on our nearly perfect relationship for what could have all been a simple misunderstanding? The answer, every time a new doubt would creep in, was always a resounding no.

The realization settled like a stone in my chest, and it took me almost a full minute to find my voice. "You're right. I did accept all of it because I loved you, and I trusted you, and you played me for a fool."

Adam remained quiet, maybe trying to strategize his next play, or perhaps he was simply out of moves. When he finally spoke, all he could manage was, "No, the love I felt . . . feel for you was always real, even if the rest wasn't." Now it was his turn to stare at me through tear-rimmed eyes.

I glared back, daring him to claim he loved me again. Clearly, he wouldn't know love if it poked him in the eye. Between the uncomfortable truth and my vicious glare, Adam remained silent. My ears grew hot, and looking at his pathetic face only made me more irate. "No! Deceit and manipulation, those things don't equal love, Adam, they equal greed. You put value in all the wrong things and now, you have nothing."

I stood up, securing my purse on my shoulder and pushing back from the table, the chair legs scratching loudly against the linoleum floor.

Adam jumped to his feet, knocking his chair to the ground. "Avery, no, please don't go!"

The guard quickly hollered, "McDaniels! Calm yourself down or visitation's over."

I backed away from the partition, indicating I would not be rejoining Adam at the table. "No, sir, it's okay. Visitation *is* over." I looked straight at Adam, who was still standing with his hands locked in front of him, his feet shackled together at the ankles. "Goodbye, Adam, and happy New Year."

I hurried through the iron gates out onto the sidewalk, the brisk breeze a welcome change from the stale recycled heat inside the prison. As I filled my lungs with the fresh air, my chest inflated like a balloon, my posture straightening and vision sharpening with the deep inhalation. I somehow felt lighter, freer, and before I even could register what I was doing, I slipped the fugazi off my finger and tucked it into a zippered coin purse in my bag, a literal and figurative weight now lifted. I'd make an appointment to sell the ring this weekend and use the money to start over. It might not have been as much as I thought or hoped for, but I felt lucky to have it at all.

The same thin older security guard who had so kindly given me his MetroCard after my Gabe debacle on Christmas spotted me on the street corner and stepped out of the booth to yell over to me. "Hey, didn't I direct you to the subway a few weeks ago? Hope you haven't been looking for the station this whole time?" He chuckled at his own joke as he approached.

"Oh, ha ha, no. Got home safe and sound thanks to your generosity that night," I said. "Just back here . . . visiting . . . actually, saying goodbye to someone."

"That's nice. Well, now that your visit's over, do you need me to call you a cab?"

"Um . . ." I chewed on my bottom lip as I thought. "Actually, I'm not too sure where I'm going at the moment."

"Gotta be honest, not sure any of us really do," he offered with a comforting smile. "Sometimes when I'm not sure which direction to go, I think about what I was doing the last time I was happy and try to do some more of that. For instance, yesterday after a tough morning at work, I took a stroll to the park with my grandson . . . turned my whole day right around."

The last place I remembered being genuinely happy? It only took a second, but as soon as it popped into my head, I felt a warmth spread deep in my core and roll in waves through my limbs.

"On second thought, sir, I think I will take that cab."

Chapter Nine

As soon as the taxi pulled into the heart of Times Square, the familiar illuminated sign of Mimi's Shooting Star Diner triggered a torrent of nostalgia so vivid, I could have sworn I'd stepped back in time to a decade earlier when I was a frazzled undergrad hurrying from music theory class to work a pre-matinee shift. Back then, I reasoned that the education I was getting at Mimi's alongside my fellow waitstaff, all of whom had dreams that rivaled my own in making it to Broadway, offered me just as much as my course load at NYU.

Somewhere between singing show tunes for tips, the impromptu duets with my fellow servers, and the steadfast belief we all held that some well-known producer would wander in and offer one of us a role in their next musical, we became a kind of family. Those walls held a lot of hope and a lot of heartache, and I remembered how my pulse would accelerate at the anticipation of not knowing which one would greet me on any given day. But really it didn't matter, we had each other's backs either way. After five years and somewhere over fifteen hundred shifts, the diner became like home to me, and standing here now, it was as if I'd clicked my heels three times and recited Glinda's famous mantra.

Stepping inside and scanning the dining room, I was relieved to see little had changed. The kitschy 1950s decor, the twinkling lights that practically covered the whole ceiling, the large platform-like stage smack in the middle of all the booths and tables. Three servers, none of whom

I recognized, were standing under the center spotlight belting out "One Day More" from *Les Misérables*, doing their best to cover every single part. Even though their Jean Valjean was nothing to write home about, it didn't matter; the crowd ate up the performance, just like always.

I waited for the thunderous applause to die down and went to the hostess stand to see if they had any seats available at the counter.

"First come, first serve. Take any spot that's open. Should be plenty, the matinee crowd just left," the hostess said, gesturing to a few empty spaces.

I snagged an open seat between two couples enjoying their lunches and a performance of "Mr. Cellophane" from *Chicago* and shrugged out of my coat as the server approached to take my order.

"What can I get for you?" she asked.

"Just some coffee."

"We have a Starlight Espresso, a Phantom of the Mocha, an Americano in Paris," she said, rattling off a list of Broadway-themed drinks.

"You don't have just coffee? There used to just be coffee."

"Closest thing I can offer you is a Do-Re-Misto."

I nodded. "Sure, sounds great."

A few minutes later, she set the steaming drink down in front of me. I checked around for the sugar canister, but seeing none attempted to borrow some from the couple to my right, but they were so *razzle-dazzled* by the spectacle, I couldn't seem to get their attention.

I pushed up from the counter and leaned all the way forward. "Hey, excuse me, can I get some sugar for my coffee?"

The server whizzed by me to drop off a Don't Cry for Me Margherita pizza to another patron, completely ignoring my request. I called out to the other server behind the counter, his back to me as he ran a credit card through at the register.

"'Scuse me, can I get some sugar, please?" I repeated.

"Sure, here, no problem," he said, spinning on his heels and setting the dispenser down beside my cup.

I could hardly believe my eyes. "Charlie?"

The man in front of me stood about a head taller than I remembered, sporting a clean, short haircut, so different from the floppy-haired young guy I worked with almost ten years earlier. Charlie's face, once soft and cherubic, now had the chiseled features of a man, from his structured chin to his hollowed cheekbones. The only feature unchanged were his deep-set warm cornflower-blue eyes. He was simultaneously the guy I closed the diner with every weekend and one I barely knew anymore. My eyes widened to take him in. No question, he was still startlingly good-looking, like a professional headshot come to life.

We used to be pretty good friends. We'd psych each other up for upcoming auditions and then talk each other down after our numerous rejections. We'd help each other rehearse the small two-bit roles we'd occasionally land, spending late-night hours after Mimi's closed reading lines back and forth over slices of whatever pie of the day we had left over. There was never anything romantic between us beyond some fun flirtation and showstopping duets. It was just nice to have a work buddy who really understood what it was like trying to make it as an actor in New York.

When he saw me, his mouth dropped open. His deep voice startled me from my gawking. "My God," he sighed, "BrAvery Lawrence, is that you?!"

I'd completely forgotten the nickname he'd anointed me with after a particularly saucy rendition of "Big Spender" from *Sweet Charity* that had a group of buttoned-up businessmen losing their minds. Man, I made some good tips that night.

"You still work here?" I threw my hands over my mouth. "Oh my God, I'm so sorry, I didn't mean for that to come out as rudely as it did. I'm just surprised to see you."

He chuckled and nodded. "Yeah, still here. I am the manager though now, so you know, livin' the dream. And what about you? Off touring with the Royal Shakespeare Company doing proper th-ee-ehh-ter?" he asked in a mocking British accent.

"Not quite, more like looking for a job. And though I'm a little out of practice, I swear I still have some juice left in these pipes," I said, even though I wasn't quite sure that was true. It'd been more than a hot minute since I'd taken 'em for a real test drive, so I was hoping that, if called to it, muscle memory would kick in and I would be able to squeak out a passable rendition of something.

"I have no doubt. You were one of the few servers who could hit a high E above middle C." Charlie slowly put his receipt book down by the register, dusted off his hands, and extended an open palm toward me, his eyebrows helping to communicate the invitation. "You know, we *do* have an opening . . ."

Mimi's always had an opening. The waitstaff was exclusively made up of wide-eyed actors who'd come to New York in hopes of getting their big break, but instead would wind up having to wait tables to make ends meet between auditions. Eventually, though, a part or national tour would come along, and off they'd go, leaving a spot to be filled by the next young hopeful.

"So? How 'bout an audition?" Charlie asked and again thrust his open hand forward toward me.

I looked around, still unsure of what he wanted me to do with it. "Wait, what? Like right now? I'm not warmed up! In fact, I'm ice cold, you know, not having sung basically anything outside of the shower in the past few years."

He dismissed my concern with a wave of his still proffered hand. "Like riding a bike. I'll take it easy on you. No high Es above middle C. Not until you're ready, I promise."

Before I could protest any further, the familiar chords of *Grease*'s "You're the One That I Want" erupted through the space. My heart constricted both at the song choice drumming up memories of Adam and our spectacular engagement and the fact that Charlie was pulling me up onto the counter to sing for the first time in forever.

"C'mon, Sandra Dee, you got this. It was our song, remember?" he said, handing me a mic and a light-pink satin jacket.

He opened up the song with Danny Zuko's first lines, and I was initially worried I wouldn't remember all of the words. But as soon as he started to sing, looking at me with a handsome smile and gyrating hips, I burst into giggles and let my inhibitions fall away. When we got to the chorus, as if rehearsed, we both crooked our thumbs in our belt loops and did the iconic shuffle, complete with a little hop on the word *honey*, just like John and Olivia. It was amazing how naturally it all came flooding back: the moves, the singing, and most of all the rush of adrenaline I felt every time I'd ever stepped onstage.

By the end of the song, the room was on its feet clapping and singing right along with us, even demanding an encore performance.

Charlie squeezed my hand as we took our bows. "Well, BrAvery Lawrence, it looks like you're hired."

I stepped out of the diner and into the hustle and bustle of rush hour. Considering it was mid-January, it was one of those unexpectedly warm winter days that, even if just momentarily, reminds you spring is some-where on the horizon. I decided to walk home instead of taking the subway, figuring I could take advantage of the nice weather and get in some steps. Once Adam had hired a driver, we'd hardly ever walked, always opting to be dropped at the door of our next destination. I'd forgotten how much you can miss in New York when you aren't a part of its rhythm. It was the difference between merely appreciating a song on the radio and playing live at Madison Square Garden, your fingers tightly wrapped around the bass.

I blended into the crowd of tourists and commuters and let myself be carried along with them down the packed sidewalks, appreciating the shops, sights, and smells. I'd never grow tired of the scent of candied cashews from the Nuts4Nuts vendors perched at every corner. My stomach grumbled as the sweet aroma drifted up my nose and straight into my belly, causing me to immediately make a U-turn to buy a bag. I dug around my pocket for some change and handed the vendor four quarters.

"It's three dollars a bag, hon," he deadpanned.

"Sorry. Just give me one sec." I set my tote down, unpacked my new phone (my old one was still sitting and collecting dust in an evidence box in a precinct somewhere) and my makeup bag on the sidewalk, and fished around for another few bucks. "Here you go," I said, reaching up to hand him two singles.

He passed me the warm bag of nuts as I brushed off my knees. I stuffed my makeup bag back into the tote and picked up my phone from the ground, noticing its screen illuminated with a text message notification.

Our place at 10:00.—G.

With everything that had happened these last couple of weeks, I'd managed to push the strange encounter with Gabe on Christmas out of my mind, unsure my fragile heart could handle anything beyond that one chance meeting.

But intrigued, I read over the text again. *Our place.* A sense of overwhelming wistfulness slammed into me at the familiarity of Gabe's words. My breath caught in my throat, and, hands trembling, I couldn't suppress my curiosity at being revisited by this ghost from my past and promptly typed back, See you there.

Chapter Ten

Before our bizarre Christmas encounter, Gabe and I hadn't spoken in close to seven years, our last exchange taking place at the very same café where I sat waiting for him now. After almost five years together, our relationship hit an iceberg of *Titanic* proportions, and we called it quits the morning after what had been the most important callback audition of my career—one I completely blew, one that cost me more than just the part: it cost me everything.

At twenty-three years old, I'd only ever known the Gershwin Theatre to be the forever home of one of Broadway's most celebrated and Tony-clad shows: *Wicked*. Even though I hadn't managed to secure an agent post-graduation, I was lucky enough to secure an audition after dazzling the show's musical director (unbeknownst to me at the time) while belting my way through a rendition of "Defying Gravity" for a pre-matinee crowd at Mimi's.

After moving through the first several rounds of the rigorous process, the final audition for the national tour was down to me and only three others for the lead role of Elphaba. It was the closest I'd ever gotten . . . and without representation, likely would get. I'd tried like hell to dismiss the negative self-talk and the niggling anxiety I always battled when I stepped in front of a panel of producers and directors, but standing and waiting in the wings for my turn, flashes of me choking at Tisch's senior talent showcase and botching every subsequent audition bloomed from a small bud to an invasive weed that creeped and crawled through the fertile soil of my mind. Sweat prickled on my palms, and I wiped them down the flowing black cape I'd brought with me to wear for my big number.

Right before it was my turn to go on, one of the techs walked me through the mechanics of how the flying lift for "Defying Gravity" worked one final time.

"It's pretty simple. When you're ready to go up, just step back and onto the platform, evenly distributing your weight on both sides. The safety latch will lock, and off you'll go," he said as he checked the seat belt–like contraption that was meant to snap closed as soon as I followed his instruction.

I nodded to him that I understood and waited for the swell of the orchestra to cue the big moment. But as soon as the time approached for me to join in the song where I would need to take in the deepest breath I could, nerves caused me to shift my weight a little too quickly, and the mechanism snapped shut around my middle before I was ready, snatching from me the long pull of air I'd just drawn into my diaphragm.

Instead of a beautiful long E at the end of the word "*Meeeeeeeee*" as I soared through the air, the jarring jolt produced more of an "*Ooooooo!*" that, paired with the jerk of the belt, created a sound more like a cow would make than the triumphant declaration of the show's verdant heroine. The image of me dangling in the air mooing at a panel of Broadway's elite still haunts me to this day, the expression of horror and embarrassment on the musical director's face like a GIF that plays on a loop in my brain.

After that, like the Wicked Witch of the West, I pretty much melted down, never quite recovering—in (or from) that audition or how much it damaged my confidence.

As soon as I took my final bow and offered a quick "thanks" to the panel, I raced backstage eager to get out of that room, out of that theater, and as far away from my epic failure as I could. Tears of frustration streamed down my face as I tightened my grip on my small duffel and maneuvered through Times Square toward the subway and back home. I tried to call Gabe, in need of a supportive voice or word of comfort, but instead, it just continued to click over to voice mail, indicative of him silencing my call. *Seriously? He knows how important today is. Is he really too busy to even pick up and see how it went?*

Jamming my phone back into my pocket, I slipped in my AirPods, hoping to drown out the world, and the noise, and all of New York for just a minute. *How could I have blown it so damn bad?!* The echo of my lowing "moo" reverberated in my mind, causing me to physically shudder in spite of the warm summer air. My senior showcase. Every single audition since. Was it self-sabotage?! Didn't I always know that auditioning is a key part of life as an actress?! In spite of the number of hours I spent preparing, the number of times I'd put myself out there, it wasn't getting any easier, and I didn't seem to be getting any better.

This was supposed to be it. My big break, my one chance! And after my parents scraped by to help me pay for NYU, and all the years I'd dedicated to honing my craft, maybe I just didn't have what it takes. Maybe I just wasn't cut out for it? I was really something in No-Name, Connecticut, but as for the Big Apple, I wasn't hacking it. There was a reason people believed if you could make it there you could make it anywhere, right? Sinatra never bothered to sing about what happened if you couldn't. The song was called "New York, New York" after all, not "New York or Bust."

The entire way home, rocking side to side on the air-conditioned subway, I vacillated between giving myself a mental pep talk to carry on acting come hell or high water and giving myself permission to abandon it entirely, without guilt. But by the time I'd finally made it back to Gabe's apartment, nothing had been settled, and all I wanted was a hot shower and a warm, supportive hug.

I let myself in, allowing my coat and bag to slide off my shoulder to the floor, before crumbling to the ground right along with them.

Gabe, startled, covered the receiver with his hand, and looked up from his laptop. "Hey, Ave," he whispered. "You okay?" Gabe's face twisted in confusion. I could see he was still trying to pay attention to the voice on the other end of his call, while also trying to discern why I was lying in a heap on the ground. As if I wasn't fetal, he continued, "You'll never believe it, the Clintons *are* going to be able to make it to the fundraiser after all. I've been on the phone with their secret service and the venue organizing details for their security protocols all morning."

My body remained still but my eyes shifted to him, expressionless and flat. I waited another moment for a response, a question of concern, for him to check my pulse, *anything*, but instead, he swung his chair back around and spoke again into the phone's receiver as he hunched over the desk to scribble a note. In a daze and at the speed of a roving sloth, I picked my bag and coat up off the ground, hung them both up on a hook by the door, and slumped down in the seat beside him. Without so much as a glance in my direction, he pressed on, "Yes, Susan. Sounds great. Don't worry, we'll get it all sorted when I arrive. No, it's okay, I'll come over sooner so that I can take care of it, and I'll just change there . . . yup, sounds good. See you in twenty."

He closed his laptop and finally turned to face me. "Okay, I'm all yours. For the next two minutes anyway, and then I need to get over to the event space. What's going on? How was your audition?"

I expelled a sigh, hoping it would say all the things I couldn't. "I don't know where to even begin. Actually, I do. I'll begin at the part where I *mooed* at the entire casting team."

"What does that even mean? You *mooed*?"

"It means I bombed. It means I won't get this part or any other part—not today, not tomorrow, maybe not ever."

He picked up his phone and scrolled through a few emails, finally landing on the one he was looking for. "C'mon, I'm sure it wasn't as bad as all that," he said without looking up.

"No, you're right, it was worse."

He peeked up from the phone. "Exactly! It could have been worse."

"Gabe, that's not what I said."

"Sorry, I *am* trying to listen to you, I'm just . . ."

"Distracted. I know." I stared at him blankly, unable to even conceive the idea that he was so completely oblivious to what a huge deal this was to me. My voice constricted as my frustration mounted, and I did my very best to fight back the tears gathering behind my eyes. "Hey, didn't you tell Susan you'd be there in twenty? You're going to be late."

He glanced down at his watch. "Oh shoot, yeah, I need to get going. Av, I really am sorry. I promise to give you my undivided attention as soon as we get home from the fundraiser tonight. We can talk about all this later. But really, don't worry, I'm sure you'll get a final callback. It sounds like you did great!"

I opened up my mouth to rebut—*It sounds like I did great? I mooed for God's sake!*—but before I could even squeak out another syllable, he pressed a kiss to my forehead, snatched his tux from the hook on our bedroom door, and rushed out of the apartment.

"This *was* the final callback," I muttered to myself, now alone in the space where I had been hoping to find support and comfort. But like usual, he was off on his next crusade.

It took me almost a full two minutes to pull my jaw up off the floor and move from the spot where he left me. I was utterly dumbfounded. Not an ounce of empathy or sign of understanding. For what felt like at least the hundredth time over these past few months, my feelings not even a blip on his radar.

Chapter Eleven

At precisely 9:59 a.m., Gabe strode into our café clutching a black-and-white marble notebook, wearing the same green canvas crossbody bag with eclectic patches he had almost a decade ago. The punctuality, however, was a welcomed change. Before finding me in the crowd of tables, Gabe placed an order with the barista and picked up two steaming mugs after tossing a few bucks into the nearby tip jar. The barista's face lit up as she leaned over the counter to thank him, flashing a flirty smile and more than a hint of cleavage, neither of which he seemed to pay much attention to.

Gabe popped up on his toes to survey the room. Our eyes met, drawing me in like a siren song, and he made his way through the sea of people over to where I was seated. He set his bag on the ground and eased into the chair across from me.

Sliding one of the mugs over without missing a beat, he said, "Tall drip with two shots of espresso, oat milk, and one sugar."

The thoughtfulness of the gesture was one thing, but the fact that he hadn't forgotten how I took my coffee caught me completely by surprise. "Thank you. I can't believe you still know my order."

"By heart," he responded, never breaking eye contact as he took a sip. He leaned in closer to study my face, and suddenly, I forgot how to breathe. "So, Avery Lawrence," he said, chewing on his bottom lip, "I guess you weren't an apparition after all. You look beautiful, by the way. I've always loved your hair like that." He studied me as if trying to recognize someone he'd known a lifetime ago.

My fingers instinctively moved to tuck a wisp behind my ear. "Well, it's a far departure from the mess I was when I showed up at your door," I joked, inwardly cringing at the memory.

"The thing I haven't been able to work out, though, is how you knew where I lived? It's a sublet, and I only moved in a few days before," he said.

"You probably wouldn't believe me if I told you," I answered.

He raised his eyebrows, crossed his arms over his chest, and said, "Try me," his gravelly voice intensifying the challenge in his words.

Le sigh. That look. That face. With his smoldering intensity so singularly focused on me, my knees buckled even though I was sitting. His magnetism was undeniable, and I knew I would relent to whatever he asked of me, every . . . single . . . time. "It was Christmas Day, and I couldn't find a taxi to save my life. I stepped into a phone booth in search of a cab company, picked up the receiver, and it switched over to an operator who, for some reason, gave me your address instead."

He shook his head, clearly mystified. "That doesn't make any sense." He stayed quiet for a moment, lost in his own recollection. "And what's even stranger is I had just been thinking about you *literally* that very day, and then poof, there you were, standing in my doorway after almost seven years of radio silence."

I put my hands up to emphasize my own defense. "Gabe, I swear, I didn't come looking for you that night. I was just as surprised to see you standing on the other side of that door as you were to see me. I can't explain it. I wish I could. I was going to pretend like it never happened, but then you sent me that text, and I don't know, I wanted to see you again."

He grabbed for my hands and tucked them into his own. They were warm and comforting and familiar. "I wanted to see you again too," he said, his admission intoxicating.

His phone rang from inside his bag, cutting through the words he left hanging in the air between us. He let go of my hands to scramble to find it amid his notebooks and papers, but instead of answering, he quickly hit the silence button and tucked it away, before promptly turning his attention back to me.

Surprised, I couldn't help but ask, "Did you need to get that?"

"Whatever it is can wait."

Who was this person? He certainly *looked* like the same Gabe. About a head and a half taller than me, wild dark hair and that beautiful face . . . from his scruffed chin to his familiar hazel eyes fringed with thick lashes any woman would envy. But now, the tension he used to carry in his jaw and shoulders had given way to a more relaxed posture that conveyed a sense of ease he never had before. The old Gabe would have never let a work call roll to voice mail. This was brand-new territory.

"There's so much I've wanted to say to you over the years," he continued, "but you'd moved on, and I figured maybe it was all better left in the past. Then there you were on my doorstep, and I thought maybe I was being given the chance to say all the things I never did."

Though it was the last thing I expected, I couldn't keep my heart from swelling at the idea that he'd left things unsaid too, and that after all these years, we were somehow getting a chance to lay it all out on the table.

He continued, "I was a different person then. I didn't appreciate what we had, not in the way I should have. You were my best friend, and I let you walk right out of my life. I'm sorry, Avery. I was so consumed with my own ego to believe I could somehow fix the world for everyone around me, all the while hurting the one person who mattered the most in mine."

His finger crooked under my chin and gently lifted it so I could look into his eyes. His voice was soft, almost a whisper. "But don't think for a minute that I walked away completely unscathed."

Before I could exhale, he rubbed his thumb over my cheek. His expression radiated a hurt I wasn't aware I'd caused. And after the disastrous *Wicked* audition and our subsequent breakup, the last thing I ever imagined was that I'd be sitting across from him in this small café, a bistro table, two steaming coffees, and seven years of silence between us.

I stared into his apologetic eyes and could tell he was truly sorry that he hadn't appreciated our relationship more. Hearing Gabe lay out his regrets so openly had been the last thing I expected when I agreed to meet him today. Over the years, I'd managed to convince myself Gabe was fine with our breakup—one less thing to distract him from his social crusades. Now, finding out he'd been as heartbroken as I was shook me to my very core.

At the beginning of our relationship, it was Gabe's unwavering passion that drew me to him. Growing up with a single mother, always just skirting the poverty line, he committed himself to doing his best to even out the playing field for everyone else. I couldn't help but be impressed by his altruism, the same way everyone was. But there was a good reason most superheroes stayed single. Turns out, when you're all consumed with saving the world, there's very little room for much else. After all this time, I couldn't help but wonder if Batman had finally hung up his cape, or at least tucked it into the drawer?

I shifted my gaze, after realizing I'd been staring at him for a few seconds too long, and said, "So, I have to ask, you mentioned you were thinking about me on Christmas. About what, exactly?"

He flashed a grin and nodded. "Yeah, I was trimming the tree with some old ornaments in my new apartment thinking about that ridiculous hovel we shared—"

"The one in Hell's Kitchen with the bathtub in the living room! We had roaches so big we named them and almost bought them their own stockings."

"That's the one! Yeah, I was thinking about that apartment, and that first Christmas Eve we spent there. Remember, you came home with all those bags of groceries after a particularly lucrative shift at Mimi's," he reminisced.

"People couldn't seem to get enough of my Auntie Mame, and it was the holidays so maybe they were feeling extra generous." I smiled at the memory.

"We cooked a feast, remember?"

"All I remember is every time you stuck your finger in the pot to taste what was cooking, you'd yell out—"

"'It's a Christmas miracle!'" we both shouted in unison with our pointer fingers thrust toward the sky.

We laughed at the recollection, and for as much heartache and time that had passed, it didn't take long for us to fall back into our natural rhythm.

"You'll be happy to know that before I took this new apartment, I insisted that my bathtub actually be *in* my bathroom—no 'half bath' situation," he said with a wink and smile.

I clasped my hand over my mouth to stifle a laugh. "Remember how excited the super was to show it to us in that first apartment? Exclaiming something like, 'It has a half bath . . . half of the bathroom just so happens to be beside the couch. Pretty great, right?'"

He flashed a mischievously sexy grin. "It was *pretty* great."

I thought back to our Sunday night wind-down ritual. Gabe would draw a warm bubble bath, and we'd climb inside the tub with a box of pizza and a cheap bottle of pinot noir to watch *Game of Thrones*, staying curled against one another in the water through the whole episode, not even caring how much the temperature dropped over the sixty-minute show. When it was over, we'd hop out of the bath, water puddling at our feet onto the hardwood floors, and flop onto the couch wrapped up in terry-cloth towels with every intention of watching whatever show followed. But . . . we rarely made it past the opening credits before we lost the towels and then ourselves in each other.

I blushed. "Who would have thought a bathtub could actually be better than a couch? Unless you count that time we watched *Titanic*."

"Oh, right? That was a little *too* immersive of an experience. That movie clocks in at what? Close to four hours? We were the icebergs by the time it ended."

I had just taken a sip of my coffee before his retort, and it threatened to shoot out of my nose as I fought back a giggle at the memory. Once I swallowed, I added, "My favorite was when I made you hold my arms out, us naked and perched at the front of our tub, as I shouted, 'Jack, I'm flying!' We were laughing so loudly Mr. Quinta was knocking on his ceiling from below with his broom, shouting at us to turn it down."

"Oh my God, he almost put a hole through our floor with all that banging," Gabe recalled.

I held my hands up, conceding. "Okay, okay, not one of my better suggestions."

"No, it was great. You were great." His tone shifted from the light mirth into something more somber and wistful. "I'm just sorry I didn't appreciate you more."

With a thousand thoughts and memories competing for my attention, I didn't know what to say, so I remained quiet.

Gabe took my silence as a cue to continue, cupping his hands over my own. "So tell me, how are you doing? What are you doing?"

"I'm back working at Mimi's. To put it mildly, my last relationship imploded, and now I guess I'm starting over again." I lowered my eyes with embarrassment, a little overcome with emotion at having to admit the setback aloud.

Gabe reached for my chin with a finger and lifted my face to look at him. "Starting over can be a good thing."

I wasn't sure if he was talking about my last relationship now or our own. The truth was, I wasn't ready to open my heart to anyone after what happened with Adam, but Gabe wasn't just anyone . . . he was Gabe. My Gabe. The Gabe I dated for five years who always made me feel safe and loved. And unlike Adam, Gabe was a good person, had always been a good person, even in the moments when we didn't see eye to eye.

We'd met young and had competing priorities that created what, back then, felt like an insurmountable barrier. But with time and distance, maybe those deep cracks had started to spiderweb down the wall, and I couldn't help but imagine what would have been waiting for us on the other side if we hadn't given up on one another and instead, tried to break through it.

"You really think so?" I stated both as a question and plea.

He grazed his thumb along my palm, and my skin tingled at his touch. "I really do."

I smiled warmly, unsure of what this all meant. Why did the universe or phone booth (or some combination of the two) direct me to Gabe that night? It was something I still had no rational explanation for. Had it been a rare solar flare? Or maybe the Earth had tilted off its axis? Maybe I should simply chalk it up to just one more strange event in a series of strange events that day. But it was all too odd. The fact Gabe had been thinking about me? The phone operator talking about regret and making amends for life's misused opportunities?

My phone alarm sounded in my bag, and I was glad I'd set it after realizing how distracted I'd become in our conversation. "I'm sorry, I should get going. I'm meeting with a real estate broker to look for an apartment. I have to be out of mine in about two weeks," I said, standing up from our table and slinging my purse across my shoulder.

"Yes, of course. But . . ." He stood too, now peering down at me from beneath his thick lashes. "When can I see you again?"

I adjusted my bag nervously and remarked, "Um . . . I'm not too sure that leggy blonde from your apartment would like that very much."

Gabe jerked back, a look of pure confusion plastered on his face. "Wait? What leggy blonde? Who?"

"The one who answered your door on Christmas. In the Valentino."

"Oh, that was my cousin, Chelsea. She was just picking me up to go over to Marisol's for Christmas dinner. You remember Chelsea?"

"Like Aunt Deedee's Chelsea? No way. The Chelsea I remember was a thirteen-year-old with pink hair who practically lived in her One Direction T-shirt. And wait, back it up some more. Marisol? Hosting Christmas dinner? She used to think shoving a Trader Joe's frozen burrito into a toaster was cooking. Remember when she almost burned down our apartment trying to heat up the Chinese takeout because she didn't realize the aluminum containers shouldn't go in the microwave? We couldn't get the burned smell of moo goo gai pan out of the kitchen for weeks."

Gabe smiled warmly and nodded. "Months. Thankfully, she's come a long way. And actually, Christmas Day dinner has become her thing ever since she had her first—"

"Her first what?"

He looked at me quizzically. "Bonsai tree," he deadpanned. "Her first *baby*, of course. She's married with two kids now and living in Franklin Lakes."

"She's married? A mom?! New Jersey? She used to say she'd sooner die than move to the armpit of America. Her words, not mine." I held up my hands in mock defense.

He laughed and touched my arm. I was surprised by the warmth of Gabe's fingertips grazing over my skin, the gesture so subconscious and natural. "Time, distance, and a little self-reflection can really change a person's perspective."

"Yeah, I can see that."

The phone alarm I'd snoozed before sounded again, pulling us from the moment.

"Shoot, I really should go meet my Realtor. I'm on a tight deadline to find a new place to live, and Mindy doesn't seem the type who'll stick around to wait for me."

"By all means, don't keep Mindy waiting on my account," he said with a sheepish grin.

"It was really good to see you, Gabe."

"You too, Avery."

As I turned to leave, I glanced back at him one more time, wondering if this was all an absurd coincidence or maybe, just maybe, it was the universe offering up a second chance with my first love?

Chapter Twelve

Panting and sweating after climbing the equivalent of Everest, Mindy, my real estate broker, threw herself against the apartment's front door until the lock gave way, and she practically fell into the hallway, catching herself on a nearby coatrack.

"That lock always sticks," she said, brushing off her pantsuit and putting her blazer back on after abandoning it about four floors into our nine-story walk-up. At that point, I hadn't really been sure how she was going to make it up another five flights.

Still fighting for breath, Mindy continued, "Just needs some WD-40. I'm sure the super can take care of it. Okay, so as you can see, this is a south-facing unit with lots of natural light."

I glanced around the shoebox of a living room and couldn't find a single window. "Where?"

"Normally, the sun just pours in from the kitchen and really brightens up the whole space," she said through a pained smile as she continued to speak between gasps.

I peeked my head around to the kitchen and saw a tiny window over the stove that looked directly out to the brick wall of the building next door. "That window there?"

She opened the blinds. "Well, it's a little darker than usual today because of the clouds that just rolled in, but trust me, when they part, you'll see such a difference."

"Okay? And the listing kept referring to this as a modified one-bedroom? What does that mean exactly?" I asked.

She stepped farther into the kitchen to display a large flat panel hinged to the wall. "You see, this comes down like so . . ." She unhooked the top and opened the legs to reveal a Murphy-style kitchen table.

Hmm . . . that's a clever space saver.

"*Annnnd*, here's the best part." She moved to a pantry closet, where tucked inside was a thin twin-size mattress that looked like something a person would use for camping. "This then becomes"—she hoisted the mattress on top of the table—"TA-DA!" She gestured complete with jazz hands. "Your primary suite. And *so* good for the back. I wish my mattress was this firm."

"My primary suite?! I'm sleeping on my kitchen table!" I'd been as patient as possible through the first five dumpster-fire showings, but I was at my wit's end and could no longer hide my exasperation. "What kind of insanity is this, Mindy?! I have to be out of my place in two weeks! Fourteen days!" My voice was reaching new octaves as I threatened a total meltdown.

Mindy's voice stayed even, as if she spent her life dealing with exasperated clients, and she explained, "Without a cosigner, credit history, and W-2s, your options are really limited."

Limited, sure, but there had to be something better out there. This was the sixth apartment she'd shown me and the only one that had an actual stove, a full-size refrigerator, and a window (even if it was facing a brick wall). Table-bed aside, maybe I had to at least consider it?

I huffed, defeated. "How much is this place anyway?"

Mindy glanced down at her clipboard. "Twenty-four hundred a month. Of course, you'd also have to put down first and last, but don't worry, my commission gets paid by the rental company so you won't owe anything there."

"Twenty-four hundred a month?! For something the size of my old closet and doesn't even have space for a bed? That's ludicrous!"

"Ludicrous it might be, but that's the Manhattan housing market, hon," Mindy responded with a shrug, her sweet facade crumbling more and more with each exchange.

"There has to be something else. This can't be it," I begged.

Mindy tapped her toe against the burnt orange carpet under her suede Gucci loafers. "This *is* it. This is the best you're gonna find in this neighborhood, any neighborhood with your long list of conditions."

"What conditions?! All I want is a reasonable space for an *actual* bed, not to be sharing my apartment with rodents that look like they came out of *The Princess Bride*, and not to have to strap on an oxygen tank to bring my groceries upstairs."

My mind drifted back to the first time Adam brought me to see our Park Avenue Upper East Side classic six. Never in my life did I think we'd be able to afford an apartment in the quintessential New York limestone-clad building directly across from Central Park and the Metropolitan Museum of Art. There were only seventeen units, and rarely did one ever come up for sale. Despite the enormous price tag, the Realtor convinced us to go look at one. As soon as she pushed open the apartment's double doors, any reservations I had melted away, and I could imagine the incredible life Adam and I would build inside those walls.

The living room had floor-to-ceiling like *actual* windows on three sides and a marble wood-burning fireplace I knew would make the perfect backdrop for a Christmas tree. French doors led to a large wrap-around terrace with the most epic views of Central Park. And the cherry on top, a formal dining room with a table that *wasn't a bed* with more than enough space to host friends and family for the holidays. It was perfect. Adam put in an all-cash, full-ask offer on the spot, and less than two months later, burly movers were carrying in sizable pieces from the Restoration Hardware spring catalog.

Anger I believed had dissolved over the past weeks stirred anew within me as thoughts of blame and hurt over the position in which

Adam had me reawakened. He'd not only left me penniless, but I'd recently come to discover he'd forged my name on half a dozen leases. Even though I wasn't implicated in the crime, my credit score would remain in the toilet until the whole mess got sorted out, leaving me with even fewer options.

Mindy crossed her arms over her chest in defeat. "I just don't know what you want, Ms. Lawrence. I can't fabricate an apartment tailored to your wish list and on your budget within the confines of your credit score out of thin air. It's simply impossible."

I pulled a chair out from the Murphy bed / kitchen table and, utterly overwhelmed, flopped my head onto the rubber coating of the thin air mattress and allowed my hands to dangle lifelessly by my sides. My voice came out garbled as I spoke into the plastic. "I'm sure you think I'm an idiot, right? Some gold digger who got what she deserved? But I loved Adam with my whole heart, and he duped me right along with everyone else. Worse than everyone else because I knew him. Or at least I thought I did." I peeled my cheek off the bed and raised my head. "I won't ask my parents for money. I have a job now, and I'm getting ready to start auditioning again . . . I mean, I hope to. But either way, I know I can make it on my own two feet. I just need a little help getting started."

Mindy looked around the apartment like she was hoping someone would come and rescue her from awkwardly consoling this stranger, but with no one to help, she shifted her papers against her chest into one bent arm and extended a hand out to me, patting me stiffly on the shoulder. "Look, maybe take another glance at your finances and revise your list of nonnegotiables, and then reach back out to me. Until then, you may want to consider roommates. Just an idea."

A roommate. Marisol's face immediately popped into my brain. We'd shared an apartment in Brooklyn Heights the year between my breakup with Gabe and when I started dating Adam. Looking back, those were probably some of my favorite days I'd spent in New York.

Though we were both single, we didn't spend much time dating. We went to sample sales, ate our way through Smorgasburg, and kept a very serious scoring system on the best pizza in each borough. We spent hours wandering the Met and entered ourselves into the lotto for seats at all the biggest Broadway shows, actually managing to score front-row seats to *Hamilton* with the original cast (still one of my biggest claims to fame). We watched *Sex and the City* on a loop in our tiny living room and tried out every crazy new exercise fad—my favorite, the Bounce N' Burn trampoline workout, hers, Turbo Aqua-Cycling.

Sometimes if we were feeling particularly in need of a good laugh, we'd take an improv class at this small underground theater in Williamsburg. Marisol had absolutely no background in performing, but that never stopped her. In fact, even though it was completely out of her wheelhouse, somehow she always came up with the funniest, most clever material—the best lines, the most ridiculous facial expressions. It was amazing to watch her be so uninhibited and confident in everything she did. I admired that most about her. Maybe that was why it'd always stood out to me as so remarkable?

A roommate was a good idea, actually. It would help a lot with rent and offset some other expenses too, and considering my rapidly depleting savings, it seemed to be the soundest option. And who knows, maybe it would even be fun?

Mindy lowered the kitchen blinds and turned to me. "Can you close the bed-table back up again? I have another showing in an hour."

And with that, Mindy turned on her Gucci loafers, waited for me to shove the mattress back in the closet, and ushered me out the front door, closing it firmly behind her as we started our epic trek back down the nine flights to ground level.

Chapter Thirteen

The next morning, Charlie waved me in to Mimi's for my first day back at work with a warm and welcoming smile and handed me my old name tag.

I fastened it to my shirt. "Where'd you even find this?"

"Name tag graveyard. We hold on to them in case the person hits it big one day."

"*Orrrrr* comes crawling back after because she's desperate and destitute," I teased.

"Well, tom-A-to, tom-AH-to. We don't judge here at Mimi's Shooting Star Diner," he remarked with a snicker. "Go put your coat away, grab a copy of today's set list off the counter, and meet me in the back."

I followed him into the long hallway leading to the kitchen, taking a moment's pause in front of the audition-call bulletin board that had been a well-maintained staple of the diner dating back to even before my earlier days working there. I scanned it, checking for any upcoming non-equity calls, when Charlie realized I was no longer trailing behind him and doubled back.

"Anything catching your eye?" he asked.

"No, I'm not quite ready yet. But I'm hoping after a few more weeks of shifts here, I will be?" As much as I hoped that would be the case, the statement came out as more of a question.

"No better Broadway boot camp in the world. Here you go, this one here's yours," he said, pointing to the last door in a long row of lockers. "Make sure to actually lock it, though. We've had a few servers with sticky fingers."

"Got it." I nodded, mentally noting to buy a lock on my next trip to Duane Reade.

"Here's where you clock in and out. Binder's on the *deeeeeesk*." He elongated the vowel as he reached across his work space to grab for the time sheets. "You stamp 'em and then return 'em to that same spot when you're done."

"All right, easy enough. How does it work with the song selections? Same as before? We get to choose our own for each set?"

"Pretty much the same drill. You perform one song every hour over the course of your six-hour shift. Generally, it shakes out to two solos, two ensemble numbers, and two duets, but that depends sometimes on staffing. I assign the ensemble and duet numbers, but you can choose your own solos. We don't mandate costumes or props, but nothing's changed—the more you're willing to commit to the role, the bigger the tips. Speaking of . . . ," he said, pointing to a short, curvy young woman in a dark wool coat that almost hit the floor and a large black hat adorned with two Hasidic curls fastened to its sides.

The girl took her place at the center of the diner's stage and began performing the famed bottle dance from *Fiddler on the Roof*. I was more than a little impressed to see that she, unlike so many dancers before her, did not glue the bottle to the hat and instead actually mastered the balance she needed to perform the full choreography without any added assistance.

When the song ended, she tipped her hat as she took her bow, illustrating that the bottle wasn't fastened to the top, and was met by even louder applause and a hailstorm of dollar bills from the crowd. She collected her tips and exited the stage to where we stood watching in awe.

"That was amazing," I gushed.

"Another great set, Lyla. And this here is a new server, well . . . a new old server, Avery Lawrence—"

"Ouch," I teased.

"Oh my God, *the* Avery Lawrence? Like high E above middle C Avery Lawrence?!"

"Wait, you know who I am?" I asked, certain I'd misheard her.

"Of course I do. Everyone does. Your range is legendary. So excited to meet you," she said, extending her hand toward me.

"Likewise," I said, offering mine in return.

"Well, I better get changed and check on my tables. Hey, Charlie, care if I head out a little early? I have to run home for another appointment."

"No problem. I've got my fingers crossed for you this time."

"Please! Fingers, toes, I'll take any luck we can get." Lyla laughed and turned to face me. "Great meeting you, Avery. Can't wait to catch your set next shift."

"Thanks, and same."

Over the next few hours, Charlie reacquainted me with the diner's opening and closing procedures, introduced me to all the new menu items, and walked me through the updated computer system. When most of the dinner tables cleared out to catch their eight o'clock curtains, leaving just a couple of diners, we finally took a break.

"Are you hungry? You must be. Let me grab us something from the kitchen," Charlie offered.

I nodded, the sudden thought of food making me salivate, and pulled out a chair to relieve the pressure from my throbbing feet. He returned not long after, carrying a triple-decker sandwich stuffed high with turkey, lettuce, bacon, and juicy bright-red tomatoes, plus a bubbly soda. "A Kit-Kat Club and a Climb Every Mountain Dew," he said as he placed them down and pulled up a seat opposite me.

"Nothing for you?" I asked, already starting to pick at the fries from the small basket.

"Nah, I'm good. I may grab a fry or two, though," he said.

"My Edel-fries are your Edel-fries," I joked and pushed them closer to him so that the plate resided evenly between the two of us.

"Danke," he said with a grin and punctuated his gratitude by snagging a crispy fry from the top of the pile. "So, I can give you Mondays, Tuesdays, and Fridays for now. As you know, weekends are the most desirable shifts, so I don't have any Saturday or Sunday slots at the moment, but that'll most likely change in the spring."

"I'll take as many shifts as you can give me. And feel free to pass my number to the other servers in case they need any last-minute coverage. I'm in hustler mode," I joked with a half-hearted chuckle, flexing my wannabe muscle from my pathetic excuse for a bicep.

He narrowed his eyes, catching the anxiety in my voice. "Everything okay, BrAvery?"

"Just trying to rebuild my life, that's all."

He raised his eyebrows. "That's all? Six years ago, it seemed like you had it all figured out."

"I guess I was a better actress back then."

Charlie laughed. "Yeah, what happened? You were so good. Why'd you give it up?"

"I didn't mean to give it up, but the longer I stayed away, the harder it felt to jump back in. So instead, I threw myself into a new life and ended up playing a part I didn't realize I'd even auditioned for. But it feels like maybe the universe is giving me a second chance to get it all right this time."

"I'm not sure I'm totally following," he said.

"Right, sure, sorry. I just . . . I've been having a hard time keeping all my thoughts straight lately. This is going to sound crazy, I know, but I just have to tell someone about this thing that happened to me a few weeks ago that I'm still trying to make some sense of?"

"Yeah sure, lay it on me," he said in a way that I couldn't tell if he was concerned, curious, or just playing it cool.

I leaned in closer to him and lowered my voice. "For reasons too complicated to explain right now, I found myself fresh out of spending a few awful hours in a holding cell . . . in jail . . ."

His expression darkened and concern loomed in his eyes. He drew closer, so close his voice turned into only breath, and asked, "Murder one?"

I barked out a laugh, delightfully surprised at how off guard the joke caught me. "Funny, it wasn't for murder, but I'd be lying if I said the thought hasn't crossed my mind a few times since that night . . . Anyway, so I was outside the um . . . the *jail*"—I whispered the word and then resumed a normal volume—"in need of a ride home . . . mind you, it was Christmas Day, so there were no cabs in sight *and* I didn't have a dime on me. So, I went to ask for some help at a nearby security booth, and this guard, who incidentally I later discovered may or may not have been dead for the last fifty years, directed me to the very last phone booth in New York."

"Wait? The guard was a ghost guard?" he said, his eyebrows halfway to his hairline.

"Yes, I think so. Well, maybe, I don't know, but that's not even the strangest thing, if you can believe it."

"Oh, I can believe it."

"I picked up the receiver, and this voice on the other end gives me an address. Only it wasn't to a cab company like I'd expected. When I knocked on the door, Gabe answered. My college boyfriend Gabe. The same Gabe I hadn't spoken to in seven years. On the same night my life fell apart landing me in that holding cell, some mysterious ghost lady sent me to a phone booth, which directed me straight to my ex-boyfriend. That's weird, right?"

"Yeah, I would categorize that as weird. Maybe not like *Twilight Zone* or *The X-Files* weird, but definitely strange. So was that it? The one chance encounter with Gabe?"

"Well, actually, he invited me to meet him for coffee the other day and you know, he was just . . . so different. I mean, the same in all the best ways, but grown up, more mature. As much as I loved him and I know he loved me, he always put his work first, and I knew we'd never land on the same page. But there was still something there between us. I think he felt it too."

"Look, I don't know about ghosts and phone booths, but I do believe that the universe has a way of setting things right that need to be set right. Call it karma or spirituality, whatever you want. I don't think you're crazy. I think we're given signs and clues all the time, but we're not always in a place to pay enough attention and recognize them. Sounds like on that particular day, you were."

"I hadn't thought about it like that. Thanks for the perspective . . . and for not calling to have me carted away."

He tilted his head to the side, his light-blue eyes flashing with a devilish smirk. "I would never."

I laughed. "I should probably get going soon. I'm checking out a sublet on the Lower East Side. I have to be out of my apartment soon, and I'm freaking out. I can't find anything in my price range or that wouldn't double as a set for *American Horror Story*. For example, the ad for the apartment I'm headed to now describes the place as 'sub-terranean,' but I've learned that's probably shorthand for 'dungeon,' right? I don't know if I can take any more of these showings. Each one's been worse than the last, and trust me, my standards have come down. *Waaaaaay* down."

"You're looking for a place to live?" Charlie asked. "What about that friend you used to live with . . . what was her name? Melody? Monica?"

"Marisol, Gabe's sister, actually," I corrected, amazed he'd even remembered her at all.

"That's it! Yes, Marisol. You two were thick as thieves. Can't you bunk with her or another friend for a few weeks 'til you find something? Or what about your parents?"

"Marisol and I lost touch a while ago, and my parents are in the throes of planning their big retirement and move to Florida."

Charlie nodded in understanding and graciously shifted the conversation. "Well, you know Lyla, the bottle dancer from earlier? She's been looking for a roommate. I'm pretty sure she lives *above* ground in Bushwick."

"How far 'above ground'?" I asked skeptically, my mind jumping back to the ninth-floor walk-up I trekked with poor Mindy, who almost didn't make it.

"Not sure? But I'm happy to tell her you're interested."

"Oh, um . . . wow, yeah. Actually, that'd be great. The sooner, the better," I said.

"I'll go text her now, which is good timing because I have to finish making up tomorrow's set list schedule." He motioned to my plate. "But take your time, and you can clock out when you're done. You did great today."

"Thanks." I held up a fry. "And thanks for dinner and the talk. See you Friday."

I sank my teeth into a corner of one of the neat triangles of the turkey sandwich, the tomato juice dripping down my chin, and sighed as I chewed gratefully and grabbed for a napkin. I'd been so hungry that I almost forgot how hungry I was until the first bite hit.

Raucous giggles from the far back corner of the diner shifted my focus from my sandwich to two young women, probably somewhere in their early twenties. Their belly laughs continued to ring through the space, growing louder with each eruption. Spread out across their table was half of the appetizer menu in all its deep-fried glory.

I couldn't hear their conversation, but it didn't matter. Their uninhibited chatter and comfortable body language indicated these were two friends sharing uncounted calories and a relaxing day out . . . and I was jealous. The friends I made after Marisol went our separate ways were superficial at best, hanger-on-ers who were only there for Adam's jet-set lifestyle—and once it was gone, they quickly were too. I didn't see it then, but now, I had to wonder if Adam preferred it that way, nobody ever getting close enough to know what was really going on behind the curtain.

It'd been a long time since I had a moment of real, genuine friendship. Short of that nice conversation with Charlie a few minutes ago, my list of close confidants had dwindled to almost nil, and truth be told, I couldn't remember the last time I'd really laughed . . . like *laugh-laughed*! Like tears in your eyes, snot down your face, side-splitting, ready to pee your pants kind of laughter. A special kind you really only get with good friends. The kind I could count on anytime I hung out with Marisol.

That last fight we had, I'd replayed it over and over in my mind the better part of this last decade. Marisol, my closest friend, was now living in New Jersey, a married mom with two kids. How had that happened? And worse, how did I let myself miss it all?

Chapter Fourteen

I thought back to that last fight Marisol and I had on a girls' weekend Adam planned for us at a chic hotel in Montauk. At the time, I thought he was trying to win her over since she was not only my best friend, but also happened to be Gabe's sister. Looking back, though, I wondered if the real reason was to distract her with smoke and mirrors, what I would later come to understand was his MO whenever he believed someone was starting to catch on to his true nature.

Maybe he knew that Marisol, a New Yorker through and through and as brutally honest as they come, would very clearly see through his bullshit. I'm sure he was worried she'd ask too many questions (which, of course, she did), but I was so dazzled by the light show that I couldn't see Adam for who he really was. Instead, I ended up pushing Marisol away because she had seen it all along.

That particular weekend, Adam pulled out all the stops, booking us the private deluxe oceanfront cottage, not to mention spa treatments and surf lessons. At first, Marisol seemed to be enjoying herself, but as the weekend went on, things started to feel more and more strained between us. By the time we got to dinner the second night, she was barely speaking to me. Things finally came to a head when the waiter brought over a pricey bottle of Dom Pérignon.

Instead of a bright and grateful smile, Marisol's face morphed into a scowl, more annoyed than appreciative.

"Okay, what's your problem? You've been acting like a petulant child since breakfast, so speak up. I've never known you to hold back before," I spat.

Marisol sat up straighter, emboldened by the challenge. "Is this really who you are now? C'mon, eight-hundred-dollar bottles of Dom Pérignon? Is this a joke?"

"No, it's a gift. You're my closest friend. Adam's just trying to impress you."

"No, he's just trying to impress *you*, Avery. It's weird. Why does he feel like he has to work so damn hard?"

I leaned forward in defiance, countering her stubborn gaze. "Admit it, you just don't like him. Not because he's Adam. But because he isn't Gabe. You were the one who said, even though Gabe's your brother, the breakup wouldn't affect our friendship, but clearly, it has."

Marisol rolled her eyes. "You don't want to be with Gabe? That's fine. Don't be with Gabe. But you're too smart to fall for all *thissss*," she said, gesturing wildly—at the table, the room, the champagne. "I never took you for the kind of girl who could be so easily bought."

I slammed my hand down on the table between us. "No. Adam makes me a priority, something Gabe couldn't do. Something neither of you have ever been good at."

She narrowed her eyes and squared her shoulders. "What's that supposed to mean?"

"Just because you've never been in a relationship long enough to understand how to put someone else first . . ."

She snorted. "You're not putting Adam first, you're hiding—the same way you allowed yourself to be absorbed by Gabe and what mattered to him. What about what matters to you, Ave? You broke up with my brother, claiming that he didn't *see* you, but do *you* even see you anymore?"

Her words stung like a slap, but even worse was that they were kinda true. I did blame Gabe, at first anyway. For not being supportive enough. For not pushing me hard enough. For not believing in me when I needed him to the most. And maybe it wasn't fair, but it's how I felt at the time. And then, of course, Adam galloped into my life like an unexpected white knight. Though we'd met briefly at one of Gabe's fundraisers, it wasn't until a year later when we ran into one another again that he started to pursue me. I wasn't interested at first. Of course, I thought he was handsome and charming, but I wasn't ready. We became friends but it didn't take long for him to sweep me off my feet in a way that only Adam could. He'd chosen me as his leading lady, so it stopped feeling so bad that casting agents didn't. I kept auditioning here and there for a while, but my heart just wasn't in it anymore. It'd been broken too many times, and there was Adam ready to mend it with both hands.

"Adam has nothing to do with my career," I insisted.

"Or lack thereof," Marisol bit back.

It was a below-the-belt strike, and I fought to find something equally hurtful to hurl in her direction. But my racing thoughts kept me from finding the perfect retort. After a moment of silence, all I could muster was, "I love Adam, and I love our life together."

"You mean his life, don't you?" she fired, not relenting. "You gave yours up when you moved out of our place and into *his* penthouse on Park Avenue."

"*Riiiiiight*, I forgot the only place worth living is ten feet from Grimaldi's Pizzeria. Just 'cause I crossed the Brooklyn Bridge doesn't mean I defected. I was drowning—in failed auditions and in self-doubt. Meeting Adam was like being thrown a life raft. When you're drowning, you don't question the help, you just take it, grateful your head's above water again."

Marisol softened a bit, her expression growing more worried than angry. "I'm not trying to fight with you, Ave . . . I just . . . I don't recognize you anymore. What happened to the girl singing and dancing on tables at Mimi's ready to take on the Great White Way? You gave up on her too easily. Where's your fight? Where are *you* in any of this?" she asked as she again gestured to the opulent chandeliers, luxurious decor, and tuxedoed waitstaff.

Why couldn't Marisol see that I didn't want to stop fighting—I just didn't have any fight left. Doors can only be slammed in your face so many times before you start looking for a new one. I sighed. "I'm still me, Marisol."

She grabbed for the bottle of champagne and waved it in front of me. "Could've fooled me."

I held up my hands, tired of running in circles that seemed to have no finish line. "Maybe we were stupid to think that after Gabe and I broke up our friendship could go on like nothing happened. You chose your side. I get it." I ceremoniously picked up my glass of the $800 bottle of Dom Pérignon and lifted it in a cheers motion. "And I chose mine." I pulled a long sip from the flute before resting it back on the table between us. "There's nothing more to say. I guess we're done."

The corners of Marisol's eyes were wet with tears, but she cleared her throat and threw some cash down on the table as she rose from her chair. "Until you see this has nothing to do with Gabe or Adam and everything to do with you, I guess we are done."

Chapter Fifteen

True to his word, Charlie texted Lyla, and we arranged to meet the next day at her apartment in Bushwick, Brooklyn. Climbing out of the M Train, I pushed through the throngs of early-morning commuters until I reached the Knickerbocker Avenue exit. I closed my eyes and inhaled deeply, the air crisp and fresh, fragrant with the scent of pizza mixed with the sweet, herby cloud blooming from a nearby vape pen. I looked for an address, scanning the streets and signs, but after a few seconds of confusion, I ducked into the first shop I saw in search of someone to ask.

Pulling open the heavy glass door, I was assaulted by the thick, dank stench of weed and gave a little cough as I made my way to the counter through a haze of smoke. A lithe young hipster stood behind the counter, which displayed glass tubes and thingamabobs that I couldn't even identify. A thin gray thread floated up past his lips as he asked, "What can I get you? We have a special on Gorilla Punch and also Marshmellow vape carts."

"Oh, I'm not . . . um . . . I don't need that today. Thanks. But I was wondering if you know where I can find Morgan Avenue. Is that close by? I just got off the subway, and I'm a little turned around."

He hiked up his pants with a shimmy and pushed his glasses farther up his nose. "Morgan *Avvvveee*." He dragged out the words as he thought out loud. "You came up on the M, right? Then you were parallel to Morgan. You just took a wrong turn when you left the station.

Head back, and it'll be on the other side. Just cross over at the main intersection, can't miss it."

I threw a few bucks into his tip jar as a thank-you and stepped back into the fresh air, a little dizzy from the possible contact high. I retraced my steps back to the subway and started heading north on Morgan, checking the numbers as they descended until I found myself standing in front of Lyla's apartment building. I hurried up the front steps into the lobby and pushed the ringer for apartment C3.

Suddenly, a bright voice from inside the intercom said, "Come on up," followed by a click and a loud, vibrating buzz. I pushed open the vestibule door and started my ascent to the third floor, which incidentally was a breeze after the Mount Everest–like climb I made with Mindy.

A young woman with smooth dark skin, a round face, and wide, excited eyes answered the door with a smile. "You must be Avery. Come in." She swept the door open and gestured widely with her arm to enter. "Girls, Avery's here," she called, her voice echoing down the corridor. "I'm Oaklyn, by the way. I go by Oak. Lyla's just finishing getting ready, she'll be right out."

"Yo, what's up?" one of the other roommates added as she approached us.

Oak put her arm around the girl's waist. "This is Sevyn, and she is clearly a woman of many words."

Sevyn shrugged and barely registered the slight. "Emotions are overrated. I either eat 'em or yeet 'em."

"Ooh, love that. That should be a T-shirt slogan," Lyla said, coming out of her room to greet us. "Hey, Avery. I was so happy when I saw Charlie's text yesterday. We've been interviewing a lot of randos and one's literally been weirder than the last."

"You're telling me. The last apartment I looked at was advertised as being subterranean. It was more like sub-subterranean. No windows. Just concrete cinder walls. I kept waiting for the guy from *The Silence of the Lambs* to pop out and offer me some lotion," I joked.

Lyla, Sevyn, and Oak all looked at me quizzically. *Okay, note to self: if I was going to move in here, no pop culture references before the year 2000.*

"Anyway, so it's just the three of you who live here together?" I asked.

"Not quite. We have one other roommate, Ass, who travels a lot for work. She's hardly ever home, so she has the smallest bedroom in the back," Oak said.

"Her name is Ass?"

"Aston," she replied.

"Right . . ."

Oak continued, "She told us that as long as you weren't sus, she trusted us to give the green light."

"I . . . I don't *think* I'm sus."

Lyla said, "Great! That's the vibe I get from you. Actually, I consulted my tarot and crystals about your aura this morning before you arrived, and it seems like you'll be a decent fit, according to my cards. And the universe, no cap. And my favorite psychic on the Tok."

"The Tok?"

"TikTok, obvi," Lyla answered.

"Obvi, right. Well, that's good news," I offered, still a bit overwhelmed by the Gen-Z lingo being hurled in my direction. Living with four Gen Zers in Brooklyn was a world away from the life I'd been living on the Upper East Side only a few weeks ago, but compared to the limited options I'd seen, this seemed far and away the best one. Not to mention that there was something comforting about my less than six degrees of separation from Lyla and the fact that Charlie had vouched for her.

Trust wasn't something I had much of these days, Adam's cool deceptions still haunting my thoughts and decisions like a looming shadow. If I could be that foolish once, was it out of the realm of possibility to think I could be that oblivious again? I hated him for robbing me of my ability to trust my gut . . . because look at where it got me.

Lyla continued, "Great. We all have pretty crazy schedules, but Oak is the only one that works from home and she usually takes her

MacBook to the park or a WeWork a few blocks away. We don't host crazy parties or anything, but we do love a good night out. The rent is nine hundred dollars. Think you can swing that?"

I did a quick tabulation of the average of what my tips might be and added it to my paltry savings . . . carry the one . . . it was certainly more affordable than the other apartments I'd seen but would still be tight. I definitely would need to increase my big belting numbers at the diner and start working on hitting that high E above middle C pronto. My pulse quickened at the thought of having to possibly drum up a rendition of "Defying Gravity" (which had always been my most lucrative and crowd-pleasing showstopper). But since every time I thought of it, the sound of me mooing made my insides turn into molten lava, I hadn't been planning on bringing it back into rotation unless I was desperate.

Damn.

I answered, "I can manage the rent. So, I'll take it, that is, if you'll have me." I smiled politely and then remembered I hadn't even seen which room would be mine. They could be putting me in Harry Potter's under-the-stairs closet for all I knew. But did it really matter at this point?

"Wonderful," Lyla answered. "When can you move in?"

"Yesterday. Seriously, though, I need to be out of my apartment ASAP, so the sooner the better. I don't have much, just a few suitcases of clothes and a couple of boxes."

Lyla nodded and continued. "Our last roommate moved abroad. All her old furniture's still in the room, so it might take us a minute to offload it, but then we can prorate the rest of the month. Unless you'd want us to leave it for you?"

The repo men had already come to collect pretty much everything of value from the Upper East Side apartment and Hamptons house, including almost all the furniture. After spending the last few nights in a sleeping bag on a parquet floor, even the Murphy-style kitchen-table bed in the ninth-floor walkup was starting to sound pretty damn good to me. Anything my new roommates were willing to provide would be a total godsend.

"That's perfect. It would be a real help if you could leave it."

"Awesome, you can move in tomorrow, then!" Lyla exclaimed.

"That's great. My shift doesn't start till four, so I'll be here in the morning." I pulled my phone out of my pocket and looked up at Lyla. "I already have your number, should I get the two of yours?" I asked Oak and Sevyn.

"Oh, here." Oak proffered her hand, her lime-green manicure meticulous.

I stared at her outstretched palm, her fingers kind of dangling there. I took them in an attempt at some kind of awkward limp handshake.

"No, no!" she exclaimed with a laugh and pulled her fingers from mine. She stuck her thumb in the air and said, "My nail. I had a QR code inlaid into the gel polish with all of my socials. If you open your camera, you can scan it and voilà!"

"Are you kidding me?" The words escaped my mouth before I could even stop them.

"No! I kid you not! It's all the rage. It's like a portable business card, but even better."

"Aren't business cards already portable? Never mind." I stopped my line of questioning. I was clearly an alien on this planet of Gen Zers, and I had *a lot* of learning to do if I was going to keep up.

Oak lifted her hand again, and I opened my camera app and scanned her thumbnail, which instantly populated all of her social media handles into my phone under her contact info. Dude! That *was* kinda cool.

"Okay, so we will reach out to our landlord immediately to let him know, and barring any issues with the background and credit check and whatever, we'll see you tomorrow," Lyla said.

I stuck my finger in the air to pause the conversation. "Oh, I almost forgot I um . . . kinda had a bit of a run-in with a temperamental detective and sorta got arrested for assaulting an officer. The case was dismissed, though."

"Honey, please. I had a similar arrest like four years ago at a Women's March in DC that turned a bit hairy. Par for the course, am I right?" Sevyn offered in a self-satisfied tone and extended her hand for a fist bump.

"Great! I think this will be . . . great," I said, even though I wasn't actually sure if this was going to be an epic train wreck or the experience of a lifetime.

Chapter Sixteen

Having gotten the hang of my new commute over these last few weeks, thankfully, even with recent delays on the M Train, I managed to make it from my new apartment in Bushwick to Times Square for my shift. A look of relief washed over Charlie's face as soon as he spotted me. "Oh good, you haven't morphed into Elphaba yet. After your last shift, I had to wipe green fingerprints off half the place settings."

"You know I make double the tips when I sing 'The Wizard and I' in *full* makeup."

Charlie tilted his head to the side. "You wouldn't have to do the makeup at all if you'd just get up the nerve to sing 'Defying Gravity' instead. If memory serves, that number's your real moneymaker." This was maybe the tenth time Charlie had mentioned this in just as many shifts, and I was running out of ways to dodge his urging. He didn't know a thing about the *moo* heard round the world and the complicated history I had with that song, so he thought he was being helpful.

"We'll see. So, what can I do around here?" I asked, desperately trying to change the subject for the second time today.

Charlie tossed me a cloth from inside his apron pocket. He motioned to the rest of the booths that still needed a wipe down, while he placed freshly laundered linens atop the clean tables.

"Can you take sections one and two today? Paula has a callback and won't be here 'til the late afternoon," he said.

"Oh really?" I lifted my head, shifting my focus from wiping the table. Apparently, my voice was unable to hide my disappointment.

"Why? What's wrong?"

"Paula was supposed to be the Joanne to my Maureen in our 'Take Me or Leave Me' duet." I pulled my set list from my back pocket and scanned it over. "It's fine, just means I'll have to rework the *Rent* medley."

"If you need me to stand in, just let me know," Charlie offered genuinely. "I thought I filled the Anne Boleyn hole in the *SIX* megamix pretty well, if I do say so myself."

I laughed at the memory of Charlie with two space buns slapped over his ears and a bedazzled *B* choker around his neck. Truth be told, his rendition could've given Tom Holland's iconic *Lip Sync Battle* a run for its money. "Teamwork makes the dream work, right?" I teased. "Is there anyone you won't play?"

He tapped his upper lip and thought for a moment. "My line in the sand *was* Little Orphan Annie. Actually, no," he said, scratching the back of his neck, "I take that back, a seven-year-old's birthday party came into the restaurant a few years ago, and the mom offered two Benjamins if we could throw together an *Annie* mash-up. And for two Bennies in our tip jar, you can bet your bottom dollar I was out there belting out 'Tomorrow' like there wasn't one, red wig and all. I don't know how many other men would be up to the challenge," he joked.

"Not to mention have the range to pull it off," I teased back, tossing the damp dishrag into the linen bin.

"But that's the gypsy life, though, right? We all help each other out, have each other's backs, cover for one another when we have a real gig or audition. Everyone here understands the dream, and we hustle hard so we can each pursue our own version of what that looks like. That's why I'm still here all these years later."

Carrying over a bin of clean silverware and a stack of paper napkins, I slid into one of the booths and began rolling them together into sets.

"So, what's the dream now? Still composing? If I remember right, you were writing a show of your own. Did you ever finish it?" I asked.

Charlie scooted into the booth across from me and grabbed some forks and knives to join in. "I finished that one, and three others to varying degrees of success, but nothing Lin-Manuel Miranda–level yet. My biggest hit had a three-week run at The Public a few summers ago, which was pretty awesome. And I'm working on something now I think might have some potential."

"That's incredible. You'll have to tell me a bit more about it sometime." It was refreshing to talk with someone who really understood how the desire to create lived like a supercharged layer just beneath your skin. I'd set my eyes on being an actress ever since I was a little girl in Miss Mildred's basement theater class, singing and dancing in front of anyone who would watch and listen. That same drive I'd felt since the age of five may have been dormant for a while, but with each shift at Mimi's, I was realizing it wasn't entirely dead like I'd thought, just hibernating.

I continued to roll silverware sets, my fingers working industriously as we chatted with ease. "So just biding your time here like the rest of us?"

"Mimi's is my day job. Sometimes, my night job," he joked. "But it gives me the stability to be able to pursue my passion."

He'd hung in there all these years, believing in himself and his dream, and I couldn't help but admire him for it. "But what if that big break doesn't come? Doesn't that scare you?"

He shrugged, and his bottom lip protruded in an expression that conveyed *oh well*. "It might not. And that's all right. Through my *maaaaannnny* failures and relatively few traditional successes in this business, I've realized it's not about the big break for me . . . not anymore. I guess in my youth it used to be, but I'd still do it all the exact same way even if I knew there would never be a pot of gold at the end of my rainbow. The art of making art, right?" He paused for a moment and grabbed another handful of silverware. "What about you? You ready to tell me what really brought you back to Mimi's yet? Actually, let me guess, a magical toaster told you it was your destiny?" he teased.

"Very funny. Did I ever tell you I got a scholarship to Tisch? I was *that* girl. The one who always landed the leads in community theater and in high school. I guess I thought I would come to New York and it wouldn't be long before I made my mark. But as it turns out, everyone at Tisch had been the lead in their community theater's production of *West Side Story* or high school performance of *Our Town*. I started out so confident, so sure of myself, but over time I let nerves and self-doubt take hold. I began comparing myself to everyone else around me. Except when I was here at Mimi's. Here, I could slap on some makeup and a silly costume and just perform. Not for a grade, an agent, or a part, but because I loved it. I guess, I just missed that. When performing used to be . . . I don't know . . . fun?"

"It still is and can be. But it's all a frame of mind. If you make it about the agent or the part, that's when it stops being fun. You need to make it about the performance, the thrill of the audience, the character you're playing. You need to get out of your own head and just live it. But either way, whether you start auditioning again or not, you were born to be onstage. I haven't met many actors in my life for whom I can say that with such certainty. So I hope that you continue to use Mimi's as your chance to practice and take risks and get yourself ready to get back on the horse because I think—no, I know—that though you've taken a few wrong turns along the way, you ended up back here for a reason."

Charlie reached over and grabbed for my hand, uncurling my fingers from around the silverware I was currently white-knuckling. I hadn't even realized how tightly I'd been grabbing the cold metal utensils.

I set them down, smiled up at him, and gave his hand a squeeze in return, grateful for his support. "Thanks for giving me a second chance. I wouldn't have blamed you if you had sent me *easin' down the yellow brick road*," I sang, trying to joke my way out of my pity party.

"You're welcome, and besides, it wasn't *totally* altruistic. You're too damn talented to not be given a second chance." He glanced at his Apple Watch, and realizing the time said, "Speaking of yellow brick roads, don't you have some green makeup to go slap on?"

I nodded and slid out from the table, grabbing my bag and slinging it over my shoulder as I turned toward the dressing room.

"Hey, Dorothy?" he called.

I smiled and turned back to face Charlie. "Yeah?"

"I'm glad you're back."

"Well, you know what they say? There's no place like home."

As the diner was filling up with a hearty matinee crowd, I tucked my makeup case away right behind the trusty green Elphabear stuffed animal Marisol gave me before my *Wicked* audition. And while it wasn't a good luck charm exactly, I couldn't seem to part with it. I glanced at the clock and hurried to coat my verdigris in one extra layer of setting spray so as to not leave any green smudges behind this shift.

Checking the full-length mirror, I adjusted my witch's hat as Lyla—in a bright-blue dirndl dressed as Maria von Trapp—waddled in after her set. Tangled in a mess of marionette strings from her tour de force performance of "The Lonely Goatherd," Lyla firmly announced to the dressing room, "I am *never* performing that song *ever* again." Her face was growing redder and redder with each swipe at the mess of fishline and puppets clinging to her lederhosen.

She looked like she was trapped in an actual catfight, and I couldn't help but giggle. "Girl, you say that every shift. But then you count your dolla dolla bills, and before we know it, you're out there yodeling for your supper again."

"Look who's talking!" she clapped back with a laugh. "But, you'd know better than anyone, *no good deed goes unpunished*, right?" She tried to throw her arms up in a see-what-I-mean sort of motion, but instead, one of the marionettes jerked up, a wooden foot clocking her square in the forehead.

I burst into another fit of giggles, extending my hands hesitantly toward her. "I want to help you so badly, but . . ." I held up my jade-colored digits.

"No, I get it. It would take a hefty dry-cleaning bill to de-greenify this dirndl." She pointed to my ensemble and continued, "By the way, they have been talking about your 'Defying Gravity' around here for *yeeeeears*. I seriously thought you were an urban legend until you actually walked through the door and I heard some of your other sets. Oh crap!" A contorted look of concern struck her face as she spoke. "Are you performing it today? Like right now? Oh man, I'll never wriggle out of this circus in time to see it." She started to try to maneuver the cords and dolls over and around her limbs but seemed to only get more stuck with every hasty movement.

"Whoa, whoa, don't get your puppets in a panic or else we're gonna need to cut you out of that thing. I'm just doing 'The Wizard and I' today. I think I still need a little more time before I'm ready to get back on the 'Defying Gravity' broom."

"Whew!" Lyla exhaled. "Okay then, well, when you head out there can you ask someone—Charlie or Keesha or Kai or whoever—to come back here and help get me out of this costume?"

"You got it," I said with a wink. I took a deep breath and made my way down the small corridor between the dressing room and the restaurant. On my way, I caught Kai and sent him back to rescue Lyla, and then I continued to take my place in the wings to wait for my cue.

Charlie came to check to see if I was ready and smiled widely upon seeing me.

"What?" I asked, my hands instantly flying to my face.

"Nothing. It's just that I think that green is your color."

I stood a bit taller at his compliment, and a swirl of confidence engulfed me like a cyclone. "Thank you, but you've seen me in this getup before."

"I know, and it suited you then too. I just didn't get the chance to tell you," he offered.

"That's sweet, and I'm glad you think so because if I keep doing this bit every shift, my skin may be stained like this permanently," I joked.

He flashed me a smile and then checked his watch. "Okay, BrAvery," he said, giving my arm a supportive squeeze, "little change of plans . . ." As if on cue, I heard the opening chords of—not "The Wizard and I"—but to my surprise and horror, "Defying Gravity."

"Wait, no, Charlie. I . . . I . . ."

"You got this, BrAvery! I believe in you. Just go out there and stop overthinking it . . . it's supposed to be fun."

I silenced my instinct to flee back to the dressing room or right out the front door, and instead, straightened my pointed hat, nodded firmly, and strode out to the stage, drawing in a few deep breaths in preparation. Sweat now beading at my hairline and rolling down my temple as my hands trembled by my sides, I was grateful for the extra coat of setting spray I'd applied before coming out.

As I hit my mark, I was assaulted by a barrage of bright lights and fog I hadn't been prepared for. Charlie was pulling out all the stops and I fought to focus, continuing my duet with an exuberant Glinda who flitted about the stage around me.

The audience was enraptured, and with each note, my confidence burbled up from a place I'd stuffed it down long ago. I planted my feet, ready to attack the final belting note of the showstopper. I sucked in a breath, fully inflating my diaphragm, and as I opened my mouth to let out the wall of sound I was ready to unleash, I spotted Gabe in the doorway of the restaurant. And at the shift in my concentration, my voice epically and impressively cracked—just like I had again, under the pressure.

Chapter Seventeen

From behind a bouquet of brightly colored peonies, Gabe walked through the door of Mimi's just in time to hear the disastrous final note of "Defying Gravity." I blushed fiercely at the gaffe, the rouge of my cheeks mixing with the caked-on green makeup, and I imagined myself looking more like the rusted Tin Man than the Wicked Witch of the West. I glanced over at Gabe, expecting to see him wincing or his jaw dropped to the floor, but instead, a huge smile erupted across his face.

He backed into a seat at the counter, his eyes never leaving mine. As the crowd broke into a light smattering of applause, Gabe's loud, raucous hooting overpowered almost everyone in the room. Gabe couldn't have *possibly* heard the same train wreck of a final note that everyone else did? I mean, I guess it wasn't a *moo*, so that was an improvement over the last time, but still it was pretty terrible. I awkwardly curtseyed and scurried off the stage, hopping down and making my way over to where he was seated.

"Wow, that was fantastic," he gushed.

He looked so handsome, so put together, my ridiculous getup made even more apparent by the contrast. "Gabe, I'm so surprised to see you. What are you doing here?"

"Ever since you told me you were working at Mimi's again, I've been looking for an excuse to stop in. But I don't have one other than just wanting to see you. And bring you these." He handed me the lush bouquet, and I bent my head down to inhale the soft floral scent. "Peonies are your favorite, right?"

"I . . . I can't believe you remembered that." I took a second sniff, and somehow they smelled even sweeter than they had moments before.

He smiled and nodded. "I remember a lot of things. For example, I remember that our favorite French bistro is only a few blocks from here, and I made us reservations. I was hoping we could grab a late lunch together if you're free? Please say you are?"

I thought about the charming French bistro we used to visit several times a month when we dated. The delicious Chablis that paired perfectly with their unforgettable fondue, the candlelit atmosphere, and the Parisian-style accordion player who worked Thursday through Saturday nights. It was *our* place, and I hadn't been back in at least a couple of years. Even still, I could smell the garlicky seafood broth of their moules frites special, and the flakey baguettes they served with it.

"That's really thoughtful, but I still have about two hours left in my shift. Maybe we can do it another time?" I still wasn't sure what to make of Gabe's unexpected presence in my life. The scars from Adam had barely started to heal, and it was hard to imagine ever opening myself up to someone again in that same way. But Gabe wasn't just *someone*.

Reading my hesitation, his face fell slightly, even though it was evident he was trying to hide the hurt. "You showing up at my door like that on Christmas can't just be coincidence. And I'm sure it's hard for you to trust me again, probably to trust anyone. But, Avery, I know what I lost, and I'm not prepared to let that happen a second time. So, if it's okay, I'll wait for you, right here, until your shift is over. I need you to know how much I've changed."

"You want to wait for me? Here?" I tried to suppress a smile, his resolve winning me over.

"Yeah, I'd like to see a few more of your numbers."

Flattered, I glanced around the busy diner and relented. "Well, you're welcome to wait, but uh . . . you'll need to order something if you're going to occupy a space at the counter."

"Great! I came hungry for lunch anyway. What's good here?"

I passed him a menu. "Well, the Ham-ilton and Cheese is fairly popular. So's the Holdin' Out for a Meatball Hero. We also have a Fried Chicken Breast Side Story that's really good."

"I'll take the Holdin' Out for a Meatball Hero, and since I'm playing the long game here," he said, scanning the back page, "the Bend and Gingersnaps for dessert."

"Great choices." I nodded. "Anything to drink? How about a Fanta of the Opera?"

Gabe scrunched up his face. "Is it possible to just get an iced tea?"

"Of course, one Sweet Chari-tea, comin' right up." I winked at him and scribbled his order on a notepad I pulled out from my pocket.

With the bouquet tucked in my arm, I turned to leave, but Gabe caught me by the elbow and said, "Has anyone ever told you that you look good in green? Beautiful, actually."

"Maybe," I said with a cheeky smile, then hurried away before the blush igniting in the apples of my cheeks started to turn my face a ruddy brown again.

After punching in Gabe's order, I headed back to the dressing room to take off the green makeup for the rest of my shift, a little easier said than done. Without access to a shower, I balled up a handful of remover wipes and did my best to rub off as much as I could.

Minutes later, Charlie came up behind me. "You have a little something there," he said, pointing to my hairline before I swatted his hand away, still annoyed he hadn't given me a heads-up about his last-minute adjustment to my set list.

I leaned forward toward the mirror and scrubbed my forehead harder. "Thanks," I huffed, then tossed the wipe into the garbage can and spun around to face him. "Why'd you change the song? I told you I wasn't ready."

"Actually, you never said that. You said, 'We'll see.' So how was I supposed to know you were actively avoiding singing it? It really wasn't that bad. You've got the chops, now you just need the confidence."

I rolled my eyes. "Thank you for your diagnosis, Doc."

"Avery . . . I thought I was helping," he said with a shrug.

"Well, you weren't," I snapped back. I took one last look in the mirror, stood up, and tied my apron around my waist. "I should probably get back out there, I have a bunch of tables waiting on their orders."

Charlie backed away, his expression a bit wounded. "Yeah, the lunch crowd should get moving if they're going to make curtain. Oh, before I forget, Kai got called in at the last minute to cover in *The Lion King* matinee."

"So you'll be duetting me?" I asked.

"If that's okay?"

I forced a smile back on my face. "Yeah, of course it is."

"Good."

I stepped back into the crowded dining room and spotted Gabe clapping and singing along to "Dancing Queen" from *Mamma Mia!*—a sight I never thought I'd see. I twirled over to his stool and sang a few bars to him. Gabe pulled a cheesy bite from his meatball sandwich and bobbed his head along with me to the music before I shimmied over to my other tables to take their orders.

An hour later, following a Sondheim tribute that included an immersive *Sweeney Todd* moment that left Lyla covered in fake blood and minced meat, it was time for me to perform again. Charlie swung his acoustic guitar over his shoulder, and we met underneath the main-stage spotlight. After adjusting our mics, we sat down on two stools facing the audience. Lifting his pick, Charlie strummed the opening notes to "Falling Slowly" from *Once*.

As he and I sang about redemption and second chances through the airy and delicate notes of the ballad, I let the music overtake my soul, and this time, my voice didn't crack—it soared. Our tight harmonies and the apropos lyrics about sinking boats and concepts of home swelled through the diner as Gabe's eyes settled firmly on me, full of pride and admiration. He was seeing me, *really* seeing me.

I glanced at Charlie, who was beaming as we took our bows. He slung the guitar behind his back and grabbed our stools to exit the stage. Nodding in the direction of all the dollar bills spilling out of our tip jar, he said, "You sounded fantastic. Looks like you found your new showstopper."

"*Our* new showstopper," I replied. "We sounded fantastic together!"

"Yeah, we sure did," he agreed.

"Look, I'm sorry about earlier. I guess I'm just getting my sea legs back and haven't been feeling all that sturdy lately. I didn't mean to bite your head off," I said, squeezing him on the shoulder.

"I'm sorry too. I didn't mean to put you on the spot. I just . . . kinda selfishly, couldn't wait to hear you sing it. It was good, you know. You were good."

The words signaled an unspoken truce, any awkwardness from earlier evaporating with their sound into the coffee-scented air. Taking us out of the moment with his excited voice, Gabe found his way over to where Charlie and I were standing together.

"Avery, that was incredible. You sounded amazing. You too, man," Gabe said, jutting his arm out for a handshake. "I'm Gabe."

"Hey," Charlie said, reaching for Gabe's proffered hand, "it's good to finally be able to put a face with the name."

Gabe's eyebrows furrowed and his eyes shot to me, clearly confused by Charlie's comment.

I interjected, "Charlie and I waited tables together back when I used to work here during college. He's the manager now."

"That's right. I remember," Gabe said.

Charlie's eyes zeroed in on him. "Yeah, I remember you too. Avery used to talk about you a lot."

Gabe lowered his head and nodded. "I can imagine that they weren't the most flattering things back then, if we're being honest. But a lot of time's passed"—Gabe shifted his gaze to me—"and I'm not that same guy."

Charlie repositioned the guitar on his back and glanced between me and Gabe, suddenly aware he was now the third wheel. He looked at his watch, cleared his throat, and said, "You only have a few minutes left in your shift. If you want, you two kids can take off. I'll clock you out."

"Thanks man, appreciate it," Gabe said.

"Gabe, just give me a minute. I have to grab my things and put this apron away. Be right back."

I scurried to the dressing room, shoved my apron in my locker, and grabbed my coat and purse. When I rejoined Gabe in the restaurant, he took my hand and led me, not to the door, but instead to the dance floor in front of the stage. Surprised by the gesture, my face broke out into a wide grin as he twirled me around and then pulled me into his broad chest, his arm wrapping around my waist. I put my head on his shoulder, and we swayed to "Tonight" from *West Side Story*, and for just a moment, he was Tony and I was Maria and nobody else existed in the diner, New York City, or the whole damn world.

A sudden vibration from his phone rattled all the way up to his chest, and I pulled my head back to look at him. "Do you need to get that?"

He slid his hand into his pocket, once again silencing the ringer like he had at the coffee shop, and drew me into his embrace. With an alluring smile and attentive gaze, he caressed a hand over my back.

"No, my dear, it's only you tonight," he said, and pulled me in a little closer.

Chapter Eighteen

Hand in hand, and without any real destination in mind, Gabe and I found ourselves strolling up Fifth Avenue, window-shopping at the luxury stores and marveling at their ornate window displays. Since Gabe was still full from his meatball hero and I'd grabbed a few too many handfuls of Edel-fries in the kitchen between sets, we skipped the French bistro reservation and headed out into the late-afternoon air and setting sun. It was cool but not cold, just enough chill to keep me snuggled up to Gabe's side as we walked.

"I was planning to win you back with your favorite vintage of Chablis and Loic's rendition of 'La Vie En Rose,' but now I'm at a loss. I mean, how's a guy supposed to compete with moules frites?" Gabe smirked playfully with a shrug in my direction. "But I am determined to salvage this date somehow, so we can do anything you want. Anything at all. Just say the word and we're there."

I thought back to when I first met Gabe. He was my New York passport, showing me all the best spots and hidden gems only "real" New Yorkers knew about. I remember one time we took the subway all the way down to Essex Street so he could show me what used to be "Pickle Alley," aptly named for the dozens of pickle vendors who could once be found there. Only a few stands remained, but we spent our afternoon on a "pickle crawl," tasting and critiquing the briny delights and laughing at our ridiculous mock assessments.

With our snootiest accents we mocked, "Hmm . . . good girth, but the hint of dill makes it less than exemplary." "Ah yes, this one's a bit too sour for my refined palate." The proprietors of the stands were not as amused as we were.

That's what it was like to be with Gabe—he kept me on my toes by always managing to find the extraordinary in the ordinary. Unlike Adam, who made every occasion flashy and lavish, Gabe kept it simple. Straightforward. There was no pretense or underlying motive. He was who he was, and there was something comforting in that, especially after finding out Adam had ten different aliases and probably an entirely different set of lies built around each one.

Gabe's authenticity and genuine heart were why I fell in love with him as hard as I had. He always made me feel safe and protected, and at the diner (and even now), I was surprised by the calm ease of my body melting into his, relishing in the familiar curve of his neck as I nuzzled my head under his chin during our impromptu slow dance.

I said, "I do have this one idea. Oak, one of my roommates, was talking about it last week." I widened my eyes in his direction as a challenge. "That is, if you think your electric boogie is good enough?"

"Oak? Electric boogie? I have no idea what any of that means, but please, I'm intrigued. Lead the way," he said, gesturing toward the sidewalk.

I took Gabe's arm and we zigzagged through the crowded Midtown streets until we reached the entrance to Central Park and a sign for Wollman Rink.

Gabe tapped his pointer finger to his chin. "Ice skating?"

I smiled broadly. "Nope, not ice skating."

We crossed over the Gapstow Bridge, past the pond and the Central Park Zoo to where more and more people were beginning to funnel into a wide, gated entrance.

"So we aren't skating . . . but we're at a skating rink? Curiouser and curiouser," Gabe said, still trying to work out the big reveal.

I grinned mischievously and pointed to the neon sign welcoming the crowds to DiscOasis: An Immersive Roller Skate Experience. Happy couples and families with small children continued to usher past us, their Afro wigs and bell-bottoms now even more apparent. "So, are you game to 'Get Down Tonight'?" I asked.

His smile gave way to a sexy grin. "C'mon girl, 'Let's Groove.'" He took my hand, and as we walked in the direction of the entrance, Gabe chuckled. "By the way, how many more of these disco puns do you think we have in us?"

"The night is young, and I'm here 'til the 'Last Dance,'" I said, singing the Donna Summer hit.

He retorted with a quick, "Well then, let's get in there so you can 'Shake Your Groove Thing.'"

We walked up to a ticket window and paid for the "Le Freak" passes, which got you two costume rentals and two drinks, before we were ushered over to the "Funkytown" tent. Inside were racks and racks of fringed vests, polyester jumpsuits, and tie-dyed tees.

I triumphantly held up a pair of hot-pink flared pants with sequins down the front of them. "I must wear these!" I said, and continued rummaging through the racks. "Ooh! With this!" I held up a patchwork bandeau top and a fuzzy white faux-fur jacket, one in each hand, and squealed at my finds.

Gabe looked simply lost. "Um . . . ," he mumbled.

I nudged him playfully. "I gotchu, hot stuff. Gimme a sec," I said, handing him my finds and diving back into the racks.

The minute I spotted the outfit, I knew it was the one. I wrenched it off the hanger and handed Gabe an almost exact replica of John Travolta's *Saturday Night Fever* white leisure suit, complete with fitted vest, bell-bottom pants, and wig. His eyes darted from the garment back to me, to the garment again, certain I was joking. When I shook my head and thrust the suit a little closer, he sighed in amused defeat and took the getup from me to go and change.

A few minutes later, both of us looking like we just stepped out of Studio 54, we went over to grab our roller skates from the rental counter. Though the leisure suit was an over-the-top, slightly ridiculous costume, the cheap polyester somehow hugged him in *all* the right places, and he was making that suit look good. Maybe it was this new, go-with-the-flow attitude I wasn't used to seeing in him? Or maybe it was my childhood crush on John Travolta, but between the ease of his smile, the occasional flash of his dimples, and this new sexy silliness, my heart was practically palpitating, and we hadn't even started the cardio yet. We flashed our "Le Freak" passes, and a young guy wearing a suede fringe vest and dripping in gold chains handed us two pairs we quickly laced up on a nearby bench.

Before standing, Gabe turned to me. "I haven't done this um . . . maybe ever. So apologies if this night gets rerouted to the ER."

I tilted my head. "You've ice skated, and didn't you used to play roller hockey as a kid? You'll do great." I stood up, took his elbow, and helped him to his feet. Shaky on his legs like a newborn colt, the white polyester of his suit gleaming in the lights of the glittering disco ball, Gabe, usually so stable and self-assured, looked beyond adorable trying to get the hang of things. After a few laps around the rink, he finally caught on and was able to successfully stay on his feet while doing "The Hustle" along with the enthusiastic crowd.

Settling into the motions, everything seemed to be going well until the DJ cued up "Y.M.C.A.," the crowd erupting into cheers. We skated, hand in hand, to the opening verse, groovin' and movin' to the brass beats, and just as the Village People launched into the famous chorus, Gabe and I threw our still clasped hands up in an all-too exuberant Y, sending us off balance and knocking us flat on our bedazzled behinds.

Gabe's faux-fro flew off his head and launched into the middle like an errant missile with no regard for its victims. A group of teens, too consumed with taking selfies to pay attention to the scene, rolled straight into the tumbleweave and quickly became a mound of polyester and gold lamé on the floor, causing a multiperson pileup on the disco freeway.

In an effort to not cause any more casualties, Gabe and I army-crawled toward the wall for refuge, not bothering to stifle our fits of laughter. Gabe pulled himself up, and once steady he turned to offer his hand to me, which I appreciatively reached for. I was about halfway to a standing position when he lost his footing for a second time, pulling me down on top of him, and we once again fell to the floor like a pile of bricks.

Through giggles and tear-streamed faces, Gabe managed to squeak out, "I guess it's *not* so fun to stay at the Y.M.C.A.," which sent us into another round of belly laughs.

We sat up, and I slid my jacket down past my elbows and rotated my shoulder, which was throbbing a bit, to see if I'd done any real damage.

Gabe's voice turned more serious. "You okay? Did you get hurt?" He gently took my arm and grazed a thumb over my skin, the touch sending tingles to the tips of my fingers. "Here, let me take a look."

I stretched out my hand and then made a fist. "No, nothing too serious. I'll probably just have a monster-size bruise tomorrow . . . but so worth it," I said with another laugh and wiped again at my still-tearing eyes.

He ran his hand down my back, stopping midway. As he pulled me closer, only inches apart, I closed my eyes and inhaled the sweet smell of Gabe's clean aftershave. My heart sped up remembering just what a *good* kisser he was. The fullness of his soft lips. The way his mouth would cover mine as our breath fell into an impatient rhythm. The way his fingers delicately wove through my hair, causing goose bumps to form up and down my arms. The thrill of the memory was almost as exhilarating as having Gabe inches from me now.

With his eyes locked on mine and my pulse thudding in my ears even louder than the disco beats echoing through the rink, I leaned forward in eager anticipation, and just as we almost kissed, I felt the stopper on the front of a roller skate nudge forcefully into my hip, pulling us out of our spell.

"Thss'cuse me, can I get by, pleassthe?" a young girl relying on the wall for balance asked with an annoyed huff and prominent lisp through her missing top front teeth.

Gabe and I snapped back into the reality of sitting on the floor in the middle of a speedway. "Sorry," we mumbled and pulled ourselves fully up to a standing position.

"Let's get these things off before we really hurt ourselves . . . or somebody else," Gabe joked, already leaning down to untie his skates midstride.

"Agreed. I don't have collision insurance at Mimi's," I jested back. "Or any insurance for that matter!"

We exited the rink, changed back into our own shoes, and headed to the snack bar for a drink.

Gabe glanced down at our passes. "Our choice of beer, soda, or hot chocolate? What'll it be?"

"Hmm . . . a hot chocolate sounds good."

He nodded. "Be right back."

I found us a small table overlooking the rink underneath a few propane heaters, pulled a couple of chairs close to one another, and settled in to wait for him. A few minutes later, he approached with two steaming cups piled high with whipped cream and set them down on napkins before taking the seat beside me.

"I had a really great time tonight," I said, wrapping my hands around the warm Styrofoam. "You said you changed and I wasn't sure, but you do seem different somehow. Or maybe we're both not the same people we used to be. Either way, this feels nice—to be here with you." And it did feel nice. Surprisingly normal, as if no time had passed, let alone seven years. For the first time in weeks, it didn't feel like an Adam-size elephant was sitting beside me. I was realizing I could actually have a life post-Adam, and that maybe I hadn't lost *everything* after all.

Gabe nodded, eyeing me over the hot chocolate he'd been blowing on. "It feels more than nice. It feels . . . right. You know, Mom would've gotten such a kick out of seeing us here together like this. She never stopped talking about you. Asking about you," he said, his voice dropping off at the end of the sentence. He cleared his throat and continued, "Anyway, how are *your* parents doing? Still selling antiques in Woodbury? Other than the fact they're such diehard Red Sox fans, I always really liked them."

I had heard Gabe's question about my parents, but couldn't answer, too distracted by what he'd said. "Mom *would've* gotten such a kick out of seeing us here together." The fact Gabe was speaking in the past tense and trying to change the subject made the hairs on the back of my neck stand on end—*no*—"Wait, Gabe, your mom . . . ?"

His face turned more serious. "She passed away two years ago."

All the air whooshed from my lungs, and black spots speckled my vision. I hadn't even imagined Elise could be gone. She was such a force of life. I could still smell the floral notes of her overwhelming perfume, hear the echoes of her contagious laughter, and taste her unparalleled paella. I reached out and covered Gabe's hand with my own.

I was surprised to feel my eyes wet with tears and quickly lifted my hand to conceal them. "I'm so sorry, I had no idea."

"Even in those final days, she begged and pleaded with me to call you. She never gave up hope we'd end up back together. But the problem, you see, was that I never told her I was the reason things ended, that I put my career and goals ahead of my heart. Ahead of you. And that I chose wrong."

"Seems we both did," I offered.

Gabe smiled, took another sip of his hot chocolate, and said, "It was amazing seeing you perform at Mimi's. It's been a long time since I've had a chance to check you out onstage, and it was like nothing changed, still as talented as I remember. So, have you been in anything I'd know? Working on anything new now?"

I shifted uncomfortably, suddenly unsure of how to answer the question. It was hard enough to consider the fact I'd ended things with Gabe because he didn't support me enough in my career, only to have willingly sacrificed it once I got pulled into the impossible draw of Adam's magnetic force. "After we broke up, I kept at it for a while, but I wasn't booking any jobs. I started seeing Adam, and the opportunities became fewer and far between, and then one day, I just gave it up altogether and never looked back. Sometimes I look around Mimi's and wonder what I'm even doing there, but this is all I know how to do." I took a deep breath, unsure if the admission made me sad or proud. But either way, Gabe was still listening, attentively for that matter, finally interested in my career. Maybe things really *had* changed?

I continued, my mouth a bit dry, "I've even started auditioning again."

"And?"

"*And* I still have some work to do on my belt and my confidence."

"Not sure I can help much with the belt, but as for the confidence," he said, pushing a hair out of my face and tucking it behind my ear, "I've never known a woman who has such a bright light within them. It could light up all of Manhattan if you'd just let it."

A flush of warmth worked its way under my faux fur, competing with the orangey heat lamps above us. The rest of the rink faded away behind us, and we may as well have been on the moon.

The poet Robert Frost wrote about a man encountering two roads diverging in the woods. My watershed moment wasn't so different, only it happened in the concrete jungle of New York City, between city blocks in a bustling metropolis. Happy as I thought I was with Adam, I never could shake the feeling there was a whole other life I could have been living. But now I had the chance that so few, if any, ever got—somehow finding myself back at the crossroads and able to explore the path of the choice I didn't make.

Without another word, Gabe seized my waist, pulled me against him, and kissed me hard. My hands gripped the lapels of his white leisure suit like I would never let them go. I melted into his arms as fireworks erupted in my brain, and a disco ball of bright lights and colors flashed before me. I could hear the faint sound of "Upside Down" by Diana Ross echoing in the background, and I too felt like Gabe had spun my world off its axis with that one kiss.

Back in the arms of the man I once loved and once knew so well, it was almost like meeting him for the first time, but also not at all. Like when you meet a stranger you feel like you maybe knew in a past life. We had this whole rich and complicated history, which should've felt like an anchor weighing us both down, but it didn't. Instead, that anchor was the thing rooting us in place, forcing us to re-examine one another using fresh eyes and gained perspectives. With the past crashing into the present, just like that, we had the chance to start again.

Chapter Nineteen

In spite of the fact that it was almost 1:00 a.m., I swung my front door open with the abandon of a silly schoolgirl with a wild crush who had just been on her very best date. Then, remembering I no longer lived alone on the Upper East Side, I quietly closed the door behind me, securing the dead bolt in place, and tiptoed in the direction of my bed, eager for my dreams to pick up where my date with Gabe ended. But laughter and commotion wafting down the corridor from the living room stopped me in my tracks. I followed the sound and was surprised to see all my roommates were not only still wide awake, but were elbow deep and eyeball high in containers of Chinese takeout.

Like a kid in trouble, Lyla cooed, "*Ooooooh, Grandmaaaaa.* Someone was out past her bedtime. We were getting ready to deploy Search and Rescue."

"Yeah, you're never out this late! Who's the lucky guy? Or girl? No judgment!" Sevyn waggled her perfectly sculpted brows at me as I kicked off my shoes, smiling dreamily from ear to ear like a rom-com heroine, and flopped down next to Oak on the couch.

Without moving the rest of my body, I lifted my head and dodged her question by asking, "Were you guys waiting up for me, or do you normally order food at one in the morning?"

"Oh, this? Yeah, this is a pretty common occurrence, but you usually miss out since you're tucked in by ten," Oak teased.

Lyla gestured to the table full of egg rolls, dumplings, and three kinds of noodles. "Are you hungry? Want some dim sum? We got plenty. Ass was supposed to be home, but her work trip got extended," she said, shaking a white paper container in my direction.

"Forget the dim *sum*! I wanna know, did you get *some*?"

"Sevyn!" Lyla cried, swatting in her direction.

Sevyn laughed. "What? With a grin like *that* on her face, I *meeeeean* . . ."

I felt my cheeks warm and waved my hands to pause their line of questioning. "No, no, nothing like that. I just . . . I had a really great date with um . . . a very old friend."

A look of shock spread across Lyla's face. "Oh my God, did you go out with Charlie?"

"Charlie?" I asked, momentarily forgetting that I even knew anyone named Charlie. "Oh no. Actually, it's a bit of a crazy story."

Sevyn lifted a wonton to her mouth with her chopsticks and took a bite. "Girl, I watch TikTok on the reg, and I have *seeeeen* some *thiiiiings*." Her eyes grew wide to emphasize her point, and then she relaxed and went back to chewing. "I don't think anything can surprise me at this point."

When I moved to Bushwick a little more than a month ago, I filled my roommates in on the whole Adam situation, explaining the reason why an almost thirty-year-old suddenly found herself in need of a flat with four roommates and was hustling in a job as a singing waitress. When I confessed how starting again seemed wholly impossible, the amount of support paired with their lack of judgment was an incredibly welcomed surprise.

Though they knew about Adam, I wasn't sure how to explain the Gabe situation or what happened with the mystical phone booth. So as quickly and uncomplicatedly as I could, I detailed my strange encounter with Gabe on Christmas Day and everything that came after.

Finally, when I got to describing the date, I told them about Gabe's surprise appearance at Mimi's followed by our Funkytown Le Freak show, all of which ended in the most earth-shattering kiss I'd had in a long while. After all these years, after all this time, when our lips met, it felt like the stars aligned to create a portal, rocketing us back to before it all fell apart. The girls sat ramrod straight perched at the edge of their seats, lo mein noodles dangling from their lips and chopsticks, enraptured by the sheer absurdity and magic of my fairy tale.

Oak pushed her thick red-rimmed glasses up on her nose and motioned with an eager wave of her hand for me to continue. "So, with chemistry like that, what happened? Why'd you guys break up?"

"It's a bit complicated, but I guess it comes down to the fact that we were on different ships sailing in opposite directions. Gabe was such a good guy, *is* such a good guy, so passionate about making the world a better place, so unlike Adam. The polar opposite, actually. I can't stop thinking about the fact that there has to be a reason the phone booth brought me to his doorstep, now, after all this time. Maybe it's because we're finally on the same page?"

"I guess it's true what they say: the greatest love stories are rarely a straight line, now are they?" asked Lyla, who looked like the human version of the heart-eyes emoji.

"Happiness is not something ready-made. It comes from your own actions," Sevyn interjected, her voice monotone and her face full of skepticism.

"Tell me you did not just throw out an Ariana Grande quote and try to pass it off like prophetic wisdom?" Lyla called out.

Oak chimed in from beside me. "Actually, Ariana Grande may have repeated it, but that little nugget of wisdom belongs to His Holiness the Dalai Lama."

"Really? Well, whatever, it felt fitting whoever it was that said it. My point is there is no preordained love story; these days you gotta write your own." Sevyn shrugged and crammed another heap of noodles into her mouth.

Lyla tossed a decorative pillow at Sevyn, who deflected it like a ninja and sent it flying into the kitchen. "Don't listen to her, Avery. She's a salty Gen Zer who's been on one too many bad Tinder dates. She's cynical of all happy endings."

"You'd be cynical too if you went out on a date with the Tinder Swindler," Sevyn snapped.

Oak clapped her hand to her mouth. "OMG, I totally forgot you went out with the Netflix guy!"

"And amazingly, he wasn't even the worst of them," Sevyn deadpanned.

My eyes went round. "*Worse* than the Tinder Swindler?"

"Lyla, tell Avery about the guy who constantly clogged our toilets." Sevyn threw up her hands dramatically. "I just can't do it. PTSD."

For the next ten minutes, Lyla regaled us with tales of Clog the Toilet Guy, an investment banker Sevyn dated for a few months who, for reasons still unknown, liked to flush random objects down the toilet.

"You have no idea, Avery. It was crazy-town. He flushed magazines . . . shoes . . . his *own* iPhone. And then, one day, I noticed my pet turtle had gone missing," Lyla said, her tight voice holding back emotion.

Upon Lyla mentioning the turtle, everyone, between gasps of laughter, cried, "OHHHH HAAAAANNNKKKKK!!" in unison. And then they really lost it. Their laughter was contagious, and after a deep snort from Lyla, Oak spit out her matcha, spraying the couch and me with a mist of green tea, causing me to break into a fit of hysterical giggles along with them. The apartment was near silent except for the squeaks and wheezy breaths of side-splitting laughter. And the strange sounds emitted from our mouths caused us to laugh even harder.

Tears streaked down my face, and I grabbed for some paper napkins from under a container. But being unable to see through my wet lashes, I instead stuck my hand right into the fried rice, sending me almost to the floor in a whole new fit.

When I could finally see straight and my lungs reinflated, I sighed heavily and shook my head. I hadn't laughed that hard in God knows how long. Actually, I did. About six years. The unadulterated joy felt fantastic, as if a weight I didn't know I'd been shouldering since my fight with Marisol suddenly lightened.

After Montauk, I should've called her and tried to fix our friendship, but I was so enraged by her no-holds-barred disapproval of my choices, it was just easier to cut her out, like I did with pretty much any challenge I faced at the time. So that's what I did. I cut Marisol out and tried to pretend her absence hadn't left a big gaping hole in my life. But my new roommates reminded me of how essential female friendships were for those belly laughs, the tough times, and everything in between.

"Oh girl, Sevyn's bad dating stories make me grateful to identify as asexual. And if her nightmare dates crack you up, then you are in for an eternity of giggle fits just like this," Oak remarked, working to blot out the matcha spattered all over the leather couch with her sleeve.

"Well, that sounds nice, actually," I admitted, smiling at the girls as I surveyed the living room. With unexpected clarity, I was beyond grateful—for the laughter; the whole silly, comfortable moment; the bliss of the day with Gabe; all of it. My heart felt remarkably full for the first time in a long while, and I allowed myself to just settle into the sensation and relish in it as long as I could.

"Whew, I haven't laughed like that in a *very long time*," I admitted.

Sevyn wiped her eyes in agreement. "Me either. But it seems like a good way for me to end the night. I have an early-morning Zoom call for work that I'll be sleeping through if I don't get to bed."

She grabbed her plate, put it in the sink, and blew us kisses as she made her way to her room.

"How about you, Avery?" Oak asked. "This is a far departure from your usual bedtime. Don't you have work tomorrow?"

"Thankfully, I have the day off. Good thing too, I need to give my cords a rest. I've had some real brutal sets at the diner followed by even more brutal open calls this week. A day of physical, mental, and vocal rest sounds like just what the doctor ordered."

At the comment, Lyla's face brightened and her eyes grew wide. "Actually, if you are looking for help with your vocals, I know this amazing Reiki master downtown. She works with a lot of the servers at Mimi's. I can shoot her a text in the morning and see if she can squeeze us in."

As had become typical with my new roommates, I needed Urban Dictionary or Google Translate to figure out what was being said, but not wanting to blow my coolness cover, I just nodded and said vaguely, "I don't know. Um . . . that's not really my thing."

"Come on, Avery, open your heart chakra and mind. Trust me, Reiki is amazing."

Still not completely sure what I was agreeing to, I finally caved and said, "Okay, okay, you don't have to Reiki me over the coals, I'm in."

Chapter Twenty

The next morning, I followed Lyla out of the subway and into the heart of Alphabet City, the area of New York that extended roughly from Avenue A all the way to the East River.

"I used to live on Avenue C," Lyla said, motioning to the street sign overhead, "but my scummy super wanted to raise the rent over twenty percent. That's when I decided to move to Bushwick. But I suppose everything worked out the way it was supposed to, or else I never would have met my besties."

"I still get confused. Who was friends with whom first?"

"Okay, let's see," Lyla said, chewing her bottom lip. "Oak and Sevyn went to The New School together, so they've been friends the longest. They're the ones who originally found the apartment. I used to go out with Sevyn's ex-best-friend's cousin Toby, which is how we met. And as for Ass, before she decided to go the freelance route, she used to work with Oak's ex-girlfriend."

"Got it," I said with a nod, even though I didn't really get it at all. "Seeing as you've never mentioned Toby before and the fact that you're going on a date later, I assume you two broke up?"

"Yeah, that ended a while ago. Now, I date mostly for fun, and between you and me"—she lowered her voice—"sometimes for the free meal or drinks. I'm not looking for anything serious. I have to put all my energy into my career. As you know, the struggle is real, the hours are insane, and the chances are slim. I used every single penny I had to move from my little corner of Decorah, Iowa, to get here, and I am not going back unless I am able to parade through the streets waving my Tony Award in my hands. Or a Grammy, I'm not picky," she joked.

"I didn't realize you were from Iowa? You seem like such a New Yorker."

Lyla stopped dead in her tracks and put her hand over her heart. "Really? Thank you. I think that's the best compliment I've ever gotten. You should've seen me when I first moved here. I was terrified of literally everything. The subway, the crowds, the sewer rats."

I scrunched up my nose. "To be fair, everyone's terrified of the sewer rats. They're no joke. I saw one the other day the size of a Chihuahua. So, what's this place we're going to again?" I asked.

"Achy Reiki Heart. Oh my God, you're going to love it. I swear, Miss Tilly is like one part Reiki master, one part hypnotist, one part masseuse, one part chiropractor, one part therapist, and one part total *goddesssss.*"

"That's a lot of parts."

"I know!" Lyla exclaimed. "It's like a one-stop shop for your soul."

"And you really think she can help me with my range?"

"Are you kidding? Everyone at Mimi's swears by her, not to mention her Insta Stories are chock-full of the Broadway elite. Sutton Foster was there just last week, and Patti LuPone the week before that. Miss Tilly will get you hitting that high E above C again in no time."

"Sutton Foster? Really? I mean, I guess if she's good enough for Sutton, she's good enough for me," I joked.

"No, seriously, Avery, she's the real deal. I went to see her last year when I was hit with a particularly wicked case of laryngitis before my callback for the national tour of *Mean Girls*. I mean, I didn't get the part, *buuuuut* practically overnight, my voice was in top shape for that audition."

"That sounds promising," I said, hoping that the small threads of skepticism in my intonation weren't detectable.

We walked through the shop door and climbed down a dark and narrow staircase until we were inside the studio space. Almost instantly, my nostrils were assaulted with the smell of burning incense so strong my eyes began to water. Colorful pillows were scattered around the room, and next to a large gold Chinese wind gong was a rock fountain that took up almost the entirety of the back wall.

Miss Tilly, a heavyset woman dressed in a flowery caftan who was twisted up like a pretzel doing some version of Lotus Pose, spotted us and sprang up from the floor. "Lyla, my sweetheart, perfect timing, I just finished my morning transcendental meditation session," she said.

"You practice twice a day?" Lyla asked.

"Absolutely—morning and evening. It's the only way to maximize its benefits—a more alert mind, increased energy, clearer thinking, not to mention a *roaaarrrring* libido."

Lyla molded her hands into two claws. "Me-ow!"

Miss Tilly chuckled as she slipped on a silk robe. "Exactly. So, who's your friend?" She motioned in my direction. "I don't recognize this one."

"A new roommate. Avery. She's a singer too. She works with me at Mimi's."

Miss Tilly waved her hand around. "Say no more, you've come to the right place. So tell me, what's been going on?"

I shifted my weight, unsure of how to start. "Well, my range isn't what it used to be."

"As I said, you came to the right place then. Miss Tilly's gotchu covered," she said.

Over the next few hours, Miss Tilly led me through a series of alternative and energetic medicine meditations, crystal and Tibetan sound therapy, Reiki sessions, and aromatherapy treatments. I wasn't sure any of it was actually helping my voice, but I had to admit, I did feel significantly more relaxed than I had in months.

"You carry a lot of tension in your shoulders. Has anyone ever told you that?" Miss Tilly asked as she finished up my spine adjustment. "We're just about done here. Let me go and grab your complimentary crystals from my office."

Miss Tilly went into the back room, leaving Lyla and me alone in the studio.

"How do you feel?" Lyla whispered.

"I feel good, but is it odd that she didn't have me sing a single note? How do I know any of it worked?"

Lyla pointed her finger in the air. "Oh, it worked. Trust, girl. Trust."

"All right," Miss Tilly said, clutching a small brown suede bag in her closed fist. "I have the most fantastic assortment for you." She motioned for me to hold out my hands and gently shook a rainbow of crystals into my cupped palms. "The garnet kick-starts belief in personal power, the kunzite encourages forgiveness and helps ease emotion, and finally, the sapphire reaffirms purpose and direction. The amethyst reduces anxiety, helps reestablish boundaries and a sense of control, and most importantly, strengthens confidence and self-empowerment."

I closed my fingers around the stones. "I need like literally all of these. How did you know?"

She lowered her voice. "If I'm being honest, you don't need any of these. You possess all their powers inside yourself. The crystals are just a way to help you manifest them a little quicker."

Though hard to believe considering I'd taken directions from a mysterious phone booth, the truth was I had never been a particularly spiritual person. Marisol was the one who believed in all this stuff—psychics, fortune tellers, and tarot cards. I liked to see things with my own two eyes, not some mystical third one. But, for some reason, I trusted Miss Tilly and her new age methods. I mean, what did I really have to lose?

Miss Tilly reached into the pocket of her robe, pulled out a receipt pad, and started scribbling out my list of treatments. When she got to the third page, my palms really began to sweat. Finally, she presented me with the bill, and my eyes nearly fell out of my head. In total it was a little over $600 and that was *with* the friends and family discount. Without any tangible proof that any of it actually worked, regret and images of overdraft alerts were racing through my panic-stricken mind, and I mentally calculated how many songs from *Wicked* I'd have to perform at Mimi's to make up that amount of money.

"I take cash or credit. But not Amex," Miss Tilly said.

I reluctantly handed over my bank card and prayed the charge would go through, breathing a heavy sigh of relief when I saw the word ACCEPTED flash across the small screen of her Apple Pay. I pushed the suede bag of colorful crystals into my tote but held on to the amethyst one, tucking it deep into the front pocket of my jeans.

Miss Tilly handed Lyla a few samples to try, and we started our ascent up the narrow staircase back to ground level.

"I'm not meeting my Bumble date until way later if you want to grab a quick bite or something?" Lyla said.

"Yeah, sounds good. Nothing too bougie, though, I just donated a small fortune to Miss Tilly's retirement fund."

"There's this falafel spot I've been dying to try in the West Village. The lines are always super long, though." She glanced down at her watch. "But it's after one, so we might've already missed the lunch crowd? And it's not too cold today. What do you think?"

With little to no wind, the mid-February day, warmed by rays of the unobstructed sun, felt more like a day in March. "Sounds perfect."

We walked up to Union Square, which was even more crowded with people taking advantage of the unseasonably nice day, and hopped on the 6 Train to Bleecker Street. We got out of the subway and used our phones to navigate our way to the restaurant. When we got there, the line was still wrapped halfway around the block.

"You've got to be kidding me," Lyla grunted and turned to me. "What do you want to do?"

I backed up and surveyed the line, my rumbling stomach vying for a vote. "I'm game to stick around. I mean, we're already here."

Lyla nodded and opened up her TikTok app. "I'm working on increasing my followers. I'm up to like 5,700! When you hit 10K, that's when the brands start sending all the free swag to advertise. I'm gonna try to grab some new content while we're waiting."

Almost twenty minutes later, Lyla returned to where I was still standing in line, having only moved up a few feet from where she'd left me.

"How'd it go?" I asked. "Did you get anything good?"

"Some cute stuff. Snapped some pics for the Gram and put together a reel asking people waiting in the line what they 'falafel about.'"

I leaned in, certain I didn't hear her correctly. "Huh? What they falafel about? What does that even mean?"

"Yeah, a play on words. What they *feeeeel* awful about. Get it? 'Falafel about?'"

"Ohhhhh, I get it now. Funny."

"Most were just hungry, but a few gave more thoughtful answers. Let me get you."

"Me?"

"Do me a solid. When I ask you what you 'falafel about,' just don't say hungry." She held up her phone to face me before I could protest. "So, we're standing outside the West Village's newest hotspot eatery, Chick Pea, tell me, what do you falafel about?"

"Today or generally?" I asked.

"Generally."

"Auditions," I admitted.

Lyla stopped filming and lowered her camera. She sympathetically placed a hand on my arm and said, "That's great you're putting yourself out there again. You're so good, Avery. Really." Her eyes suddenly lit up. "You know what you should do? You should audition for *The Voice*. They'd hear you sing, swivel their chairs around, see what a babe you are, and boom, record deal in no time."

I appreciated her words of encouragement, but I wasn't sure *The Voice* was my chosen path. "I should have mentioned it sooner, but I was already feeling the pressure and just . . . didn't want to have to tell you all and Charlie and everyone how I didn't get cast again, and again, and again. My stats are pretty awful. Seven auditions so far, no callbacks."

"Seven? That's nothing. I do seven in my sleep," she joked in an effort to be supportive. Her voice turned more serious. "Avery, it's the biz. But you have to keep putting yourself out there. Your break will come. Mine too. We've got to believe in ourselves, right? I mean, if we don't, who will?"

Lyla was right—no one was going to do it for me. This time I didn't have a scapegoat or another road I could hide down. I had to either face the challenge or abandon my dream altogether—and was I ready to do that? Throw in the towel completely because it was what . . . hard?

Mom liked to say, "Mistakes are meant for learning, not repeating." So, what *had* I learned? That I missed the hell out of performing. That I'd lost myself somewhere between my senior showcase and the moment the feds practically kicked down our front door. And that it was time I got out of the damn passenger seat and back behind the wheel of my own life.

Chapter Twenty-One

After close to another forty-five minutes of waiting, we were beyond ravenous and certain we wouldn't see any falafel before we collapsed from hunger, so we begrudgingly abandoned our places in line and went in search of a classic New York hot dog cart. Although they could usually be found on every street corner, for some reason we were having a hard time locating a single stand and found ourselves wandering aimlessly in pursuit of one.

"If I pass out right here, just make sure to take care of Hank II for me," Lyla said with her hand dramatically on her forehead.

I took her by the arm and dragged her up the sidewalk. "Come on, I see something at the end of the block."

"It's probably just one of those guys selling knockoff purses," she whined.

"No, there's an umbrella. It has to be food."

We hurried up the sidewalk, and just as we rounded the corner, a voice called out to us, "I got your Gucci, Chanel, Prada, YSL, Bottega, and Hermès right here, ladies. If you don't see what you like on the table, I got more in the truck."

Lyla threw her head back. "I told you!"

"Okay, okay, but look over there," I said, pointing across the street. "Either I'm hallucinating from hunger or there's a wiener on that umbrella."

"Yes, it is!" Lyla said gleefully. "Oh," she sighed. "I've never been so happy to see a wiener in all my life! C'mon, let's go." She barely finished her sentence before grabbing a fistful of my sleeve and hauling me in the direction of the iconic blue-and-yellow awning.

After practically shouting our order at the hot dog vendor, we finally stood on the corner, a frank covered in onions, mustard, and steaming sauerkraut in each hand. Shoveling them in at record speed, we didn't speak—just focused on not choking.

As we chewed in silence, the hunger pangs dissipated with each glorious bite, and I finally had a chance to survey my surroundings. We had been on such a tear tracking down a food cart that we wove and turned through the streets of the West Village without even paying attention to signs or landmarks.

By the time we stopped walking, I actually had no idea where we'd ended up. After inhaling the two hot dogs in record time, I excused myself to grab a few Cokes from the vendor. I waited behind a business-man who was ranting into his earpiece about a failing deal. He tossed a few bills in the man's direction and snatched the frankfurter from him without so much as a thank-you. I helped the vendor collect the bills threatening to blow away in the wind, organized them into a neat pile, and handed them over to him.

"Sheesh, glad it wasn't windier today, right?" I joked and smiled warmly.

"Some people are always in a rush. Rush rush rush. I wonder if they even notice how much of their life they're missing." He seemed to be speaking aloud to the universe, more so than to me.

"Probably not," I answered, to his surprise.

"What was that?" he asked.

"Oh, never mind. I was just agreeing with you. So, um . . . can I get two Diet Cokes, please?" I extended my arm in his direction to make sure he had a good grip on my ten-dollar bill before letting go.

"You got it," he said, leaning down to a cooler fastened to the side of his cart. He dug through the ice chips and pulled out two frosted soda bottles, fresh with drips of cold condensation rolling down their curves. He handed them over along with a pile of napkins.

"Thanks," I said, adjusting my grip so they wouldn't slip from my fingers.

"Sure thing," he responded, closing the lid of the cooler tightly and brushing his wet hands off on his pants. "Have a nice day, young lady. And remember, no space of regret can make amends for one life's opportunity misused."

As soon as his comment hit the air, my blood turned colder than the fresh sodas in my hand. "I'm sorry, what did you say?" I managed, certain my ears were playing tricks on me.

Before he could answer, I spotted the flash of a shiny silver bell pinned to the lapel of his jacket—the same exact one I spotted on the ghost guard at the jail on Christmas Day. I opened my mouth to ask him about it but was interrupted by a forceful female voice from behind me.

"Sir, you aren't a regular on this street," the uniformed police-woman stated firmly to the hot dog vendor. "Where are your permits to work at this location?" she pressed, the man now flustered by her line of questioning.

"Yes, of course, just leaving now, ma'am," he announced, and hustled away with his cart.

"No! Wait! Please! That thing you just said to me, where did you hear that from? And your pin! Where did you get that pin?" I shouted in his direction, the crowds of people swallowing him up as he rolled his rickety cart down the street. Like Alice chasing the White Rabbit, I jogged to catch up, dodging the pedestrians, getting stuck at a cross-walk, and attempting to weave around two moms pushing strollers side by side. By the time I made it around the hordes of people, the hot dog man was gone, along with whatever answers he may have had pertaining to the broach and quote.

"Dammit!" I shouted out loud, startling the crap out of a mother walking hand in hand with her young daughter. "Oh, sorry!" I offered with a small wave, but my chest felt like an agitated swarm of hornets had been released from their hive, generating a buzz of restlessness I couldn't seem to quiet.

From behind me, Lyla approached huffing and puffing as she made her way to me. She snagged a Diet Coke from my hand, cracked it open, and downed a few long gulps before exclaiming, "Avery, what happened? Are you all right? One second you were getting sodas, and the next you took off like a bat outta hell. I thought you got mugged or something, like someone snagged your phone from your hand or your purse and you took off after them. All I knew was that you started running like a girl on fire, and I had no idea where you were going!" She bent in half to catch her breath, her hands on her knees as she sucked air into her lungs.

"I'm sorry! It's just . . . well, I needed to . . ." Needed to what? Chase down a hot dog vendor to ask him about a silver-bell pin he was wearing all because I thought it was the same one worn by a guard, who may or may not have been dead? *Oh my God. Am I cracking up? Am I totally losing my mind?*

I surveyed the street. Benny's Bagels and Bialys (ooh, catchy *and* alliterative) stood on the corner, a short line weaving out the door and out of sight. A few other nondescript small businesses—an old camera store, a nail salon, a lighting boutique, and a typical New York City bodega—bespeckled the block. Stretching my neck in the direction from where I'd run, I tried to figure out how far I'd run during my mad pursuit of the hot dog vendor, and that's when I saw it, standing there in all its well-worn and dilapidated glory.

"Oh. My. God," I exclaimed.

"What now?" Lyla reeled around, searching for something to clue her in to what the hell was going on.

"That's it!" I cried and pointed toward the opposite side of the street.

Lyla swiveled her head, trying to follow my ranting, but was clearly still lost. "That's what? What are we looking at?"

"The phone booth. The magical phone booth I told you guys about last night," I exclaimed, still not quite believing it myself.

Lyla glanced over to the graffiti-covered, rusty eyesore with the sad string of Christmas lights still somehow dangling from its roof almost two months after the holiday.

"*That's* the magical phone booth?" Lyla said, unable to disguise the confusion in her voice. "It looks um . . . a little less than magical, if you ask me."

I shook my head and muttered, "How do I keep ending up here? And more importantly, why?"

Lyla raised her eyebrows and smirked. "Guess there's only one way to find out, right?" Her eyes twinkled with excitement as she grabbed the other soda from my tight grip and nudged me toward the accordion door.

The booth stood before me like some strange and fantastical monument in the middle of the city, the bright beams of the afternoon sun reflecting off its metal frame, almost creating a halo around it. Without waiting for the light to change, we crossed the street, dodging a few speeding cars as we scurried over to it. After a supportive nod from Lyla, I stepped inside, a warmth engulfing me like a hug from an old friend, and I couldn't keep my hand from trembling as I reached for the phone.

I picked up the receiver, dialed the number the ghost guard gave me on Christmas, a phone number forever etched in my brain, as my heartbeat sped up like a racehorse just before the starting shot. I closed my eyes, took a deep breath, listened for the two rings, and waited for the sound of the familiar click.

Chapter Twenty-Two

Lyla almost decided to skip her Bumble date to accompany me to the mystery address, but I insisted she go ahead and told her I'd be okay to do some digging on my own. According to my phone's GPS, the address the phone booth gave, 27 Barrow Street, wasn't far, but it also didn't give me any indication of what kind of building I was being directed to.

I rounded the corner looking down at my phone and almost caused a domino effect when I practically rear-ended a young woman who was waiting in a *verrrrrry* long line snaking up the block.

"Whoa! 'Scuse me," I blurted out, maneuvering around her.

The young woman pulled a pair of AirPods from her ears. "Sorry, what?"

"Oh, never mind," I said, continuing down the street. But with each step closer to 27 Barrow, I realized the line was queuing to enter that very address. I surveyed the people who were waiting like a line of ants at a picnic, a mix of men and women of all colors, shapes, and sizes, carrying headshots, listening to music, and muttering to themselves.

Curiosity getting the better of me, I searched for someone on the line without headphones. After zeroing in on a young guy in a long-sleeve waffle shirt, puffer jacket, and jeans, I tapped him squarely on his shoulder. He was scanning a piece of paper, putting it down and reciting passages from it to himself as I approached.

"Excuse me? Um . . . what's this for?" I asked, motioning to the people waiting behind him.

Startled by the interruption, he took a second to respond. "It's a line to the Greenwich House Theater. There's an open call today."

My ears perked up at *open call*. Open-call auditions usually meant that non-equity actors would be seen along with equity ones, and since I was still trying to get my equity card, it was currently the only type of audition I could go on.

I glanced up and down the line again, and asked, "Do you know who they're auditioning?"

"It's apparently a *very* open 'open call' for a new show coming in from the West End called *Marley Is Dead*. Do you know it?" He didn't wait for my response before continuing, "With the director's modern take and the show's twist on traditional roles, not to mention the rave reviews coming out of London, I think half of the New York theater scene is here today . . . hence, the long line," he grumbled as he gestured to the queue behind him.

Marley Is Dead?! The show I was supposed to see with Adam in London on New Year's? Was this a coincidence, or had the phone booth sent me here so I could audition? The excitement of the latter, the possibility that this audition could be something as special as my encounter with Gabe turned out to be, made my heart pound against my rib cage and my legs tingle with anticipation.

"Do you know what they're looking for?" I asked the guy now struggling to get his jacket hood back over his ears, probably in an attempt to return to his warm-up preparations.

He sighed, pulled his coat back down, and waved the papers he was holding as he said, "The usual. Sixteen bars and a short monologue. Just nothing too classic."

"Okay, well, thanks for the info. And . . . break a leg," I said.

Backing away from him and the line, my eyes scanned what looked like an endless stream of people winding all the way down Barrow Street.

Sixteen bars? I could pull something from my repertoire. Monologue? I had a few in my arsenal and, judging by the size of this line, a lot of time to settle on the right one. But, I could also end up waiting for hours and not even get seen. Either way, it seemed the phone booth wanted me here for one reason or another, and I wouldn't know what that reason was unless I was willing to stick around and find out. I jogged to the end of the line, popped in my AirPods, and settled onto the sidewalk to wait.

Close to three and a half hours later, I could finally see the front of the Greenwich House Theater, a beautiful six-story red-brick building with ivy climbing up the walls that looked like it had been transported straight out of London's West End. As the sun started to set and the temperature dropped into the forties, people slowly started trickling out of line. I thought about leaving too, but I was too torn to actually move. *Maybe if I give it just ten more minutes*, I'd reasoned—every ten minutes for the past hour. Certain the phone booth meant for me to be here, I wasn't ready to give up, but I also wasn't sure if I was putting all of my faith into a ridiculous and fantastical goose chase.

My calves ached and I desperately needed to pee. I decided I'd give it five more minutes and then call it. At this point, it didn't look like I'd be given the opportunity to audition, and I hadn't had any chance encounters while waiting in line. Maybe I just needed to accept that this time the address was *just* an address and the phone booth got it wrong? Or, I was simply delusional for having put my faith in an archaic hunk of junk. Maybe there was no bigger meaning to any of it? Considering all that transpired over the last few months of my life, I was probably just reaching out for anything to help me find my way. The disappointment settled in my stomach like liquid metal, sloshing around for a moment before it turned to lead.

Just as the series of doubts flooded my mind, the front door of the Greenwich House Theater cracked open, and a woman hugging a clipboard peeked her head through. "Okay, we have time to see eight more. To the rest of you, thank you for waiting."

I popped up on my toes and counted the heads in front of me. *Okay . . . five, six, seven, and . . . and . . . me! I was lucky number eight!* HOLY. CRAP. This was unbelievable. Un-freakin'-believable. My lead stomach lightened so quickly I practically floated up the steps like a hot-air balloon into the theater's impressive vestibule. I yanked my hair out of its elastic, gave it a shake, and tucked a few pieces behind my ears. As the eight of us moved forward in the queue toward the audition room, I started my warm-up routine.

I silently stretched my mouth to form a tall O like one of those strange Byers' Choice Christmas caroling dolls to a wide, toothy grin, the apples of my cheeks pert and round. I moved my jaw back and forth, back and forth, loosening up my face muscles. I chewed on my tongue, an old trick to help increase the flow of saliva now completely drained from my mouth, a common occurrence whenever I grew nervous.

One by one, the last of the auditioners went into the studio space while I paced up and down the hallway repeating my vocal exercises. When number seven, a woman a little older than me, exited the studio with a satisfied smile across her face, it was finally my turn.

"Next," a voice called from inside the door. I sucked in a deep breath, pushed out my chest, and strode into the studio.

The pianist seated in the left corner of the room held out his hand, ready to receive the sheet music. However, not knowing I'd be auditioning, I of course didn't have any.

I cleared my throat and stepped in close, past his extended arm, and whispered, "Hi, um . . . so I don't have any sheet music with me. Do you know 'Look to the Rainbow' from *Finian's Rainbow*?"

He shook his head, his face twisted by his lack of recognition of the song. "Sorry, never even heard of that one."

"Shoot," I said, racking my brain for a quick plan. I could sing it a cappella, but man, it'd be risky without the support and backup of some accompaniment. "Okay, so um . . . what do you know?"

His eyes grew wide, almost confused by the question. "You want me to name all the songs I know?" His voice now rose above mine.

"No, no, of course not," I said, trying to bring his tone back down to a quiet simmer. "I just need something in the mezzo range. Any ideas?"

"Well, I've been pretty much playing everything from *Hamilton* all day."

"Err, I don't want them to just see me as another Schuyler sister . . . ," I mumbled as I thought aloud. "Anything else?"

"Well, for a mezzo, I'll give you a few options—I can do 'The Worst Pies in London' from *Sweeney Todd*. Really, anything from that score. I played in the pit during the national tour."

"Um . . . any chance you know anything less . . . wordy? Sondheim's tough even on a good day."

It seemed the clock had run out on our sidebar conversation when I heard a loud clearing of a throat from the table of casting agents and producers. The pianist too was clearly growing tired and with a huff said, "Look, I got 'I Dreamed a Dream' from *Les Mis*, or 'Defying Gravity' from *Wicked*, take your pick and let's go, I need to get to another gig."

No. Really? All the songs in the entire Broadway canon, and here I was face-to-face with the song that stole my *moo*ment . . . I mean, *moment*?! My brain raced through my Sophie's Choice as I became increasingly more aware of the growing impatience of the panel on the other side of the casting table.

"I Dreamed a Dream" would, without a doubt, be the safer bet, but there were no big moments to really show the power of my belting voice. "Defying Gravity" had a much bigger payoff—*if* I could just hit that high E above middle C and not sound like a barnyard animal. I reasoned that without a flying contraption to contend with and after $600 spent at Miss Tilly's, the odds might be slightly in my favor. I fumbled for the amethyst I still had in my pocket and channeled the energy from the small stone to help me make the decision I knew I had to make.

I glanced back over at the casting table, the agents' restlessness now palpable. I was the last audition—the only thing standing between them and a cocktail at the end of their very long day—and if their nerves weren't already frayed, my little exchange with the pianist had likely pushed them over the edge. I had no choice but to pack it in or knock it out of the park. There was no in-between.

So, though it was risky, I let the accompanist know my decision and stepped center stage. To their astonishment and mine, with the help of Lyla's advice about believing in myself and Miss Tilly's Reiki magic, I smashed that final note right out of the room and into the stratosphere.

Chapter Twenty-Three

I had barely made it past the threshold of the theater's exit door, practically bursting at the seams with excitement about how well the audition had gone, when my phone vibrated in my pocket. I pulled it out and smiled (even wider) to see Gabe's name and number flash across the screen.

"I know I just saw you last night, and I'm sure I should be playing this way more cool, but I was just thinking about you and had to hear your voice," Gabe said before I even got the chance to say hello.

"You were thinking about me?" I asked, mockingly coy.

"Like a lot. What are you doing right now?"

"Actually, I just had a killer audition. I have no idea if anything will come of it, but it's the first one that's felt . . . I don't know . . . like I actually may have impressed them."

"Sounds like you knocked it out of the park. Let me take you to dinner tonight? To celebrate. Anywhere you want *just* so long as roller skates aren't involved," he teased.

I tucked the phone under my chin to free my hands to dig around in my purse for my MetroCard. "Still recovering from DiscOasis I gather?" I joked as I slid the pass over the turnstile and navigated my way through the underground maze of tunnels to the platform for the M Train to get me back to Bushwick.

"I should tell you that I feel great and didn't ache at all the next day, but I'd be lying."

I lowered my bottom lip into a pout, hoping he could hear it in my voice. "Everything hurts, huh?"

"Oh, just my knees . . . and . . . hips . . . and back . . . but totally worth it."

I laughed. "How do you figure that?"

"Well, I got to spend time with you, didn't I?" The smile in his voice turned my insides to butter. "So? Dinner tonight?" he asked again.

"I wish I could, but I can't tonight. I'm catching a morning train to Connecticut to visit my parents and I'm not even packed yet. I haven't been home in . . . God, I don't know how long it's been? With everything that happened, it was simpler to keep our phone calls short and the details vague to protect them from really knowing just how much of my life had been tied up in Adam's. I just couldn't face their disappointment. Honestly, I'm still not sure I can," I said, realizing that all these weeks later, it likely wouldn't be any easier. "Hey, do you want to go in my place? They always liked *you*," I offered as a sad attempt to lighten the mood.

"I don't know about going in your place, but I'm happy to go with you, if you think that would help."

"You would really come with me to my parents'? Don't you have like a thousand things you could be doing with your weekend?"

"Meh, whatever else I'd find to occupy my time probably wouldn't be as fun. And definitely wouldn't be as cute. Besides, in all the times I visited Woodbury during college, we still never made it to Flapjacks, Connecticut's oldest pancake house."

"I hate to be the one to have to tell you, but it's not the oldest pancake house anymore. The Connecticut Historical Society found out there's an even older one in New Haven. Stripped the town of our plaque and everything."

"They *even* took the plaque? Those bastards. Well, I'd still like to try it. With you. If you want."

"Well, I *do* want. I'm grabbing the 10:10 from Grand Central. Meet me underneath the gold clock at 10:00?"

"I'll bring the coffee. Tall drip with two shots of espresso, oat milk, and one sugar," he recounted by heart.

"Sounds perfect." Both the coffee and his plan to join me for the weekend.

◆ ◆ ◆

True to his word, Gabe met me at precisely 10:00 a.m. underneath the big gold clock located in the center of the famous train terminal. He looked adorable in his casual weekend wear: gray hoodie, fitted black track pants, his unruly dark hair tucked underneath his well-worn Yankees cap, the same one I was pretty sure he had back in college. He had a small brown leather duffel slung over his shoulder and was clutching a steaming cup of coffee in each hand.

We boarded the train and a little over three hours later pulled into the Woodbury station, a single platform between Main Street and Maple Boulevard. My parents' antiques store was located on the north end of Main, just a twenty-minute walk through town. I glanced down to check Gabe's shoe situation, and when I confirmed he was wearing sneakers, asked if he was game to take the scenic route.

"Lead the way," he said, picking up my bag and slinging it on the opposite shoulder from his own.

We came down the platform steps and crossed over the road, heading into the busiest part of the street. Although Gabe had come home with me maybe half a dozen times while we were dating, I'd never taken him to some of my favorite haunts, a bit embarrassed by our no-frills, Podunk town compared to the bright lights of the big city where he'd spent his whole life.

"So, coming up on your left," I said, pointing to a small building with large glass windows and a pink-and-white awning, "is the world-famous Woodbury Tutu School, where after hundreds of hours of dance practice, Miss Natasha declared I simply did not have the feet or turnout needed for ballet and encouraged me to pursue tap and jazz instead. God, the amount of money my parents must've spent on those lessons. Money I'm sure they didn't have."

"Parents do that, though, for their kids. Many don't, I guess. But the ones who do do it because they want to. That's a pretty special thing, and I think I appreciate, more and more every single day, that my mother did the same for me and Marisol."

A small smile crept across Gabe's face as he reminisced for a moment about Elise until the expression tightened into more of a wince. From the way his jaw clenched, I could tell he probably didn't open up very much about losing her. Though March was peeking just around the corner and spring not far behind, the February air was still brisk, turning even sharper as an occasional gust whipped through the streets. I tucked in closer to Gabe, snaking my arm around his and resting my temple against his shoulder as we strode in sync, side by side.

"I'm sure you really miss her."

"Mostly when something I know she would think is really funny happens. I pick up the phone to call her and realize I can't. It's weird, the same thing used to happen right after we broke up. I'd read an article or see a movie or hear a song I knew you'd love and want to call and tell you about it, but I couldn't."

"You could've. Maybe you should've. You know I always wondered . . ."

Gabe stopped in his tracks and turned to face me, his hands reaching up and rubbing down the length of my arms to warm them. "We don't have to keep tiptoeing around this. No matter how it happened, after all the time that's passed and all the twists and turns we've endured, we ended up back here together . . . maybe now, the timing's finally right. Maybe we both needed to learn a few lessons and grow a little bit before we were able to appreciate what we had, and work harder this time not to lose it." He punctuated his point with a gentle squeeze and stroked the smooth fibers of my camel peacoat with the pads of his thumbs.

I looked up into his hazel eyes, and my stomach dipped when he moistened his full lips with the edge of his tongue. He slid his baseball cap from his head and ran a hand through his thick dark hair before securing it back in place. He glanced up and down Main Street to survey what was where. "Okay, my dear, so which way?"

I crooked my arm in his again and we restarted our stroll, admiring the cute facades and window dressings of the shops that lined Main Street until finally we were standing in front of Lawrences' Antiques, my parents' store that had once belonged to my grandfather and his father before him. I pushed into the shop and was immediately hit by the familiar musty odor of well-worn leather-bound books, furniture polish, and dust.

"Mom? Dad?" I called out and motioned for Gabe to follow me inside, surprised that I had to maneuver around the open door and mountains of trinkets and gadgets prominently displayed around the store. There were about a zillion items everywhere, seemingly even more than the last time I'd visited—which was ironic given the fact that 80 percent of *that* trip had been spent talking about their big plan to downsize everything once they sold the business and retired at the end of the year.

"Mom? Dad?" I cried out again. "Oh God, what if they got wedged in behind an armoire or something?" I turned to Gabe. "I told them we'd be getting in right around now."

"Ave, that you?" Dad called from the basement. "Be right there."

A few minutes later, he came huffing up the stairs. "Sorry, sweetie, we had a gorgeous Biedermeier side table delivered from an auction this morning, and I was just snapping some photos for the website."

"The website? That's new. Um . . . when did you get that going? I didn't even know you knew how to do that."

"Just a little something we put together recently. Have to join the twenty-first century sometime, right? Your mom even wants me to get a TikTok account. Has a handle picked out for me and everything: @ AntiquesJoeShow. Get it? Like *Antiques Roadshow* but with my name, Joe."

I snickered, finding my dad's "dad jokes" so adorably typical. I rolled my eyes and gave him a kiss on the cheek and a quick hug, relishing in the familiar scent of the same cologne he'd been wearing since I was five. "No,

I mean, I get it, but I just don't like *get* it. Why are you learning how to TikTok? What's with the push to revolutionize the business in its last half a year of life? Trying to go out with a bang or something?"

Dad ignored my question and pushed past me and over to where Gabe was still standing in the doorway holding our bags. He opened his arms to him and said, "Gabe Salgado, aren't you a sight for sore eyes. How've you been, son? Judging by your baseball cap, I can see you're still the eternal optimist. The Yankees haven't had a good turn since '98. Now, *that* team had some amazing chemistry."

Gabe's eyes swept over to me. "What can I say? I don't know if it's so much that I'm an optimist, but I like to think if something was that great once, it can be again."

Dad nodded. "Well, up here in Red Sox country, I'd prefer to believe that '98 was the end of an era. Speaking of, don't let the missus see that hat in the house . . . she's liable to incinerate it in our wood burning stove! I don't know if you remember, but she's more die hard than half our neighborhood."

"Oh, I remember," Gabe teased back.

"Hey, since I got you both here, want to help me film a few Insta Stories and post the Biedermeier on the Gram?"

I narrowed my eyes. "Insta Stories? The Gram? Who are you and what have you done with my father?"

"Just trying to keep pace with the rest of the world, is all."

"If I'd known, I'd have offered to bring along my roommates. Now *they* could really give you a crash course in social media. I'd say next time, but you guys'll probably already be off living the RV life by then."

Dad offered a small laugh and turned away. "I'll grab the ring light and tripod attachment for my phone from downstairs and meet you in the back. I think we have some time before we need to head out. Hope you're hungry. Mom has her world-famous lasagna waiting for us for dinner back at the house."

Chapter Twenty-Four

During a deliciously carb-filled dinner full of four-cheese lasagna and fresh buttery rolls, Gabe filled my parents in on all his accomplishments since they last saw him. Now, as a director working for the New York Urban League, Gabe was living his dream of ensuring those in underserved communities had a seat at the table. If there were obvious differences between Adam and Gabe before, recent revelations made that contrast starker than the bright light of day and pitch black of night. Mom, famous for her ability to hold a grudge, had spent the better part of the last decade referring to Gabe as the "bleeding heart who broke my heart," so it was a relief to see her rewarming up to him. I could only imagine how she'd refer to Adam moving forward. Judas? The Grinch? Or just "that greedy asshole"?

After dinner, Mom showed Gabe to the guest room on the second floor that doubled as Dad's office. She picked up a decorative pillow, shook it out to fluff it, and said, "I added a featherbed topper to the pullout to make it a little more comfortable." She pointed to the sofa bed that had to be at least as old as I was that she'd made up with fresh linens before we arrived.

"This will be great, Mrs. Lawrence," Gabe said graciously and moved inside to set his things down on the floor next to the bedside table.

"I'm gonna go drop my bag in my room. When you're done settling in, just come down the hall. You remember which one it is, right?"

"I think I can find my way."

A few minutes later, Gabe knocked lightly on my bedroom door and popped his head through the doorway. I motioned for him to take a seat while I finished unpacking my toiletries.

"Come on in, nothing to see here but a Barbie Dreamhouse and my collection of Troll dolls. My parents haven't touched this room since the day I left for college. It's like a strange time capsule full of One Direction posters and hot-pink emoji throw pillows. Mortifying."

"No, it's great. Is that an *actual* DVD player over there?" Gabe, en route to the bed, took a brief pause to scan through my bookshelf, which housed a handful of DVDs among tattered paperbacks and old play scripts. "Ooh, *Good Will Hunting*? Great movie," he commented, running his finger along the spines as he read aloud.

"Ben and Matt are a New England institution. Well, Boston, but New England by extension, so I feel like we can claim their success as our own. Oh! Wait, stop looking! I've got it!" I yelled and bounced off the mattress to reach around him to grab the romantic classic I hadn't watched since before we broke up.

He glanced at my selection, and his eyebrows danced in delight. "Is that who I think it is?! Mr. Leonardo DiCaprio?! And the heart of his ocean, Dame Kate Winslet?!"

"Should we? I know this is *just* a twin bed and not a bathtub in Hell's Kitchen, but I guarantee we'll be a lot warmer snuggled under these covers than we were freezing our icebergs off in that tub!"

"'You jump, I jump, right?'" he said, quoting Rose's famous line from the movie.

We hit play on the DVD and dove under the covers. Within seconds of the haunting first notes of the eerie melody, Gabe was cocooned around me, his breath warming my neck, the intermittent rush of air like the rhythmic rolling of ocean waves.

Somewhere between Rose living it up in steerage and the steamy make-out scene in the back of the classic Coupe de Ville, Gabe fell asleep nestled up against me, his arms holding on to me tighter than Rose was clinging to her floating door (which totally had enough space for her and Jack, not even a question!). I carefully peeled Gabe off my shoulder, wiggled out from his embrace trying my best not to wake him, and went downstairs for a glass of water.

I carefully tiptoed through the house, but it didn't matter. Squeaks and creaks reverberated out of the old maple floors, bouncing off every door and window. Bernadette (Peters), our grumpy basset hound, asleep in her usual spot by the fireplace, slowly raised her big droopy eyes to see who was there before curling back into her dog bed completely unperturbed.

I grabbed the handle of the refrigerator and wrenched it open, the small bulb inside bathing me in a cool white light. Catching my eye were two large Tupperware containers filled with some of our dinner's leftovers stacked next to the pitcher of water. *Maybe just a little snack?* Grabbing one container with my left hand, I wedged a fork between my teeth, and grabbed a cup of water before making my way to the couch. Only, just as I leaned back into the cushion, a loud and resounding *yelp* sent me at least two feet into the air and the Tupperware of lasagna, as well as the water, flying across the room.

I slowly lifted the blanket off the couch. "Mom, is that you?"

"Of course, it's me," she said, kicking the blanket off her legs.

"Jeez, you scared the hell out of me. What are you doing down here?" I asked.

"The RLS makes your father impossible to sleep with. I end up on the couch at least four nights a week," she managed through a yawn.

"I thought the doctor said Dad didn't have restless leg syndrome?"

"What do they know? I'm the one who's been sleeping next to the man for the past forty years." Mom pointed to the far corner of the room. "Hey, Ave, you might want to pick the lasagna up off the floor before Bernadette finishes it all."

I turned to look behind me. Bernadette had slurped up most of the mess and was polishing off whatever remained in the Tupperware.

"*NOOO!*" I cried, and rushed over to scoop up the leftovers until I realized that Bernadette was doing a better job of cleaning it up than I could, so I just let her go to town, while I found a spray bottle of disinfectant and some paper towels to do a final wipe down after she was done.

Without even having to be asked, Mom tightened the tie of her faded navy terry cloth robe, pushed up from the couch, and headed into the kitchen. Reaching into the fridge, she pulled out the second Tupperware and set the microwave to three minutes. When it finished, she pulled out the piping-hot dish and set it on the table. She poured a tall glass of milk, placed it beside the plate, and pulled a chair out, gesturing for me to take a seat.

"Thanks," I said, giving the floor one last swipe before balling the dirty paper towels in my fist and tossing them into the trash. "You didn't have to go to any trouble. I was planning on eating it cold."

"Trouble? What trouble? I used the microwave." She eased into the chair across from me.

I took a few bites of the lasagna and pushed the milk away from my plate.

"What's wrong? You don't like milk anymore?" Mom asked. "I can get you something else? I think we still have that bottle of wine you sent us for Christmas last year." She went over to the sideboard, bent down, and shimmied a bottle out from the back. "*Ahh*, here it is. You like red, right?" she asked, holding it up.

"Mom, that's an eight-hundred-dollar bottle of wine."

She jerked the bottle away from her to examine the label, as if there was a price tag she'd somehow missed. "Why on God's green planet would you ever send us an eight-hundred-dollar bottle of wine?!" Her voice shrieked to a whole new octave, clearly bowled over by the ridiculousness of the purchase. But it hadn't been frivolous when we bought it, or so I thought. It was our attempt at a gesture of well wishes after having to reschedule yet another set of holiday plans with my folks.

"Well, you know Adam," I said offhandedly, until the irony struck me between the ribs. "Knew Adam . . . Well, actually, turns out we didn't, eh?"

Mom shifted her gaze, clearly uncomfortable at the mention of Adam, and turned back to where she kept the alcohol. "Here," she said, pulling out a second bottle from the cabinet with a nondescript duck on the label, "this is an eleven-dollar bottle of wine. You can't feel bad about drinking an eleven-dollar bottle of wine."

I tilted my head to the side. "An entirely different kind of bad." I waved the bottle toward me. "But go ahead, bring on the pain."

Mom laughed and poured us both a glass of the cheap merlot and settled back down at the table. I took a sip and glanced around the living room, taking in the knickknacks, tchotchkes, and antique trinkets practically spilling off every shelf and stuffed into every cabinet. My parents weren't exactly hoarders, their clutter more of an occupational byproduct, but no question Marie Kondo would have a field day in this place.

"I'm surprised you and Dad haven't started selling any of this stuff yet. You know like less than a quarter of it's going to fit into an RV, right? Unless you're planning on renting a storage unit . . . or half a dozen? And I passed by the store today. It too is still crammed with inventory. Don't you need to start unloading it all soon?"

Mom nodded. "I know, this house has become like a second showroom over the years. There's a lot to go through."

"I can help you tomorrow for a bit before I head back to the city? We can figure out if any of this stuff *actually* sparks joy."

"It all sparks joy, that's the problem," she joked.

"You'd be surprised how easy it is to pare down when you don't have any other choice."

Mom rubbed my shoulder. "Oh, honey, why didn't you take us up on our offer of coming home when you first told us about everything a few weeks ago? We could've helped. You know our door is always open to you for as long as you need it."

"No, I'm a big girl. I needed to figure out some of this on my own. And I did, plus, I know your door is always open, but space in an RV is pretty limited. Seriously, let me help you at least get started," I offered.

"There's no rush. You have a lot on your plate. Another weekend you can come and Kondo me, it's a promise."

There was a tinge in her voice, like she was holding something back. It was the same warble she had when I was eleven and she had a hard time telling me my pet rabbit, Mary Hoppins, died while I was away at a two-week theater camp. "What's going on? I thought you and Dad planned to be settled in Florida by the summer?"

"It's no big deal. Really. But, we have to push things off a bit."

Are her hands shaking?

"What? Why? Are you okay? Is Dad?" My heart suddenly felt like it had plummeted to my stomach, beating like a ticking time bomb deep within my core. Dad was diagnosed with stage one prostate cancer two years ago, but as far as I knew, it hadn't progressed beyond that.

"No, no, it's nothing to do with anyone's health, thank heavens. Guess that's always the silver lining. Aside from the RLS and a bit too much flatulence outta your dad for my liking, everybody's doing great," she joked with a half smile that didn't quite meet her eyes.

"So, what is it then?" I tried to remember the last time I'd seen my mother upset like this. Angry, sure. I'd seen her lose her shit a few too many times after one thing or another throughout my high school and college years. You know, the normal stuff for a mom trying to make ends meet while raising a moderately mouthy teen. But this distracted, distraught version of my mom was altogether foreign.

Her hands trembled and only stopped once she rested one elbow on the table and her forehead into her palm, closing her eyes like she was warring internally about how to tread next. "I wasn't planning on telling you this. I figured you were dealing with enough as it is but, we . . . your dad and I . . . we were . . . well, are victims of Adam's too."

I exhaled with relief. "Oh, Mom, I know you loved him like a son. I mean, none of us could have seen that coming—" I started as an attempt at consolation until Mom jutted her hand out to stop me.

"No, Avery, I mean, we're *actual* victims. A few years ago, Dad was talking to Adam about how we needed the store to turn more of a profit if we were going to be able to retire before we turned sixty-five and he convinced us to invest some money into one of his online marketing packages."

"No," came out of me as a whoosh of air as Mom's words struck like I'd been pummeled in the solar plexus by a battering ram. My vision narrowed, creating a blackness around the edges.

Mom placed her hand on my arm and stroked it comfortingly. "Luckily, it wasn't as much as your father originally wanted. I've always been a bit more conservative where our finances are concerned, but it was enough to derail our plans. Not entirely, but just . . . for the moment anyway."

Up until now, Adam's victims had been nameless. Nameless and faceless. It was still unimaginably awful, but not knowing them made it easier to somehow compartmentalize it all. The speeding pace of my thoughts competed with the hammering of my heart. Adam did this to my parents. *My* mom and dad. All those years we'd visited them for holidays together. All the plans we'd talk about when we'd talk about the future, like taking our children to visit Mimi and PawPaw in Woodbury. It was truly the worst kind of betrayal, and the news of it hit me even harder than the initial knock of the FBI team on our door Christmas morning.

My mind flashed to the $800 bottle of wine, the designer brand names that I started to drop into conversation like they were actual friends, the lavish Upper East Side apartment, the house in Quogue, all of it. Did she think that I was in on it? That I knew what he was up to and turned a blind eye out of self-interest?

"God, Mom, I didn't know. You have to believe me. Maybe I was naive, but I swear, I had no idea who he really was. What he was really capable of. I can't believe he took advantage of the two of you. I thought he loved you."

"And we thought he loved you. And sweetheart, we never—not for one second—believed you had any inkling of what Adam had done. Not only because you were barreled right off your ass just as hard as we were, but more so because you are my daughter and you have one of the very best hearts of anyone I know. As for him? Well, none of it makes a lick of sense beyond sheer greed. Greed and hubris to believe he could swindle so many people and just get away with it." Mom stood up, licked the pad of her index finger, and dabbed at a rogue crumb from the table before pushing in her chair. "But he didn't get away with it in the end, did he?" She offered me a crooked brow and a knowing-mom-style satisfied smile.

I lifted my glass in a mock toast. "No, no, he didn't."

"We'll still be able to retire, it just may take another year or two. I promise you, sweetie, we'll be okay, and I know it may not feel this way now, but in time, so will you."

I picked up my plate to clear it from the table. Mom took it from me and said, "You look exhausted. I'll finish cleaning up. Why don't you head back upstairs and try to get a good night's rest?"

I carefully stepped over Bernadette, now snoring in a carb coma at the bottom of the stairs, and crept back to my bedroom where Old Rose, her hair blowing in the sea breeze as she climbed up the railing under the night sky, was just about to toss the Heart of the Ocean *into* the ocean, and Gabe was still sound asleep. I climbed into the bed and nuzzled my way back into the crook of his arm.

Gabe stirred and groggily kissed the top of my head, mumbling, "Did they hit the iceberg yet?"

His eyes were still closed.

"Close to an hour ago. Don't worry, though, I won't tell you how it ends."

He breathed a laugh into my hair and pulled me closer to him, his legs entangling with mine, my cold feet searching his for warmth. "What's wrong?" he asked. "Can't sleep?"

"No. Maybe. But this is perfect. Can we stay like this? You wrapped around me just like this?" An errant tear slipped down my cheek. I hadn't even realized I'd been crying.

"For as long as you need me."

I drew myself into him and closed my eyes as his arms tightened around me like armor, like a shield that would keep the world at bay, at least for a little while.

But the next morning, the world came knocking in the form of a phone call. To my total astonishment and utter delight, I'd received a callback for the title role in the upcoming Broadway production of *Marley Is Dead*. The question was, though: Was I ready to answer it?

Chapter Twenty-Five

My weekend at home illuminated so much. However, the fact that my parents had been victims of Adam's too was the very last thing I ever expected. Over all these weeks, as more and more about his crimes became public, I'd managed to convince myself Adam had two sides to him. Like Dr. Jekyll and Mr. Hyde, there was the mild-mannered gentleman shadowing the presence of an unimaginable monster. The Adam I knew was generous and loving. I didn't think I'd ever met Mr. Hyde, but maybe I had?

My thoughts darted back to that year we first started dating. I was still auditioning, still trying to get my foot in the door, even though my track record was abysmal, my confidence wavering with every casting agent's dismissal from the stage. Adam never outright discouraged me, but instead liked to highlight all the ways I could be happier. How he could make me happier.

I didn't back then, but now I understood all the small but subtle tactics he used to chip away at my dreams, convincing me his were better. But they weren't. And I could see that now.

On Monday, I returned to the city ready to dive into preparing for my callback for *Marley Is Dead*. Just like the old days, Charlie generously offered to stay after his shift to help me work through the material.

"Okay, first of all, I cannot believe that you have a callback for Marley. I mean, you're one of the most talented actors I know, but the fact the phone booth sent you to *that* audition? It's really kinda wild," Charlie said nonchalantly as he swung a stool around to the working side of the counter, now closed. The only people left in the restaurant aside from us were a few bussers finishing up in the kitchen before they too headed out for the night.

"I know, I'm still not sure how the pieces of this crazy phone-booth-mystery puzzle all fit together, so for now, rather than make myself crazy trying to get to the bottom of it, I've decided to just kinda go with it."

"You know what they say, it's the small pieces that make the big picture, and I'm sure yours will show itself in due time," Charlie answered thoughtfully. "Half the fun is the big reveal, isn't it?" He reached across the counter and patted the top of my head. "*Ahh*, patience, young grasshopper."

I grunted dramatically. "You know patience has never been 'My Strongest Suit.'" I sang the last words to the tune of the snappy *Aida* hit.

"Okay, okay . . . back to your audition. You are 'not throwin' away your *shot*,'" he said, riffing on *Hamilton* before leafing through the pages I'd set down on the counter.

He was right. I only had two weeks to learn three scenes and two songs, and I couldn't let myself get distracted by the magnitude of the opportunity or discouraged by nerves.

"The casting director sent these over last night. I haven't even had a chance to look at them yet," I admitted as I fanned out the pages I'd printed off from my email message. There was a scene from act one, one from act two, and a monologue.

The script described one of the songs as a heartfelt ballad that comes early in the show called "The Christmas Spirit." The second song was described as an up-tempo, *SIX*-style number with catchy lyrics, unforgettable beats, and clever wordplay called "My First, My Past, My Everything."

"This is such a fun number, have you heard it? Let me pull up what I can find on YouTube. They haven't recorded a cast album for the show yet, but I think there are a few bootlegged songs hidden somewhere on the web," Charlie offered, grabbing his phone and thumbing through his apps. "Actually, with it coming to Broadway, maybe the album will be out sooner than expected?" He continued to scroll for the song, his eyes fixed to the screen. After a bit of searching and an excited "aha!" he hit play and set the device between us to listen. Though the sound quality of the bootleg wasn't great, I held the sheet music up to face us both and tried to sight-read as the quick tempo moved along at an unrelenting pace. I was winded by the time we hit the bridge.

"Holy God, when am I supposed to breathe?" I joked (quite seriously) as I was certain I was the color of a blueberry.

"Yeah, that is a tough run there. Maybe try sneaking in a quick breath between the words *chance* and *through . . . riiiiiight* here." He pointed to the measure with his finger. "It'll be more of a lift than a full inhale, but it might be just enough while Scrooge is holding his note that you can make it to the end of the line without fainting."

"Oh, yeah, I like that. Thanks." I pulled a pencil from my bag and marked the measure with a clear slash through the text. I tapped the rewind button on his phone until the song was queued up to the beginning of the run and did it again. This time as Charlie sang through the break holding Scrooge's long note, I grabbed enough air to finish out the line without issue.

"Yes, excellent, so much better," he remarked through a proud grin.

"Yeah, that felt a lot better," I said, setting down the music sheets. "*If* you have some more time, I was hoping we could do a bit of scene work? I could really use a sparring partner in order to get the feel for this character. Plus, I have to start learning my lines. Would you mind?"

"Not at all. I cleared the rest of my evening," he said, already standing and moving from behind the counter to meet me. He strode over to the stage and hopped up effortlessly, turning around to offer me some help. So, instead of heading to the steps backstage, I took his hand, hoisting myself up, and handed him a copy of the scene.

"Maybe let's do a read through first, just to get a feel for what we're dealing with?" I suggested, taking a seat on the stage and crossing my legs underneath me. It'd been a long time since I deconstructed a scene, not since my days at Tisch. But it was an important part of the acting process, and it felt good to be in the throes of my craft in this way again. Charlie lowered himself to the floor as well and sat facing me, the pages of the script in his lap.

Charlie asked, "How much do you know about the show? Anything?"

"Honestly, no, not really. I know it's been getting raves, and that it's a take on *A Christmas Carol*, but that's about it?" I said, a bit embarrassed by the admission.

"Yeah, I guess you could call it a prequel or maybe more of an origin story? Do you remember Jacob Marley from the original book? He was Scrooge's equally greedy business partner and the one who forewarns him of the three ghosts that will visit him during the night. He was left to roam the Earth in heavy chains forged from his own sinful past. But in this version, Jacob Marley is now Marley Jacobs, a woman who was once in love with Scrooge, abandoning her own sense of right and wrong, all her life's ambitions, in her pursuit of him. The show is told from her point of view and is basically a modernized allegory."

"How do you know so much about it? Have you seen it?" I asked, impressed with his knowledge of the plot.

"Last year, I went over to London to help with the opening of the Mimi's Shooting Star Diner in Piccadilly Circus. One of the servers there was in the workshop at the Norwich Theatre Playhouse before it moved to the West End. I caught an early version, but I could tell it was gonna be a big hit. The story was fun, but the music was unbelievable."

"Wow, that's incredible. Okay, so a modernized allegory. Got it. But then what happens? Same plot as *A Christmas Carol*? She gets visited by the three ghosts?"

"No, actually, she kinda *is* the three ghosts. So, what happens is at the opening of the musical, Marley arrives in purgatory and is given one last chance to see if she is worthy of Heaven. She must return to Earth as the Ghosts of Christmas Past, Present, and Future to confront all the choices in her life that led her to that moment."

"Whoa, that's clever. So Scrooge is like a secondary character then?"

"Well, no, he's a pretty big influence who sort of sets the story in motion, but don't worry about that now, it'll all make much more sense once we read through all the scenes."

Two hours later, we were ready to call it for the night. After a long shift at work and a grinding rehearsal, we were both spent.

Charlie shuffled the script in his hand, rolled up the pages, and shoved them in the back pocket of his dark-washed jeans. "Hey, it's been a hell of a day. How about a drink?"

I glanced down at my watch. "Sure, yeah that sounds great."

He hopped off the stage and headed to the back. A few minutes later, he emerged triumphantly clutching a large bottle of Patrón Silver and placed it on the counter before pulling a carafe of fresh-pressed orange juice and some cranberry from the fridge. "Cranberry is going to have to do since we don't have any grenadine, but here." He continued to mix up a glassful of this and that, before ceremoniously placing a shiny maraschino cherry on top. "Presenting my version of a tequila sunrise."

I slapped on an intentionally exaggerated pout and said, "No! This is Mimi's Shooting Star Diner—where *everything* is Broadway themed. C'mon, Charlie, you can do better than that . . . ," I challenged him with a raised brow.

"Hmm . . ." He raised his glass confidently and eyed me to lift my own to meet it. "Oh, I got this. Enjoy your Tequila Sunrise . . . Sunset."

"*Ahhh*, so good!" I laughed and mockingly bowed down to him. I clinked my glass to his and exclaimed, "L'chaim!"

"To life," he answered back without so much as missing a beat. He took a sip of his cocktail and said, "So, how are things going in the new place? Lyla mentioned you've been getting along great with the rest of her roommates."

"I still haven't actually met one roommate yet. But the rest of them have been really welcoming. It's been nice to have that kind of sisterhood in my life again."

"I'm glad it worked out. So . . . same time, same place tomorrow night? We can pick up with act two after we close?"

"Actually, Gabe asked me to be his plus-one at a fundraiser tomorrow night. I was going to see if you minded if I headed out a little early to get ready?"

"Oh, sure. No problem," he replied. We finished up our drinks and Charlie set them down on the counter to be washed. "You don't have to stick around. I have a few more things to do before locking up."

"I'm happy to help . . . you scratch my back, you know?"

"My back's good," he joked. "Seriously, don't worry about it. I'll just see you for your shift tomorrow."

"Are you sure?"

"I'm good, Avery, I promise."

"Okay then, 'So Long, Farewell,'" I sang with a salute and a bow. "And thanks again, really."

"Auf Wiedersehen, goodbye." He winked and headed back toward his office.

Chapter Twenty-Six

The next day, after a long shift where I played Elle Woods, Ms. Hannigan, and Annie Oakley, I was beyond exhausted. With my energy rapidly waning, I tossed back a double Starlight Espresso and clocked out of the diner so I could make it to my hair appointment on time.

Gabe's fundraiser was black tie and being held at the swanky Pierre hotel, and I wanted to step it up a few notches. I settled on my favorite YSL little black dress, one of the few mementos I'd kept from my life with Adam. Sevyn offered to do my makeup, and I decided to splurge on a blowout to pull the whole look together.

One of the salon assistants walked me over to the washing bowl, and I settled back in the chair, my long hair spilling out into the sink. She pumped a few globs of shampoo into her palm and massaged the soap into my scalp until it became a mountain of foamy suds.

"I might have to do a double wash. You have a lot of green makeup caked around your hairline and in your temples?" she said quizzically.

"Occupational hazard," I joked. "A double wash is great. Thank you."

After the shampoo, she led me to her station and handed me a menu of blowout options.

"My dress has a high collar, so an updo, I think? I don't know, I'm fine with whatever you think will look best," I said, passing it back to her.

"You got it. I'm going to use your natural texture for volume, but I'll twist the pieces and arrange them so that they are out of your face and look intricately woven together. Sound good?" she asked, her fingers mounting a pile of freshly spiraled curls on top of my head to demonstrate.

"I trust you," I said with a smile and closed my eyes to relax for the next hour.

"Before we get started," she said, "can I offer you a complimentary glass of champagne or a mimosa?"

"Um . . . I'm good with just some ice water." But as she turned to leave, a flutter of anxiety forced me to call after her. "Actually, you know what, maybe I will take some champagne, if you're offering."

Staring at my reflection in the salon mirror, I couldn't help but flash back to the last event I attended with Gabe, the same day as the disastrous *Wicked* audition. It'd been almost seven years, and I could still remember every detail of that cataclysmic night like it was yesterday.

As angry as I had been with Gabe for being so oblivious to my feelings, I'd set them aside and still went to support him and his cause that night. The event had been months in the making—outreach, planning, and investor meetings all culminating at a gala in support of Bigs & Littles NYC Mentoring Services, an organization Gabe had been volunteering his time at since he was in high school. The fact that Gabe had managed to get the Clintons to attend was a major coup, and the fundraiser was slated to be their biggest night of the year.

Once I'd arrived at the venue (Gabe having gone early to help with the setup), I'd positioned myself in the corner by the bar and tried to plaster a smile on my face, all the while my mind continuing to rehearse everything I planned to say to him once the event was over and behind us. In the time between Gabe leaving me standing in our apartment dumbfounded that he'd completely dismissed what could have been a huge break in my career and my arrival at the gala, my anger had melted and given way to a profound sense of hurt and disappointment at not having seen the writing on the wall all along.

Stirring me from my spiraling rabbit hole of thoughts, a handsome man I'd never seen before made his way to where I was standing, his lapels as sharp as his jawline. "Here," he said, taking an empty champagne flute from my hand, placing it on a passing tray, and subbing it out for a full one. "I've learned that the best way to get through these things is to make sure the well never runs dry." When he smiled, my stance softened, and my shoulders relaxed as I took a sip from the fresh glass, the pop of the champagne bubbles tickling my lips.

"See? Better, right?" he said.

"Definitely better," I admitted. "Sounds like this ain't your first rodeo."

"Far from it. But all for a good cause, right? One of these days, someone's gonna realize they'd do even better if they'd organize a fundraiser where we just had to send in a check and could stay home in our pj's. But until they figure that out, I'm stuck wearing the monkey suit every Thursday night of the social season," he said, gesturing to his tailored tux.

"Well, for what it's worth, you wear the monkey suit well." I reached out to touch the arm of his jacket, the gesture almost involuntary. The fabric was sumptuous under my fingertips.

Was I flirting with this handsome stranger? No, I was just making polite small talk at a cocktail party, something you apparently do with handsome *or* not-so-handsome strangers when you've basically been stood up by your boyfriend at *his* charity event, *mooed* during the most important audition of your life . . . and had three glasses of champagne. I tried to catch the eye of a passing server to see what kinds of hors d'oeuvres he was carrying in an effort to soak up some of the alcohol, but each tray turned up empty as they headed past me back to the kitchen.

Before I knew it, the stranger extended his glass to me. "Can you hold on to this for just a minute. . . ," he said, dragging out the last word as he gestured for me to fill in my name.

"Avery," I answered, reaching out to grab the flute he was handing me.

"Nice to meet you, Avery. I'm Adam. Promise you'll stay right here. I'll be back in a sec."

Moments later, he returned balancing plates piled high with all sorts of appetizers and snacks. I wanted to reach out to help him, but with the flutes still in my grasp, I was pretty useless.

"There's an open table over there. Should we claim it?" he asked. "It might be a little tricky for us to try to eat with our hands full."

I followed him to the small high-top where he set the hors d'oeuvres, and I did the same with our drinks.

"I realized I forgot to give you the other half of my fundraiser survival guide," Adam said, tapping the flute. "While you don't want the well to run dry, you also need to make sure to wrangle up some food during the cocktail portion. Once the presentations and speeches start, it's a good hour-plus before they even serve the salad. And too much champagne on an empty stomach can lead to one of two things."

"Oh yeah? What are those?" I asked, leaning in closer and slurping up an oyster.

"Either spending your whole evening praying to the porcelain god in some very posh hotel bathroom *or* spending all of your money at the event's silent auction. Trust me, I know this from experience. Though this time, I have my eye on a bike tour through Provence for two," he offered with a charming smile, a flash of one deep-set dimple catching my eye.

"Provence. Sounds nice. So are you like a professional fundraiser attendee or something? Or do you have an actual job you report to?" I asked playfully.

He chuckled and took a sip from his flute before responding. "It's a bit complicated to explain, but to put it simply, I'm in market research."

"That's interesting."

"Not really. What about you? What do you do?"

"I'm a struggling actress, and it just so happens I blew the biggest audition of my life today." The horror of me swinging through the air like the pendulum of a great cow clock repeated over and over again in my brain, and I winced at the memory.

"I'm sorry to hear that. With a face like yours and such sparkling conversation, it seems a shame for you to have to struggle as an actress when there's probably a million things that you could do and do well."

My heart sank as I realized this stranger had been more consoling than my boyfriend of almost five years. "Thanks. That's nice of you to say."

Just then I heard my name called from over my shoulder. "Avery, there you are. I've been looking all over for you. I have a bunch of people I want you to meet," Gabe said as he approached us at the table.

Upon seeing Adam, Gabe's face broke into a wide smile and he extended his hand. "Adam, so glad you could make it. And thank you again for your *generous, generous* donation."

"Gabriel, man, good to see you. Of course, it's a great cause," Adam replied.

"Avery, this is Adam Daulton. He's one of our biggest donors."

"I know. We met just a few minutes ago," I said, looking down at the mess of small plates on our table between us and hoping Gabe wasn't reading too much into our encounter. But, it seemed he was so focused on the event, he didn't pay attention to anything aside from the fact I was schmoozing with a big-time donor.

Just as I was about to continue the conversation, we were swiftly interrupted by a large redheaded man with a clean-cut beard who was sporting a lanyard around his neck (in stark contrast to his pristine suit) with the words EVENT STAFF typed in bold font. "Hey, Gabe, the teleprompter's acting up. Do you know where Simon's at?"

"God forbid we don't have a teleprompter and someone has to speak from the heart, right?" Gabe said with a huff. "Ave, can you do me a favor and tell Marcie over in the auxiliary she can open up the silent auction while I go and look for Simon? We may need to delay the speeches until I can get this thing up and running." Gabe clapped Adam on the shoulder before hurrying to follow the tall redhead through the crowd.

At the mention of dinner being potentially pushed back even later, Adam eyed me, and then his plate, and ceremoniously popped a mini egg roll in his mouth.

I chuckled at the accuracy of his earlier observation and followed suit, and we chewed together in silence behind our knowing smirks.

I swallowed and said, "Looks like I need to report for duty."

"So, are you like a volunteer with the organization? *Orr . . .*"

"Not quite. I'm Gabe's girlfriend."

"Oh, right. That whole exchange makes a lot more sense now." He stood from his chair and placed his napkin on the table. "Well, Gabe's a great guy."

"Thanks. It was nice to meet you. Maybe our paths will cross again."

"You never know." He smiled.

I grabbed my clutch off the table and offered Adam one last smile before heading off to find Marcie in the auxiliary to give her Gabe's message about kicking off the silent auction. Afterward, I made my way to our table, where I hoped Gabe would join me after he finished dealing with the teleprompter crisis. But, he never did. Two hours of speeches and three courses later, and I was still sitting there all alone.

A little after 1:00 a.m., my feet and feelings were aching to the core as I tallied up the numerous blows our relationship had taken over the past few months. There was his disregard for my audition today—really, all my auditions—his disregard for me sitting here alone now, just more examples in a series of many where Gabe was so consumed with his own passions, he didn't give much thought to mine. Deep in my heart of hearts, I knew then and there that it was time to call it quits—the night and my relationship with Gabe.

The next morning, at my request, we met at our café. Gabe came breezing in, late of course, his cell phone glued to his ear.

"No problem, I can swing by the hotel later and pick up the rest of it." He sat down at the table and raised his chin in my direction as a means of a midconversation *hello*. "Me too. Just incredible. I never thought we'd surpass our goal, and by so much. Really great job by you and the rest of the team. Yeah, yeah of course, I'll be in later." He held his finger up indicating he needed another minute or so to finish up his call.

Though I should have been used to it, in this moment, my patience and frustration grew even hotter than the steaming coffee I was cupping in my hand. There he was, as always, oblivious to the fact he was putting me on the back burner. It hadn't just been yesterday after my audition, or last night as he ignored me all evening, or even this morning walking in here fifteen minutes late and on a call. But for a long time now.

He shifted in his chair, trying to maneuver himself out of his coat while still tethered like a lifeline to his phone. "Oh, really? The *New York Times*? I'll take a look online, but if you have the actual paper, hold on to it, and we can frame the article for the office. Thanks, Susan, see you around three," he said, finally hanging up.

He set his phone down on the table and immediately started to scroll for the *New York Times* article Susan mentioned.

"Hey? Hi?" I waved my hand in front of his face.

"Sorry, give me *oooooonnnneeee* more second. Okay . . . and . . . sent." He looked up from the screen and turned his phone around to show me what he was so focused on. "The gala made the front page of the Styles section. Do you know how much more attention that's going to get us? I mean, we already surpassed our goal, but if we're able to get even a few more donations, we'll have the funding to develop the program across all the boroughs, not just Manhattan."

"That's really great news," I said, and it was. For Gabe and for all the children who would benefit from his hard work. I was truly, deep down in my heart, happy to hear the event had been such a success, but this dark cloud, this writing on the wall that I'd been refusing to read, continued to hover and thicken over our relationship, and last night made it even clearer to me our lives were heading in separate directions.

"Great? It's fantastic! President Clinton was the ace in the hole," Gabe recounted, a wide smile on his face as he opened up the menu to scan it. "Breakfast was a good idea. I never even had dinner last night. Come to think of it, I didn't sit down all evening, not once."

"I know," I remarked curtly.

He glanced up from the menu. "Hey, are you upset with me? I'm sorry I didn't spend more time with you last night, but there was a lot on my plate."

"I'm not upset, Gabe, I'm used to it," I admitted, "but I can't continue to be a total afterthought."

His hands flew into the air in exasperation. "It was our biggest night of the year, the culmination of all my hard work and time, and I needed to give it a hundred percent of my attention. What's so wrong with that?"

"Nothing. At all. That's what I'm saying. But that audition was the culmination of all *my* hard work and time, and for some reason, you dismissed it like it didn't matter. It mattered to me." I moistened my lips and prepared to say all the things I'd been hesitant to acknowledge before. "I don't think you're invested in this relationship right now. There's no room for me in your life. And I hate saying that because of all the wonderful things you do have room for, but it hurts too much not to be one of them."

"Yesterday was a whirlwind. I do want to hear about your audition. Tell me what happened, I'm ready now."

"That's the point, Gabe. You're ready now, but I needed you *then*."

"Well, *then* wasn't an option. And not because I don't love you or wasn't interested in what you were saying but because . . ."

I gave him a moment, curious to see how he would end that sentence, but even he was struggling to finish his thoughts. Deep down, I knew we were too scared to move on from one another, more in comfort than in love these past few months. But he'd been such a constant in my life that I hadn't (until recently) even considered what a future without Gabe would look like. But now it was time. You don't drown by falling in the water. You drown by staying there. I took a deep breath and filled in the words for him. "Because deep down . . . deep down we want different things. I love you, but I think we both know it's not working. Not anymore."

He sat there in stunned silence, almost as if he wasn't sure he'd heard me correctly. But when the weight of my words finally settled, he didn't contradict me. He didn't push back. Instead, he sat up a little straighter, deep lines of concentration etched into his face, no doubt considering the bitter truth we'd both been too scared to admit.

He expelled a forceful whoosh of air, and when he looked up at me, I wasn't sure if I caught a glint of light flash in his eyes or a sheen of moisture that filled his stare. "I never meant to hurt you."

"I know."

He nodded. "I'll move my stuff out of the apartment as soon as I can figure out where to go."

"We only have a month left of our lease anyway, you keep the apartment. I can stay with Marisol," I replied.

He stood up from the table and slung his green canvas bag over his shoulder, tucked his phone into his pocket, and leaned down to whisper in my ear. "For what it's worth, I do believe in you. I always have, even if I didn't always know the right way to show it."

"I believe in you too, Gabe," I managed past a thick lump in my throat.

He nodded, and with nothing more to say, turned around and walked out the door. Without looking back, he disappeared into the city, the wave of pedestrians sucking him into the crowd like a riptide. I looked once more, unsure if I'd made the right decision, but it didn't matter . . . he was already gone.

Chapter Twenty-Seven

At the sound of the apartment buzzer, I double-checked my fancy updo in the hallway mirror, and noticing my naked earlobes, hurried to find the pearl drop earrings I'd pulled out of my jewelry box. I peeked my head out of my bedroom and saw that Lyla had answered the door, ushering Gabe in, while I finished getting ready for tonight's fundraiser. I swiped on a coat of matte red lipstick, wafted through a final spritz of my favorite Chanel perfume, and checked myself one last time before sliding on my stilettos and stepping out into the living room.

As I made my way down the hallway, I could hear Sevyn's voice, more serious than playful, grilling Gabe. "So, you *don't* have a Tinder profile then?" she asked.

"Tinder? No. I've never been on Tinder."

"Grindr? Bumble? Plenty of Fish? FarmersOnly?" she pressed, continuing her interrogation.

"No, no, no, and is there really a dating website specifically for farmers? Who knew? Truthfully, online dating was never my thing," he admitted.

"Or so you *sayyyyy*." She eyed him skeptically. "So then, what *is* your thing? Flushing house pets down the toilet?"

"Excuse me?" he asked.

Lyla jumped in. "Sevyn, he and Avery have known each other for years. I don't think you need to give him the third degree."

I entered the room, joining Lyla in her plea for Sevyn to back off the interrogation. "You'll have to excuse Sevyn. She's not only fiercely loyal, which I appreciate to no end, but she has had her share of questionable dates in the past." Hearing my voice, Gabe turned to see me and sprang up from the couch when his eyes fully took me in.

"Oh my God, Avery, you look incredible. Gorgeous." His eyes were wide, and he practically had to pick his jaw up off the floor.

"Oh, this old thing?" I joked and did a little twirl.

"Here," he said, passing me a bottle of champagne. "I thought we could have a celebratory toast before we go."

Sevyn leaned over to examine the label. "Veuve Clicquot, that's really good stuff. I'll grab some glasses for everyone."

Clearly caught off guard by her assumption, Gabe stuttered, "Oh, um . . . okay. Great. Um . . . I guess we can *all* have a celebratory toast before we head out. Excellent."

I smiled at him appreciatively, assuming the bottle had been meant for just the two of us. But I was grateful for his go-with-the-flow willingness to just play along.

Sevyn came out of the kitchen balancing an assortment of mugs, glasses, and red Solo cups. "Oak," she called out, "Avery's date brought some legit champagne, come and join us."

Gabe turned to me and whispered, "How many of them are there? If I had known you lived in a sorority house, I would've brought more bottles."

I laughed. "Just one more, but Ass is hardly ever home. I've lived here for a month already and actually haven't even met her yet."

"Ass? Her name is Ass?!"

I barked out a laugh at the look on his face. It probably was the same look I had when the girls first mentioned her nickname back when I was first looking at the apartment. "Actually, it's Aston. Ass for short."

"Ah yes. Got it now," he said quickly, though clearly still trying to wrap his head around the unusual nickname.

Oak came out of her bedroom and swiped a mug from the counter while Sevyn passed around the remaining cups and glasses.

"So, what are we toasting to?" Lyla asked.

I looked at Gabe. "What *are* we toasting to?"

"Hmm . . . let me think on it for a second."

"Just make sure that whatever it is, you make eye contact when you clink or else you will be cursed with seven years of bad sex," Sevyn said. "In fact, that's how I got my name. My conception is apparently what broke my parents' spell."

"Is that really true?" Gabe asked.

Sevyn lowered her eyes coyly and whispered, "I'll never tell," with a crooked eyebrow.

Gabe's eyes widened and then locked in on mine. With a smile, he lifted his glass, still not blinking, and said, "Cheers to new beginnings," and gently clinked his flute into mine.

As we pulled up to the ornate, gilded entrance of the Pierre hotel, porters in top hats and tails opened the door of the black luxury sedan Gabe had arranged. Dozens of taxis and black SUVs lined the block, waiting to drop off the eventgoers right at the entranceway. Gabe came around the car from the other side, offered me his arm, and we were ushered into the hotel's signature trompe l'oeil–painted Rotunda Room with its double grand staircase and colorful Renaissance-inspired frescoes. Tapered candles illuminated the stairs leading up to a Juliet balcony, creating an intimate and warm ambiance in spite of the hall's vastness. It was classic New York elegance paired with sophisticated Old World charm.

Though I'd been to dozens of events at the Pierre with Adam over the years, I never ceased to be amazed at the splendor of the decor, but tonight in particular, standing here with Gabe, there was something extra magical about the space. We picked up our seating cards from a table at the room's entrance and made our way through the hall, stopping to say hello to different guests every few steps. And this time, unlike so many times before, Gabe introduced me to every donor, kept me by his side at every turn, and checked in with me over and over again to make sure I was having a good time.

"I'm fine, really. If you have to go help with something or attend to anything, I'll be all right by myself for a bit," I assured him, remembering all the events I spent on my own because he'd gotten caught up in one thing or another, sometimes forgetting I was even there at all. But this was clearly a different man, still attentive and considerate while also charming the room as one of the event's hosts.

He rested a hand on the small of my back and leaned in close. "No, I set up everything beforehand and delegated all of tonight's responsibilities to my team, so that I could enjoy the night with you." He kissed me on the cheek, smiled, and took my hand. "Let's get some crab cakes before they all disappear," he said and pulled me in the direction of the cocktail tables.

After devouring piles of amuse-bouches, fine delicacies, and several glasses of expensive champagne, we took our seats at our assigned table and Gabe pulled a few note cards from his jacket pocket. "Sorry, just give me a few minutes. I think I should review my speech one more time before I get up to speak. I'm just going to excuse myself to run through it. Will you be okay by yourself?"

"Of course I will. Go, go. I'll be fine," I assured him and shooed him away playfully. After Gabe took his exit, an older gentleman seated next to me asked if I would be so kind as to pass him the butter plate. I reached over the bread basket and handed the dish to him.

"Thank you, my dear," he said. "Are you a friend of Gabe's?"

"I am." I rested my hand on my chest. "Avery Lawrence, nice to meet you."

"I'm Javier Ibarra. I work with Gabe at the League. Great guy you have there. In the office, it's a bit of a running joke, actually."

"Um, what is?"

"The fact we'll all be able to say we knew him when. He's destined for great things, that one. We all talk about how he should run for office someday."

I smiled warmly. "He's always been really passionate about social justice."

"Passionate. Committed. With his level of drive and his charisma, he could have a big career in politics. Plus, he's not a bad-looking kid, which doesn't hurt."

I laughed. "No, it doesn't."

An echo of someone tapping on the microphone interrupted our banter, and we, along with the room, quieted and turned our attention to see Gabe front and center ready to address the crowd.

He looked so great up there. So self-assured and relaxed. No question he was in his element speaking on the issues he cared most deeply about—poverty, child welfare, homelessness, and urban development. He was a natural, and it was easy to see why Javier and the other staff members at the League believed he'd have a future in politics one day.

When Gabe finished and exited the stage, he was greeted by some of the donor bigwigs like a celebrity, and I proudly watched him revel in the attention he brought to his organization's mission. The band leader cued up the orchestra as soon as he finished his speech, and I watched the other party guests make their way to the dance floor.

I remained at the table, tapping my foot along to the beat, until to my surprise, Gabe came up behind me, and without a word offered me his hand. My eyes lifted to his, and a smile broke out across my face. I accepted his gesture, and he led me to the middle of the room and wrapped one arm around my waist, his other hand not letting go of my own.

After a bit of dancing, the tempo of the music slowed to another ballad, and he pulled me in close to whisper, his breath warm on my neck, "What do you think? Wanna get outta here?"

I lifted my head off his shoulder. "Don't you have to stay 'til the end of the party?"

He shook his head, and with a devilish grin said, "Not tonight."

We barely made it over the threshold of his apartment door when he backed me up against the wall, pressing against me, the soft fabric of his satin tuxedo lapels smooth like warm butter sliding over my skin. I sucked in a quick breath, caught off guard by the way my legs buckled under my weight as he dragged his fingertips down my arm to clasp my hand in his.

He drew my arm up over my head, pinning me between his body and the exposed brick wall behind me, and I was grateful for the force of him keeping me upright, since my limbs had almost completely given way. His other arm wrapped around my waist, simultaneously pulling me close with his hand but continuing to press against me with his hips.

Breathless, I gripped a fistful of his jacket, wrestled it from his thick arms, and tossed it to the floor. Before it even hit the ground, he kissed me hard, his lips inciting an avalanche of emotions, the earth crumbling away under my feet, causing me to fall faster and farther than I ever thought possible. Rooted in place by his body crushed against mine, I was dangling somewhere between our passionate past and the intense present, between solidity and free floating, and all I knew was that I never wanted to come down again.

Gabe wasn't my first, but he was the first that mattered. He taught me everything about my own sensuality and sexuality. Those nights we'd lie in the living room bathtub together were some of the most romantic of my life. It had been a real relationship, and it was Gabe who showed

179

me how important it was to voice my wants as much as my boundaries. We'd taken the time to get to know each other in the most intimate of ways, and it seemed he hadn't forgotten a thing.

Gabe licked at my bottom lip, and I moaned for more as I met his tongue with my own. He grazed the top of my exposed shoulder, his hand cool against my warm skin and forcing the swarm of butterflies who'd taken flight to rush *south*. I writhed against him, trying to get closer until we were sharing more than just our breaths.

He spun me around to unzip my dress, and the momentum of urgency slowed when he was met instead with two tiny buttons securing the halter top behind my neck.

"Oof, these are tough. I'm not sure I can . . ." He fumbled with the small clasps, his large hands doing him no favors. "I'm afraid I'm going to break it."

I coyly glanced at him over my shoulder and ordered, "Do it. Just rip it."

A naughty glint twinkled in his eye and he said, "Your wish is my command," tearing the collar's seams apart like an animal unleashed. The top of the dress fell to my waist and his eager hands met it there, sliding the fabric the rest of the way down my hips. In one surprisingly graceful movement, he scooped me up in his arms as I wrapped my legs around his body, and he carried me the rest of the way to the bedroom, where we didn't leave until the sun came up over Tribeca.

Chapter Twenty-Eight

Two weeks later I was back at the Greenwich House Theater, nervously pacing up and down the long hallway waiting for my name to be called into the studio room for my second audition for *Marley Is Dead*. I'd spent every spare moment over these last fourteen days rehearsing the songs and scenes, Lyla generously offering to read in for every character and Charlie selflessly staying after every shift to work with me on the material.

Since the night Gabe and I spent together, I was struggling to balance everything on my plate. Gabe wanted to spend more and more time with me, which at present I seemed to have less and less of between work shifts and audition prep. I compromised by promising Gabe we could take a weekend trip to enjoy some much-needed time alone away from the city when the audition was over.

"Avery Lawrence, we're ready for you," Joanna, the casting assistant, called out from inside the room.

I nodded, took a few deep breaths remembering Miss Tilly's advice about how to breathe in a way that opened my chakras and third eye, and stepped into the studio only to be greeted by many more people than I'd expected. A table full of faces that I recognized from the first audition plus about ten brand-new ones looked me up and down as I entered the room.

Over in the far corner was the same piano accompanist from last time. Thankfully, the audition materials were the same for everyone, so there'd be no last-minute song selections for him to worry about. As soon as I took my spot at the center of the space and gave him a clear nod, he started to play the first song, the tempo of the music just as quick as it had been on the bootlegged YouTube version I'd been rehearsing from. Though I'd been worried about stumbling over the lyrics at such a breakneck pace, all of my hours of rehearsal paid off when I hit every note and articulated every syllable in perfect time with the music.

I could see smiles and enthusiastic nods firing around the room as others were fiercely scribbling notes on legal pads.

One of the producers leaned forward in his seat. "That was lovely, Ms. Lawrence. Let's do the scenes you prepared followed by the ballad, and then we have some new pages we'd like you to take a look at."

We worked through the scenes I prepared, one going better than the last. The director provided notes and adjustments along the way, all of which I tried to implement to showcase how well I could take direction. When we finished that part of the audition, I knew in my gut it was going well.

The ballad, however, was a slightly different story. Although I managed to hit most of the showstopping notes and express the emotionality of the piece, something just felt a bit off. I didn't know if it was nervous energy or maybe the excitement from the audition having gone better than expected up to this point, but I could actually feel the adrenaline coursing through my veins, making me a bit shakier than normal. It took everything I had to hold on to the final note of the song, my voice falling off at the very end. It wasn't a complete disaster, and certainly not the *moo*-numental mishap that had been my *Wicked* audition, but I could've done better. I knew it and sensed the room did too.

When I finished, Joanna handed me the new scenes and told me I had fifteen minutes to look them over. I accepted them with trembling hands and headed to a bench outside to prepare. I slipped on my coat and made my way through a group of actors taking a cigarette break, the plume of smoke wafting through the temperate March air. I nodded a quick hello and moved to a bench along the sidewalk.

Part of me wanted to just keep walking, right past them, down into the subway, and forget about this whole damn dream. I mean, what business did I have being at a callback for a show heading to Broadway? I was over the hill (in acting years, anyway), out of sorts, and out of practice, the ballad certainly confirming at least that last point. But at the same time, I'd made it this far. So many hours of practice and even more years of failures, and here was a genuine opportunity just an arm's length away.

But then I started to wonder if the possibility of actually getting the role was more nerve-racking than even the audition process itself? *Stop it, Avery!* I was psyching myself out, like always. I needed to get out of my head, set my mounting doubts aside, and just follow through for once. Just once. And if I crashed and burned, so be it. There was too much time to make up for and there were too many times I'd opted out. But this time, I was in for a penny, in for a pound.

Exhaling a deep breath, I shook the negativity from my mind and gripped the pages with renewed vigor. I read the top of the script, noticed the scene was from the first act of the play, and scanned the paper for a description.

> Act 1, Scene 2: Marley, at the gates of Purgatory, meets an angel there who porters the gateway to Heaven or Hell. Marley is disoriented, unsure of where she is, and the angel explains that Marley cannot proceed into either Heaven or Hell until she returns to Earth to revisit three individuals from her life who she wronged and sets things

right for them. This scene rockets Marley
back to the home of a longtime friend she'd
betrayed for the love of Scrooge.

A knot formed in the pit of my stomach. There was something so
hauntingly familiar about the scene's description. As I continued to read
through the back-and-forth between the characters, their conversation felt
more like a memory than fiction, my mind swirling with my last encounters with Marisol before I cut her out of my life for the love of Adam. I
wasn't just pretending to be Marley; in so many ways I *was* Marley.

Joanna came jogging up to where I was sitting. "I know that wasn't
a full fifteen, but the team's anxious to move on. Could you be ready to
come back inside now?" she panted.

My thoughts flashed to Marisol and to our epic fight that last night
in Montauk. To Adam in his orange jumpsuit, bound in handcuffs
behind a wall of solid plexiglass. To the house of cards he'd built so carefully that all came crashing down with a forceful wind Christmas Day.
To everything I'd lost in the wake of his lies and deception, and the fact
that though Adam once dangled a shiny carrot (carat?!), I was the one
who ultimately accepted it at the expense of everyone and everything
else in my life. Filled with overwhelming regret and emotion, tears
stinging my eyes, I managed to choke out, "I'm ready."

I marched back into the studio and, with nothing left to lose, laid
myself bare. I used the pain of my own experience as fuel to ignite the
words from within, displaying a vulnerability that left me emotionally raw
and exposed. By the end of the scene, I had tears streaming down my face,
and so did many of the producers watching. There was a hushed silence
in the air as the scene closed, and it took a full ten seconds or so before
anyone said anything at all. I wasn't sure how to read their expressions, but
right, wrong, or indifferent, I'd given it everything I had.

Not wanting to break the spell of the moment, I waited for some
sort of instruction or dismissal. Finally, the director cleared his throat

and said, "Well, congratulations, we'll see you at the final callback in a few weeks. Joanna will send you all of the details."

I clamped my hand over my mouth, unable to believe I was moving on to the last round of auditions. "Thank you so much. I cannot tell you how much this means to me."

He closed the binder in front of him. "You did a really great job, especially for a cold read. I'm eager to see what you do with the material when you actually have some time to prepare. We'll have most of the show's big investors and all of the producers at the final audition. You'll perform this scene again, but this time with the song that follows. You can grab the pages from off the top of the piano on your way out. Contact Joanna if you have any questions, and we'll see you in about a month."

I managed to squeak out another gracious thank-you to the group, before giving my old friend at the piano a wink as he handed me the sheet music. I hurried out of the room, practically floating three feet above the floor, until I was outside in the fresh air and able to take a deep breath that brought me back to earth.

I could barely wait another second before glancing down at the music to see what was in store for me at the final audition, and when I did, the name of the song, "No Space of Regret," jarred me so forcefully, the air I'd just drawn in heaved back out with such ferocity I almost collapsed onto the sidewalk.

My eyes darted down to the first measure and accompanying lyrics, and though I knew what they would be before I even read the words, the hairs on my head still stood on end and a hot flash slammed into me, countering the cool March breeze. It felt like what I imagined it'd feel like to get struck by lightning.

The song began with the familiar words I'd first heard from the ghost guard on Christmas and each time I visited the phone booth since then—"No space of regret can make amends for one life's opportunity misused"—and just then a large piece of the puzzle finally snapped into place.

Chapter Twenty-Nine

Almost exploding with too many thoughts bombarding me at once, I took a moment to catch my breath on the bench in front of the Greenwich House Theater. I put my head between my knees and sucked in some much-needed air. Between securing a final audition on-site, a feat that on its own would have been enough to knock me on my ass, and then discovering the origin of the phrase "No Space of Regret," I was practically incapacitated with confusion—and, even more so, curiosity. None of this could be a coincidence. Not anymore. There were too many serendipitous occurrences that proved to me this wild ride was all meant to show me something, or maybe teach me something, but hell if I knew exactly what that was yet.

I checked my watch. I would never have enough time to make it back to Bushwick before I was supposed to meet up with Gabe for a date he'd planned for us at our favorite French bistro, the one we'd opted to skip in favor of DiscOasis. Though I couldn't wait to tell him about the audition, I hadn't told him about my second encounter with the phone booth and was hoping to let the conversation flow and see if the subject could arise organically. (Not super sure how a discussion involving a magical phone booth could come up *organically*, but at this point, I was grasping at straws.)

With some time to kill before meeting Gabe, I walked to Mimi's, about two miles uptown from the theater, hoping the fresh air and activity would help to clear my head and burn off some of the adrenaline still racing through my body. I figured I could freshen up in the restaurant's dressing room before heading off to my date, which thankfully was just around the corner from the diner.

I strolled up Seventh Avenue toward Times Square and couldn't help but imagine my name in big letters on the *Marley Is Dead* marquee that would one day (soon) adorn some theater's front entrance and could envision my face on the staged show images that usually decorated the theater's outside facade.

I swung open the door to Mimi's to hear a handful of servers finishing up their rendition of "You Can't Stop the Beat" from *Hairspray*. I clapped along with the raucous applause from the diner's patrons as I made my way to the back to search for Charlie, unable to keep the news of the callback to myself for even one moment longer.

Seeing me, Charlie did a double take. "What are you doing here? Didn't you have your callback today?"

"I did," I answered, desperately trying to keep my face even so as to not give away my big news.

He literally dropped what he was doing, tossing a handful of the menus he'd been holding off to the side to gesture for me to continue. "And?! How did it go?!"

My face split into a wide grin, hardly able to keep myself from shouting it to everyone in the restaurant. "They asked me to audition at the final callback in front of the investors and full production team. I did it, Charlie. I'm so damn close I can taste it."

"Oh my God, Avery! This is incredible and calls for a celebration! I'm going to get us a slice of The Wizard and Pie, the bright-green key lime one you like, and you can tell me all about it." He ushered me into a booth close to the kitchen door and rushed away to grab us the dessert.

When he returned a minute later, he carried two big slices piled high with whipped cream, which he set on the table before sliding onto the bench across from me. "Thank you for this," I said. "I can only have a few bites, though. I'm supposed to be meeting Gabe for dinner around the corner in a little while." I took a bite of the pie and moaned inwardly. "Hmm . . . but it really is my favorite."

"I know it is." He smiled and leaned into the table. "Okay, so tell me everything, start to finish," he said before he scooped a bite of the creamy dessert into his mouth.

I told Charlie about the first number, how well it went, and how positively the team had responded to me. Then, I told him about the ballad, how it was a little shakier but not a total disaster. "Then, they handed me a totally new scene from the show," I continued, "and gave me fifteen minutes to work on it."

"Sounds like you must've killed it if they offered you the final call-back on the spot."

"I was really feeling the material. I've never felt so connected to a character before. Like *very* connected."

"What do you mean?"

I leaned in a bit closer and lowered my voice. "Do you remember the crazy story I told you about how I reunited with Gabe on Christmas Day, and the mysterious phone booth that gave me his address and all that?"

The shift in conversation seemed to jar him but he answered, "*Yeaaah*, of course, who could ever forget a story that included a ghost guard?"

"Exactly. Well, I don't really know how to say this, but Gabe and the phone booth and this audition and this character, it's somehow all connected."

"Wait a minute. Maybe just start from the beginning, what's connected?" he asked.

"Where do I even begin?" I said, replaying the long series of strange events that had led to this moment before answering. "I was with Lyla and we stopped for a hot dog at this cart downtown. I'm handing over some cash for two sodas and look up and the guy, the hot dog vendor, has a silver-bell pin on his jacket, the same exact pin the ghost guard was wearing. And before he gets shooed away by a policewoman for not having a permit, he says to me the *same thing* the guard said on Christmas Day: 'No space of regret can make amends for one life's opportunity misused.'"

Charlie's eyes grew wide at the recognition. "That's from *Marley Is Dead*, the song 'No Space of Regret.'"

"I know! How strange is that? And I looked it up, and the line is actually taken from Dickens's original Christmas Carol story. The guard said that to me *months* before I ever even knew about the audition."

Charlie scrubbed his hand over his face and shook his head in disbelief. He opened up his mouth to speak, but closed it, seemingly not knowing what to say.

"There's more. So after the hot dog vendor was chased away, I took off after him in search of some answers, but I lost sight of him in the crowd, and you'll never believe where I ended up . . . at the phone booth. The very same phone booth from Christmas. The last phone booth in Manhattan. Only this time it gave the address of the Greenwich House Theater—"

"Where the *Marley Is Dead* open call was being held," he said, finishing my sentence.

"Yes! Don't you see? The phone booth, it's guiding me to the past and present and—"

"Future? I don't know. That sounds a bit far-fetched. Maybe you're searching for more meaning in all of this than there actually is."

"No, I don't think that's it. There are too many parallels."

"It's a beautiful thought, Avery, but fate is choice, not chance. It was your choice to give Gabe a second chance, to stay for the audition, to prepare as hard as you did for the callback. To put it all on the phone booth almost cheapens your accomplishment." He stood up from his seat. "And it'll be you who *earns* the role once you work your butt off these next couple of weeks."

Was he right? Was it simply easier to attribute all the recent good in my life to a phone booth rather than myself? I nodded. "Thank you. For the talk and the pie. Seems I really needed both." I smiled and turned to leave, but then quickly spun back. "Oh, is it okay if I just freshen up in the back before dinner?"

"My Mimi's es su Mimi's. Have fun and I'll see you tomorrow," he said as he scooted out of the booth.

I looked up at him, a flash of panic washing over me. I'd put in for that day off when he made up the schedule for this week! "No, remember? I took tomorrow off. I'm going to Vermont for a long weekend with Gabe."

"*Thaaaat's* right. Have a good time. When you get back, it's full steam ahead on the audition prep, right?"

"Yup, I'll be gone for just a long weekend, and then we can hit the ground running."

"Sounds like a plan. Congrats again, BrAvery. Remember, you *earned* this." He swiped our pie plates from the table and left me to get ready for my date with Gabe.

Chapter Thirty

Remembering just how tiny our favorite French bistro was, enough room for maybe ten or twelve tabletops, I rid myself of my jacket and tote at the coat check and squeezed past the bar and into the main dining room. Floating in the air were the sweet notes of "La Vie En Rose" played by the accordionist through the quaint, chic restaurant, the music competing for my attention against the scrumptious smells of browned butter, sautéed onions, and garlicky escargot. My mouth watered at the memory of the rich flavors, and I practically power-walked to find Gabe, who was already seated at our favorite booth—a private nook in the back, away from the hustle and bustle of the kitchen.

He gave me a sweet wave and stood to greet me, kissing me on both cheeks playfully like we were real Parisians out for a night in Montmartre, a fun exchange we shared every time we'd come.

I raised my right eyebrow. "Our table?"

Gabe shrugged sheepishly. "I requested it when I made the reservation."

I glanced around the restaurant, a flood of memories rushing back to me. The way the candles made the room glow with a pink hue as the light bounced off the crimson curtains. The way the sumptuous blue velvet banquettes felt against my skin where the hem of my dress stopped at my thighs. And the way Gabe tucked his napkin in his lap and opened the menu like he didn't already know what we were going to order.

We always got the same thing, but I loved how he pretended like he might change his mind, and how he showed off his limited high school–level French to the waiter, which turned me on a little more than he knew.

A young server approached the table, filling our glasses with mineral water from a bright-blue bottle. "Bonsoir, monsieur and mademoiselle, would you like to hear tonight's specials?"

We eyed one another, certain that whatever he said wouldn't make much difference in changing our already set minds, but we asked him to continue anyway.

"Tonight the chef is featuring foie gras cream puffs with black truffle, canard montmorency, which is duckling topped with a cherry reduction, and finally, lamb chops with a cognac dijon cream sauce served with glazed rosemary carrots."

"That all sounds très bien, but I think we are going to go with our usual: one order of moules frites, one saumon grillé, an order of escargots—tell the chef he can go heavy on the garlic—and an order of bouillabaisse, avec pain, s'il vous plaît," he said confidently, handing the waiter back the leather-bound menus. "Oh, and a bottle of . . . what do you think, Sancerre?"

"That sounds perfect." I confirmed with a nod.

The waiter nodded too. "Oui, excellent. I'll be right back with some bread and your wine."

Once he was out of earshot, I couldn't wait another second to tell Gabe about the callback. "I have to tell you—"

"I have some big news—" Gabe said simultaneously.

"Oh, okay. You go first," I said, sure that my news would dominate the rest of the conversation once I shared it.

"Actually, I have some good news and some bad news," he started.

"Okaaaaay," I said, eyeing him through narrowed lids. "Bad news first, always."

"Agreed. I canceled our bed-and-breakfast for this weekend in Vermont." My stomach dropped at the declaration, certain I'd heard him wrong.

"Wait, what? We've been planning the trip for weeks. I took time off from work. What happened?" It was hard to conceal my disappointment, that old familiar feeling of coming in second to whatever was more important in his life at the moment slowly creeping back in.

"Well, I guess that brings me to my good news." He reached around his seat and into his jacket pocket to pull out a folded-up piece of paper and handed it to me across the table.

I unfolded it skeptically and scanned it, still uncertain at what I was looking at and how it explained why we were no longer going to Vermont. "Um . . . Gabe, what is this?"

"Our flight itinerary. I figured this restaurant was the most appropriate place to tell you I booked us a last-minute trip to Paris, like we'd always talked about. Paris in the springtime . . . almost! Which, yes, I know is a bit of a cliché, but clichés are clichés for a reason, right?" He was positively beaming as he shared his news, all the while my stomach twisted in a tight knot.

"Wait? What? Paris? When? For how long? How?"

Gabe laughed at the fact he had clearly caught me so off guard I could only respond in the form of questions like a *Jeopardy!* contestant.

"Okay, let me see if I can answer all that. Yes, Paris. And that's Paris, France. Not Paris, Texas, in case you were wondering," he joked. "We leave tomorrow evening from Newark around seven p.m. and land at Charles de Gaulle around six thirty a.m. I traded in all my miles for our flights and managed to book an adorable B and B in Le Marais, right by the Georges Pompidou museum. I've read nothing but great things about the restaurants in that area. We'll go to the Louvre and the Musée d'Orsay, and the catacombs, and I scheduled us a tour through the Versailles gardens, and a French cooking class at Le Cordon Bleu. Vermont will always be there. I wanted to do something special for you . . . well, for us . . . and Avery, it's going to be *incroyable*."

He barely came up for breath as he rattled off our jam-packed itinerary, every activity he listed drumming up more and more anxiety in me. I couldn't possibly run away to Paris, especially now with the callback looming so close.

I wasn't sure when it happened, but our wineglasses were suddenly full, and I was beyond grateful for the refill. I grabbed mine and chugged it down, not leaving a single drop behind. "How long would we be gone for?" I managed to choke out after swallowing the sweet, golden liquid.

"Five days. But don't worry, you'll only miss one shift at Mimi's. I checked with Lyla and she's happy to cover for you."

"Wow, Gabe. This is so . . . unexpected. I . . . don't know what to say."

"Well, are you excited? We always talked about going. I mean, it's Paris! Why do you look so . . ." He didn't even finish his sentence, allowing his disappointment to be conveyed through the trailing off of his words.

"It's a shock. That's all." I covered his hand with my own. "I am excited. It's just that *my* news . . ."

"Oh, right? Sorry, we got so off course. What is it you wanted to tell me?"

"Well, you know how I had that callback today for the lead role in that show that's coming to Broadway?"

He blinked hard. "Oh God, yes, of course. I was just so excited to surprise you that it slipped my mind for a second. But tell me, please, how did it go?"

"Well. Great, actually. They invited me to the final auditions right there on the spot, which like *never* happens."

"Avery! That's fantastic!" He beamed with pride.

The waiter stopped by the table, delivering our first course, but I was so wrapped up in the conversation, I'd lost all focus on the hunger pangs I'd felt only moments before when my senses were inundated by the aromas of the fine cuisine.

I momentarily ignored the food and continued, "The final callback's in a month, so I'm just . . . maybe I shouldn't go to Paris right now. I mean, five days is a lot of time to lose. I'm not sure if I can afford to be away that long," I said.

He was clearly hurt by my choice of phrasing. "Time to lose?" he repeated. "I thought this would be something you'd be so excited about. I mean, it's *Paris*. We've been talking about this for . . . for forever. Our dream trip." His eyes softened and he put his head in his hands. "Maybe I can change the dates? I used miles, so I don't know?" He looked up. "Is nonrefundable like *really* nonrefundable? Maybe I can make up a dying uncle or something and try to move everything around?"

He looked so deflated and so utterly thrown. I guess five days away still left me with another twentysomething to get ready. Plenty of time. Right? Anyone else would be over-the-moon excited about this kind of fantasy trip with their boyfriend. What was I doing? It took us a decade to get here, where he was *finally* putting me first. What I'd always wanted.

He sat back against his chair, wiped his mouth with his napkin, and rested it back in his lap. "Listen, this isn't quite how I saw this conversation going. And I'm sure this isn't what you imagined either. Honestly, I was just trying to surprise you with something romantic and spontaneous. But I understand if the timing isn't right. I'm okay to do whatever you want to do. I'll figure it out."

I thought more about the callback. I mean, what were the chances of me booking the role? I bet they'd called back at least a dozen actresses, and the likelihood of them casting some no-name in the part was only slightly better than slim to none. Five days. Chances are it wouldn't make one damn bit of difference for the audition, but a world of difference for my future with Gabe.

"No, of course I want to go. A trip to Paris with you will be an experience of a lifetime. It just caught me off guard. But yes, we'll figure it out . . . together."

"Really?" he asked, perking up at my change of heart.

"Of course. I can't wait. Paris, Texas . . . ," I said with a cheeky smile. "I mean France, here we come!"

Chapter Thirty-One

After two full days of intense sightseeing around Paris, I was grateful for a chance to stand still for an afternoon at the cooking class Gabe arranged for us at Le Cordon Bleu. Though all of the sights and magic of the City of Lights were truly beyond words, I was still carrying around a small, niggling anxiety about the time I wasn't spending preparing for my audition.

I knew it was all in my head. Realistically, I had plenty of time. Even still, I couldn't seem to shake the feeling I wasn't giving this opportunity the attention it deserved. I tried every mental pep talk I could think of, yet the feeling of being divided between two things I loved was unsettling and tricky territory to navigate . . . and worse than that, it all felt eerily familiar. But, with each incredibly thoughtful surprise Gabe planned, the scale tilted just a tiny bit more in his favor, and I could (almost) push the guilt of abandoning my audition prep for a few days entirely from my mind.

Our cooking class of about sixteen participants from all over the world packed into the spacious kitchen where each pair was set up at their own state-of-the-art station. Gabe and I were placed near the back of the room but could still see the instructor's main workspace, and I was grateful to not be front and center. My culinary skills left much to be desired, especially after years of ordering takeout and fancy meals all over the city with Adam.

Gabe had registered us for a course entitled *The Art of Cooking Like a Chef*, a five-and-a-half-hour workshop that began with a demonstration followed by our attempt at recreating an impressive three-course menu. First, an appetizer of garden pineapple, tomato, and burrata with pomegranate and raspberry pesto, and smoked octopus; to be followed by the main, which was a roasted rack of lamb with a parsley crust, pearled jus, and courgette marmalade cooked with curry, garnished with fresh almonds and mint; and chocolate soufflé for dessert. It was a far departure from my usual—anything I could microwave or stick in the toaster—but it seemed too late to back out now.

I tied my apron around my waist and leaned into Gabe, who was washing his hands at the sink. "You didn't want to start with like a beginner's class, maybe?" I teased. "With my track record in the kitchen, I would hate for us to be deported because I happened to burn down the most famous cooking school in the world."

"We got this," he said confidently. "How hard can it really be?"

Just as Gabe finished his thought, the head chef stepped into the room and in a loud and boisterous voice said, "Bienvenue tout le monde! Sommes-nous tous prêts pour une journée pleine de saveurs exquises et d'aventures culinaires?" He gestured wildly to his station, which was covered in hand-tied bundles of fresh herbs and colorful vegetables.

Gabe quickly pulled up the Le Cordon Bleu course directory on his phone and scrolled frantically with wide, panicked eyes. "Did I screw up? Oh my God, is this class taught in only French? I don't think my high school–level proficiency's gonna cut it."

The chef adjusted his apron and continued, "And for those of you who are joining us from abroad, welcome! Welcome to Le Cordon Bleu! I asked if you were all ready for your culinary adventure to begin?"

A few voices peppered the air with a "Oui!" or an "Oh yeah!" and our instructor gave an enthusiastic thumbs-up, while a look of relief washed over Gabe's face. The class would be taught in a mixture of French and English. Still tough, but not entirely impossible.

"Je m'appelle Chef Audren Claude, and I will be teaching you the delicate art of French cooking over the next several hours. Let's begin—on y va!"

A sous chef slapped a slimy dead octopus on our station, and I practically leaped into Gabe's arms in horror. "What the hell is that?"

The sous chef gave me a dirty look, perhaps having been offended by my alarm. "C'est poulpe," she said and kept moving along to deliver the rest of the octopus carcasses to the other students.

I leafed through the recipe pamphlet again and scanned what else we'd be making. "Gabe, I'm not going to lie, if they bring out a whole lamb for us to flambé, I think I'll pass out right here."

"One recipe at a time. Let's deal with Ursula over here, and *then* we can worry about Lamb Chop."

I sucked in some air and turned to the appetizer instructions. "Step one. Turn octopus inside out like a pair of chaussettes and then beat it until pliable." I looked up at Gabe. "What are *chaussettes?*"

Gabe typed the word into his Google Translate, our new best friend, and said, "Socks?"

"Turn the octopus inside out like a pair of *socks?* And then beat it until pliable? This sounds so barbaric. I don't really have anything against this particular octopus. Maybe if it killed my family or betrayed our country I'd feel differently," I (kinda) joked.

We were so busy trying to figure out how to begin that we didn't notice Chef Audren at our station until he started beating our octopus mercilessly with a mallet, shouting, "C'est comme ça! Comme ça!" The octopus bounced around the countertop, and my eyes bulged more and more out of my head with each and every blow.

Chef Audren turned to me and held out the mallet. "Okay, ma chérie, your turn."

"Oh, um . . . don't you think it's been through enough?"

"Non, non! Encore! It needs to be soft like butter." He wrapped his hand around mine, which was still apprehensively holding the tenderizer, and together we started hitting the rubbery body until it looked like a deflated version of its former self.

"Bravo! Now it goes into the pot," Chef Audren ordered.

Once he left the station, Gabe looked at me, eyes wide, and said, "Remind me not to piss you off. Once you got going, I wasn't sure you were going to stop."

"It actually was a cathartic stress reliever once I put the idea that I was smashing the heck out of some poor sea creature out of my mind."

"A poor, *tasty* sea creature, we hope. It will not have suffered for naught," he said consolingly.

"Okay, but next time, you get the mallet."

"Deal."

We struggled just as much through the next two courses, our giggles eventually turning into grunts of frustration, and the five-hour workshop was beginning to feel more like a day and a half. But it was our final course, the dreaded chocolate soufflé, that almost made us abandon ship.

Chef Audren explained the process thoroughly, emphasizing that the most difficult part about baking a successful soufflé is to not over-whip the egg whites. Apparently, if you do, they don't have the elasticity needed to expand in the oven, which is the most common reason it would collapse—and according to the chef, that was a serious no-no. A sunken soufflé was almost a sacrilege, so I tried to listen to all of Audren's instructions before diving in. Meanwhile, Gabe had already started pouring things into bowls and whisking ingredients to and fro.

"I don't think you're doing that right. You need to add the sugar in slowly and mix it in in small batches, like a quarter of a cup at a time."

"I don't think it makes much of a difference," Gabe said as he continued to dump the entire cup of sugar into the fluffy egg whites, their shape collapsing under the weight of the granules.

"Yeah, I kinda think it does. Didn't you listen to Chef Audren? He said that the egg whites need to stay lifted and fluffed in order to ensure that it stays inflated while it bakes."

"It's cooking class, not rocket science. I don't think it's as technical as all that. Besides, I'm sure it will taste great regardless of if it looks like a pillow or a pancake." He grunted as he continued to whisk the egg whites together with the sugar.

I raised my hands in defeat. "*Okaaay*, but if Chef Audren starts to freak out because our soufflé looks like some roadkill found on the side of the Champs-Élysées, don't blame me."

I let Gabe take the lead on the soufflé, opting to step aside rather than argue. I grabbed a few sprigs of mint and started to chop the herbs with the new knife skills we practiced, making sure the tips of my fingers were tucked in like Chef Audren had showed us. When he came around, he peeked into our mixing bowl and instructed, "Plus moelleux," with a gesture of his hand lifting higher and higher and continued his inspection of the other students' work.

Gabe reached for his phone again, typing as he spoke aloud. "Moll-eeee-yuhz . . . fluffy? Did he say more fluffy? How am I supposed to fluff this thing any more than it already is?"

"I . . . I don't know. Like I warned, the sugar was too heavy when you poured it in all at once. I don't know if you can undo it now."

"Well, I certainly can't undo it now that it's already in there. Ugh, I'm sure it will be fine. We should just pour the mixture into the bowls and get cracking."

"I think they're called ramekins," I corrected.

Gabe glanced at the clock on the wall and huffed. "Well, let's get whatever they're called into the oven. I think I'm starting to feel a bit done with this."

Yeah, five and a half hours when you don't know what you're doing is not as fun as one would imagine. And it was clearly starting to get to Gabe, who seemed to be growing more impatient by the second. We were getting snappy at one another, and I could sense a very noticeable shift in mood. Our afternoon was somehow deflating faster than our half-assed soufflé.

When we pulled the ramekins out of the oven thirty minutes later, the sweet smell of dark chocolate cut some of the bitterness left behind from our baking battle royale, but unfortunately, our saggy soufflé still left much to be desired. The sunken top was split by a deep crevasse that should have been towering high with delectable molten raspberry filling bubbling underneath. Instead, it looked like a blob, wholly unappetizing and burned around the edges. We each took a bite, and though it was hard to believe, it tasted worse than it looked, and sadly, we ended up tossing the whole mess into the nearby trash can.

When the class *finally* came to a close, Gabe and I were mentally and physically exhausted. As we exited the school and strolled back in the direction of Le Marais, the sun was already setting and thick clouds shadowed the sky. In the close distance, the Eiffel Tower stood majestically lit, sparkling like a beacon for all of Paris to see. Gabe flagged down a taxi, and we zipped through the streets of Paris awash in the glow of the setting sun and were back at our B and B in under twenty minutes.

Gabe climbed out of the cab and turned to me to offer me a hand, looking as if he'd been through a few rounds in the ring. "I'm beat. Want to head back to the room and chill out for a bit before dinner? I think the restaurant where I made our reservations is pretty close to here."

I scanned the city, still bustling with life. For as much *fun* as cooking class had been, it had been a lot of time inside, and I wanted to just take a moment to drink in the sights and sounds of the city I'd dreamed of visiting my whole life. "You know what, I think I'm going to take a walk before I head back. But you go, relax. I'll be right behind you."

"Want me to come with you? I'm sure I can muster up a second wind," he said, even though his eyes looked heavy and his posture a bit droopy.

"Don't muster anything. Go back and relax. You look exhausted. I'll probably just grab a coffee myself and walk along the Seine for a bit. We've been cooped up in that hot kitchen all day. I could use some fresh air and maybe some time to run my lines for the final audition."

A look of relief washed over him. "Okay, well, you have your key, right? I'll see you when you get back. Call or text me if you change your mind, I swear I can rally."

We headed off in opposite directions, him back to our hotel and me down the narrow cobbled streets of fourth arrondissement until I reached the Pont Neuf, which arched ornamentally over the lazy, flowing Seine below. Black iron lampposts twinkled in the water's still reflection, and I spotted a quaint corner brasserie with a smattering of a few patrons iconically seated around the café's exterior under a wide-hanging awning. I signaled with a finger in the air that I was looking for a table for one, and the maître d' called, "Installez-vous," and gestured to a few open tables, allowing me to choose one of my liking.

When a young waiter approached, I quickly debated whether or not to try my hand at the limited amount of French I tried to cram into my brain on the plane on the way over. I focused mainly on the most necessary things I'd need: *thank you, please, where is the bathroom?*, and *can I have a glass of wine?* You know, the essentials!

The waiter flipped over my water glass and handed me a set of silverware from a tray he was holding. "Bon soir, mademoiselle. Vous avez choisi?"

My heart started to race, and I so badly wanted to default to English. But I tried to remind myself that it was polite to at least try, so I stammered out, "Oh, uh, yeah. Um . . . je voo-dray une verr de van, see voo play?"

The waiter barely missed a beat but responded in English. "Ah, oui. Red or white?"

"Oh, yes, right . . . um . . . rooj, see voo play. Mare see!"

I knew I'd butchered it, but at least I'd tried. And maybe after trying a few small, uncomfortable, out-of-character things, taking a step out on the ledge would not always be such a difficult task. I pulled the *Marley Is Dead* script pages out of my bag, slid my AirPods into my ears, and armed with the glass of red wine I'd proudly ordered myself, I dove in deep into some prep work, practically losing all sense of time until the waiter asked me if I would like a third glass of Beaujolais.

I glanced down at my watch, incredulous that it had been almost three hours since I'd left Gabe, and shot him a quick text letting him know I was on my way back. I signaled for the check as I scooped my things into my bag and rushed off in the direction of our B and B.

Chapter Thirty-Two

At close to 8:45 p.m., I burst into the room in a frenzy. "I'm so sorry, I'm so sorry, I lost track of time." I rushed right past Gabe and into the bathroom. "Give me like ten minutes tops to change and freshen up, and I'll be ready to go," I said, dumping my makeup bag upside down and rummaging around for my concealer.

"Av—" he started.

"I was walking around and listening to some music from the show, then I sat down for a glass of wine and just got swept up in the city and the smells and—"

"Avery—" he called again, trying to interrupt my rant.

"Yeah?" I popped my head out of the bathroom and spotted Gabe sitting at a small bistro-style table. Beside him was a bucket of ice with a bottle of champagne sticking out of the top, and an assortment of cheeses, meats, and fresh rolls and pastries set out on a tray. "Oh, um . . . what's all this?" I asked, and made my way back into the bedroom and sat down on the corner of the bed.

"I don't know about you, but after today, I could use a break from fancy French cuisine. I went to the market down the street and got us some of our favorites. I thought we could have a simple little picnic and just stay in." Gabe stood up and pushed the window open to reveal colorful Parisian rooftops and balconies stretching out as far as the eye could see. "We have this view, some snacks, and each other. What could be better?" He grabbed for my hands and sat down next to me on the edge of the bed. "Listen, I'm sorry about earlier. Getting snappy with you over the soufflé. Maybe it's the jet lag or all of the sightseeing, but I was just losing steam and patience and . . . it wasn't you."

"It's okay. I get it. I know I've been a little distracted, but I think that given all of the variables, we've been faring pretty well so far." I smiled and leaned into him with a playful nudge.

"Okay, good, I'm glad you aren't ready to throw me in the Seine just yet. Because I have a surprise. So, another reason for our impromptu picnic is that our dinner reservation wasn't until nine p.m., and with how leisurely French waitservice is, we could've been there until midnight, and we have an early wake-up tomorrow."

"We do? I thought we didn't have to meet the tour bus for Versailles until eleven a.m."

"Well, that's the surprise. I canceled Versailles for tomorrow, and instead booked us two train tickets on the Eurostar to spend the night in London, and we'll fly home from there instead. And one better, I bought us tickets for a Charles Dickens walking tour that takes us through the parts of the city where he grew up and based his novels."

I was speechless. The gesture was thoughtful but also a sacrifice on his part. "But you've always wanted to go to Versailles. It's been on your bucket list for as long as I've known you."

"I pulled you away from everything you have going on in New York. The least I can do is provide you with more research and insights you can use for audition inspiration when you get back home."

I pushed my hands through his dark wavy hair and pulled his face close to mine. "This is amazing . . . and you are amazing," I said, kissing the tip of his nose.

He smiled, pleased with how this surprise had gone over, and sat back against the cream-colored tufted headboard. "How about you go take a nice hot shower. We can pick on this food once you are in a fluffy robe, all squeaky clean, and then we can get to bed early."

"Well, maybe not *too* early." I motioned toward the shower. "Care to join me, monsieur?"

I've never seen Gabe move so fast. He swept me off my feet, carrying me into the bathroom, and said in an overly affected French accent, "Oui, oui, ma chérie," and closed the door behind us.

◆ ◆ ◆

We stepped out of Saint Pancras station into the morning rush of Central London, a departure from the quiet and meandering streets of Le Marais we'd left at sunup. Gabe hailed us a black cab to 48 Doughty Street, Charles Dickens's London home where we were supposed to meet up with the walking tour.

When we arrived, a small smattering of tourists was already waiting outside the house for the guide to get there. After a few minutes, an older man with a thick gray mustache, wearing a classic tweed three-piece suit, and twirling a wooden walking stick came up to meet the group.

"Where'd they find this guy? Central casting?" Gabe whispered to me.

The man cleared his throat and announced, in a surprisingly booming voice for a person of his slight stature, "It was the best of times, it was the worst of times, for those who are not here on time, because they will be left behind." He chortled (yes, actually chortled!) and clicked his cane against the pavement.

"Come, come," he said, and moved a bit farther down the street so as to not block the pathway inside. "In a few moments, we will enter Dickens's house, where he lived from 1837 to 1839. It is the only one of Dickens's homes left standing and is where he wrote the classics *Nicholas Nickleby* and *Oliver Twist*. I'll be your guide on this literary journey today. My name is Reginald, you may call me Reginald." He laughed at himself again. "Except you," he said, pointing his cane in my direction, "you can call me whatever you like, just don't call me late for dinner!" He erupted into another fit of giggles and turned to address the rest of the group again.

Gabe leaned over to me and said, "Um . . . what is happening right now?"

"I'm not sure, but you better behave, mister, 'cause it seems I have cheeky Reginald here waiting in the wings, ready to step in if you get out of line." I gestured toward Reginald with my thumbs and winked playfully at Gabe.

"I'll be sure to be on my best behavior."

Reginald continued briefing our group about the former home of the beloved English author and outlined a few other stops we'd be checking out before the tour was through.

"We start here at the Dickens Museum, and then we will make our way to an inn where Pip first lodged when he arrived in London in *Great Expectations*. We'll then head to a prefire building Dickens visited as a boy and thusly set part of his novel *David Copperfield* in as a result. We'll also pop into an old pub featured in *A Tale of Two Cities*—I do accept tips in the form of pints, in case you were wondering—and we'll end the tour at the Cratchit House, known to be a quintessential setting in Dickens's most notable and most often performed work, *A Christmas Carol*."

"Ooh, speaking of," he continued, "have any of you had a chance to see the new adaptation *Marley Is Dead* here on the West End? Splendid, truly splendid, it is."

Gabe nudged me jovially and smiled at the reference.

Reginald handed us our admission tickets to the house, now turned into a museum, and continued, "You will have the next hour to explore the five floors of Charles Dickens's former residence. The museum, which spans from the basement all the way up to the servants' quarters, is all open and houses over a hundred thousand artifacts from Dickens's personal life. I will remain in the lobby if you have any questions, but if you're ready then let's step back in time and begin our adventure!" He waved his hand flamboyantly.

Entering the house was like entering a time machine to the Victorian age, everything perfectly preserved—from the dark-red and brown leather-bound books that lined the study walls to the mahogany desk with curved legs Dickens used to write at.

"Do you smell that?" I asked Gabe.

He took a few sniffs around the room. "It kinda smells like my grandmother's apartment in the Bronx."

I swatted him with my museum pamphlet. "No, it's the paraffin wax that would be used in lanterns to make the light last longer. *Oliver Twist* is what? Like eight hundred pages? Written by hand? That's a lot of wax."

"You could not possibly still smell two-hundred-year-old wax," Gabe ribbed.

"This room is incredible. This day is incredible. Thank you," I said, kissing him squarely on the lips.

Gabe leaned down and whispered in my ear, "And it's only just beginning." He stood up straight and clapped his hands together. "Come now, chop chop, lots to see. Must move along, Hurry now," he said in his worst Dick Van Dyke from *Mary Poppins* British accent.

We finished walking through the house and then went outside where most of the tour group was already gathered and waiting for us. Spotting me, Reginald extended his arms and said, "The pain of parting is nothing to the joy of meeting again."

"*Great Expectations?*" I guessed.

"*Nicholas Nickleby,*" he corrected. "Okay, everyone, as Dickens once said, 'It is required of every man, that the spirit within him should walk abroad among his fellowmen, and travel far and wide . . .' so off we go to travel just a bit wider."

I scrunched up my nose. "*David Copperfield?*"

"My dear, it's so obviously *A Christmas Carol,*" he remarked with a twirl of his cane as he led the way down the steep cobblestone street.

Chapter Thirty-Three

Over the next few hours, we strolled through streets of the city that, we were told, had hardly changed since the days Dickens roamed them, mostly at night, chasing an elusive muse. Amid old brick buildings with angled gables and curved archways that led to narrow corridors, the sense of being transported back in time was a strange comfort after the last few days touring around Paris at warp speed. London, though busy, felt more like a comforting escape, and I couldn't help but absorb the city's charm into my skin, breathing in the sights and smells of what I imagined the city emitted in the 1800s.

My favorite part so far, aside from exploring the nooks and crannies of Dickens's home, was our stop at a pub named The Boot, which had been standing on-site since 1724. Reginald explained it was often included in many Dickens walking tours and pub crawls since it was mentioned as a "house of interesting repute" in *Barnaby Rudge*.

As members of our group continued to tip Reginald in pints of amber ale, his stories became more exaggerated, his cane gesturing wildly, knocking over empty glasses and "accidentally" whacking into inattentive bystanders. Reginald regaled the crowd with stories of Dickens the showman, much like himself, and explained that his works had always been meant to be read aloud, which is exactly what Dickens did in many pubs around the city.

I listened attentively and tried to embody the character of Marley as I listened. Would Dickens be delighted or offended by the modern adaptation of *Marley Is Dead*? I really wasn't sure, but I did take comfort in knowing that in both his original tale and in the West End's newest version, the moral of the story remained true—the protagonist was ultimately changed for the better through righting their mistakes of the past.

Gabe drained the last of his Guinness and licked the foam from his top lip. He leaned in close and asked, "I'm going to get another. Do you want one?"

"Meh, I'm not loving the room temperature style of this," I said, gesturing with my half-finished golden pint. "I mean, who drinks beer at room temperature? Bleh." I handed him the glass and asked, "Could you get me a cider instead? Anything cold would be great. Thank you."

He wove his way through the crowd still enraptured by Reginald's recitation of *Bleak House* excerpts and returned a few minutes later, handing me a frosty glass sweating with cool condensation. "*Ahh* yes. Now *that's* more like it." I took a long gulp, the crisp, sweet currents of apple cold and refreshing as the little bubbles tickled my tongue. "Oh my God, I love this. It's delicious. Do you know what it is so that I can order it again later if we hit another pub?"

Speaking in a hushed voice, Gabe's expression turned a bit unsure. "Well, the bartender said it kinda quickly and obviously has an accent, but what I heard him say was 'ass balls.'"

I practically spit my cider out in a spray, certain I'd misheard him. "Wait, you got me a cider called 'Ass Balls'?!"

"I think so?" he answered.

"I will never be able to rest until I know for sure if this cider is in fact named 'Ass Balls.' Be right back." I made my way over to the same bartender, who was mopping up the counter with a kitchen cloth. "Excuse me, sir, but my boyfriend over there"—I pointed to Gabe with my pinkie finger—"just ordered me this cider and it is delicious. Can you tell me the name of it?"

"Of course," he said in more of a Scottish brogue than an English lilt. "Ass Balls."

"Are you serious?! You guys seriously serve a cider called 'Ass Balls,' like that's not a joke?!"

The bartender barked out a laugh so loud that it temporarily interrupted Reginald's flow. "Not 'Ass Balls,' it's called 'Aspall.' It's pretty well known in the UK. But I can honestly say I have never heard anyone mistake it for 'Ass Balls' before. That may be the greatest thing I've ever heard." He couldn't stop laughing, and my cheeks grew redder than chapped *Aspalls*, knowing that I would now become a story he'd tell all of his bartender friends and frequent patrons for the rest of time.

Reginald announced it was time to settle tabs and that we'd be leaving shortly for the final stop on the tour, 16 Bayham Street, otherwise known as Dickens's inspiration for the Cratchit House. Reginald shared tidbits of information as we followed him out of the pub to the northwest neighborhood of Camden Town, about a twenty-minute walk.

"Bayham Street was about the poorest part of the London suburbs back then, and the house we're going to see is a very small, dilapidated tenement not uncommon for the lower class of the time who lived in disturbingly shabby conditions by today's standards. Dickens was struck by this disparity of classes and spent most of his life trying to raise awareness of it in his novels as a means to evoke social change," he explained.

"Hey"—I nudged Gabe's side—"sounds like someone *else* I know."

A smile crept across his face. "After everything we've learned today, I take that as the highest compliment," he said, beaming from ear to ear. Though he booked it for me, it was clear Gabe had gotten a lot from this tour too, even if only the proper way to pronounce Aspall.

We'd finally arrived at the Cratchit House, and just in time, as the sun had already started to set and the temperatures were quickly dropping, the dampness of the air enhancing the eerie vibe of the shabby street.

Reginald ushered the group onto the house's front steps and said, "'I will honor Christmas in my heart, and try to keep it all the year. I will live in the Past, the Present, and the Future. The Spirits of all Three shall strive within me. I will not shut out the lessons that they teach.' Now," he said, enthusiastically flinging open the red-painted front door, "let's go inside and learn a bit more about Dickens's most famous work, *A Christmas Carol.*"

Inside, the small living room warmed with a roaring fire within the wide stone hearth, and the house was staged to resemble Christmas Day at the Cratchits', complete with full table setting, the iconic, sumptuous (artificial) turkey center stage, and even Tiny Tim's crutches resting against the smallest chair. The mantel was adorned with winter greenery and (LED) candlelight, and the whole space, though tight, was a wonderful stage for Reginald's final performance of the day.

Reginald rested his cane against the wall and then turned to face our group. "Shakespeare is undoubtedly England's most notable writer, but Charles Dickens holds firmly as the second most famous, mainly because of the renowned success he garnered through his novella *A Christmas Carol.* Though he had earned fame and acclaim for his works up until 1843, as the year wound down, Dickens found himself in dire financial straits."

Hmm, been there . . .

Reginald continued, "His last few novels were what we would call flops today, and his publisher had all but given up on him, and many believed he had all but given up on himself, one of the worst fates that can befall an artist."

Also sounds familiar . . .

"In fact, in his most autobiographical novel, *David Copperfield,* he states, 'I had no advice, no counsel, no encouragement, no consolation, no assistance, no support, of any kind, from anyone, that I can call to mind . . .'"

Reginald interrupted himself with a loud and boisterous "BUT," startling the crap out of a young couple in front as they nearly tumbled backward into the plate of sticky toffee pudding resting beside the turkey. He stuck his index finger high into the air, further emphasizing the crescendo of his story. "This, ladies and gentlemen, was the very moment when Dickens needed to dig deep, and that he did, folks. And. That. He. Did. He produced *A Christmas Carol* in just six weeks' time, crafting notably one of the most famous and well-loved works of fiction ever written. It is with this story that Dickens became a household name and changed forever the way the Western world celebrates the entire Christmas season—emphasizing generosity and love. And with that, don't forget how much I too *love generosity*."

He flipped his hat off his head and turned it into a makeshift collection plate. "Your tips are much appreciated, as are Yelp and Google reviews. Be sure to mention me by name, it's Reginald, in case you forgot. Thank you all for coming!" he shouted to the room, and was met with a healthy round of applause from the enthusiastic and gracious group.

Gabe and I took a moment to peruse the details of the Cratchit House, all the decor and adornments they used to replicate the interior style of a typical lower-class Victorian home. I closed my eyes and breathed in the smell of the crackling fire behind us and the scent of pine from the furniture and beams. Who would have thought I would have such a strong connection with Dickens and his personal story? And even though this was *not* what I had in mind when I thought about how to prepare for my final audition, I was flooded with gratitude for the experience of it all. I had a brand-new perspective, one I knew I'd be able to uniquely draw from when portraying the character of Marley onstage.

I reached down for Gabe's hand and squeezed it, hoping to convey my appreciation through my affectionate gesture. "This was so great, Gabe. Like so, so great." I leaned against him and rested my head on his shoulder as we faced the wall looking at old photographs of Dickens and lithograph illustrations from his life's works.

"Good," he said, leaning his head to mine. "I'm glad." He gave my hand another squeeze. "Are you hungry? 'Cause I am starving. I'll be ready to eat that plastic turkey and the sticky toffee pudding on the table if we don't get outta here soon."

"Yes! Agreed! Let's just say goodbye and thank you to Reginald, and then we can find somewhere close by for dinner."

We waited in a short queue to say our goodbyes to our host as Gabe drew a ten-pound note from inside his coat pocket.

Reginald's eyes twinkled as he watched Gabe place the bill into the hat. "Much appreciated, kind sir."

Turning his attention from Gabe to me, he locked his eyes on mine and asked, "Dinner plans?"

"No, actually," I said, hoping he was getting ready to suggest a nearby favorite.

"Wonderful. Would *you* be interested in joining me for the best fish and chips in town? The best spot's just around the corner," he asked as his eyebrows danced suggestively up and down.

Still holding Gabe's hand, I couldn't help but crack a smile. Gabe's fingers squeezed mine as we shared the laugh inwardly. "I would love to join you, but unfortunately, I'm already spoken for." I lifted our intertwined hands up to eye level, and Reginald met it with a dramatic pout.

"Well, I had to try." He turned to Gabe and said, "'Love her, love her, love her! If she favors you, love her.'"

Gabe nodded. "Now that I can do," he said and kissed me on the top of the head.

I looked at Reginald. "*Great Expectations*?"

"*Ahhh* yes, my dear, and it seems all my work here is now done." He smiled and offered a wink. And with that, he emptied the bills and coins from his hat into his pockets, shimmied the cap back onto his head, and turned to leave.

Chapter Thirty-Four

We took Reginald's suggestion and went to find some dinner at the fish-and-chips place around the corner. He wasn't kidding. It must have been one of the most well-known hot spots in the city because the line was halfway down the block. It wasn't a proper sit-down restaurant—instead, you ordered your food from the café window and took your plate to one of the nearby benches or, if you were lucky, wooden picnic tables.

"How about we divide and conquer," Gabe suggested. "I'll go and secure us a place to sit and a couple of pints and you stand in the queue?"

"Sounds good," I answered, and watched him duck out of the line and make his way down the street.

Fortunately, due to the limited menu, the line moved pretty quickly. You had three options: fish and chips, bangers and mash, or shepherd's pie. It all looked (and smelled!) delicious, but since Reginald raved about the fish and chips, I decided to go with that for me and Gabe, plus a shepherd's pie for good measure.

After I paid, the cashier handed me a ticket and asked me to kindly step to the side. About ten minutes later, my number was called and I was handed two orders of fish and chips bundled in newspaper, the oil spreading farther and farther across the printed letters with each passing second.

"Don't forget about your shepherd's pie, dear," the cashier hollered as I almost walked away without it. I couldn't help but laugh—she sounded just like Mrs. Lovett from *Sweeney Todd*. I'd have to remember to tell Charlie about her when I got home.

I rose to my toes to search the nearby benches and picnic tables for Gabe, finally spotting him sitting on a bench underneath the lamplight a little bit up the road, waiting for me. I crossed the street to him, trying to not get any of the oil from the newspaper on my coat, and noticed he was talking on the phone to someone. As I made my way closer, I heard Gabe say, "Keep your chin up, okay? I'll be home tomorrow. Love you."

I cleared my throat and purposefully stepped into a crunchy pile of leaves so he'd know I was there.

"Oh, hey," he said, sliding his phone into his pocket and jumping up to help me with the food. He reached for the shepherd's pie that sat on top of the pile I was carrying and ushered me over to the bench, helping me to balance everything as I sat.

"So, um . . . any luck with the drinks?" I asked, curious if he'd fess up to whatever took him away from his original task.

"Oh shoot. Drinks. I got distracted trying to find us a place to sit. And then once I did, I didn't want to lose it. I realize now I should have probably executed the plan in reverse."

"Hey, Gabe? Just now, were you talking to Marisol? I know she and I aren't friends anymore, but you don't have to hide talking to your sister from me."

His expression was tinged with guilt at his attempt at secrecy. "I know the two of you ended on bad terms. I figured now that we're back together, best to keep those two worlds separate. At least for the time being."

"Does she know you're here with me?"

He scrunched up his face. "The truth?"

"Always."

"No, I didn't tell her. I haven't told her anything about us yet. I wanted to make sure it was all real first." He leaned back against the bench and started to untuck the corners of the newspaper to unwrap his fish and chips and popped a french fry into his mouth. "She's had such a tough time since Mom died, I wasn't sure how she'd take the news. Part of me thinks she'd be thrilled. Another part . . . I don't know. Regardless, she could use a friend like you in her life right now. But you know Marisol, stupidly stubborn, she'd never be able to admit she had any part in what exactly went wrong between you two."

"She didn't. Not really. I'm the one who was in the wrong."

Gabe set down his forkful of shepherd's pie and said, "Maybe it's not too late to right the wrong? I mean, if today taught us anything, it's that the ghosts of your past will keep haunting you until you confront them. That was the whole point of *A Christmas Carol*, wasn't it? Or do I need to go look for Reginald?"

"No, don't do that. I think you got it exactly right. He'd be so proud."

We finished our dinners, scarfing down the last of the delicious fish and chips, and wiped our greasy fingers on a handful of napkins. Gabe crumpled up his newspaper, tapped my knee, and stood up from the bench. "It's getting late. Ready to go back to the hotel?"

"Gabe, this really was amazing. This whole trip. You changing plans last minute to incorporate all of the Dickens stuff for me. I'm just . . ." I kissed him to fill in the blank and hoped it conveyed the gratitude and love that his sweet gesture incited in me.

"I know it was tough for you to get away from the city, but I really loved going on this adventure with you. I hope it's just one of many to come." He leaned in to kiss me again, pulling me in close with both arms.

The next day, we grabbed a black cab and headed to Heathrow. I rested my head on Gabe's shoulder and stared out the window for the entirety of our taxi ride, enjoying the last few glimpses of London street life before heading back to the States. As we pulled into the traffic queue at the airport, I pulled out my phone to check the time, wanting to ensure we'd left ourselves enough, and noticed an email had popped up from Joanna at the casting agency. My heart dove into my stomach.

Avery,

Below please find the details of your final callback for the role of Marley in *Marley Is Dead*.

Location: Greenwich House Theater, 27 Barrow St, NY

Date: Tuesday, April 3rd
Time Slot: 1:00PM

In the interest of full disclosure, you are one of three finalists for the title role. We will be reading all three actresses that same day, so please be prompt and prepared. We look forward to seeing you for your callback.

Best,
Joanna Kitt, *The Gerber Agency*

My mouth had fallen open and I didn't hear Gabe calling my name from outside our cab, let alone realize that the car had even stopped. I lifted my eyes filled with tears to Gabe, still waiting with an extended hand to help me out of the taxi. I wasn't one of a dozen or even half a dozen—I was one of *three* actresses left in the running for the lead.

Before this trip, I'd believed this audition was just another that would end in disappointment. Maybe it's why I didn't put up more of a fight when Gabe mentioned Paris at such an inconvenient time. But no,

I could feel it in my bones, this opportunity was mine for the taking, and I knew that, after years of ignoring my gut and my passion, I was never again going to look back and say, *Damn, I wish I'd given it more.*

Gabe peeked his head inside, his face full of concern. "Um . . . everything okay? You planning on getting out of the cab *orrr* . . ."

"Oh yeah, of course, sorry, sorry!" I said, shoving my phone in my pocket and reaching for his hand.

He slid one of his arms around me, the other pulling our suitcase in tow, and asked, "So, you ready to get home?"

"Actually," I said, more confident than I'd felt about anything in a long time, "I am."

Chapter Thirty-Five

Three weeks after returning from Paris, just days before my final audition, I turned the key and pulled open the studio door to the rehearsal space I rented for the afternoon. Inhaling the smell of freshly Windexed windows and piney waxed floors, I set my bag and water bottle on the ground and waited for the accompanist. It was an investment, but with the *Marley Is Dead* audition just two days away, I couldn't cut corners now. Mimi's had been a great place to prepare at first, but over the last few weeks, I was finding it harder and harder to focus, so I booked four rehearsal sessions at Ripley-Grier Studios in Midtown for this final push.

I pulled out my character shoes and slid them on over my stockinged feet. Hearing footsteps behind me and the door creaking open, I fully expected to see Charlie, who said he would stop by as soon as his shift was over. But when I turned, instead of Charlie, a familiar man joined me in exclaiming, "You?!"

At our simultaneous epiphany, we both jumped back to take in the other. The pianist from the *Marley Is Dead* auditions was much taller than I expected, then again, he had been seated the last two times I saw him.

"How? Why? Did you know I was going to be here?" I asked, wondering if this was more than just a coincidence? Another gift of the phone booth?

"If I knew it was you, do you think I would have been so surprised to see you?" he said, rolling his eyes. "I freelance for the studio and pick up accompanist work during my slow seasons."

"Isn't this some sort of conflict of interest? You accompanying me? I just want to make sure I'm not breaking any rules that could disqualify me from the final audition or anything."

"Actually, I'm not working the last audition. I've got a gig on one of Royal Caribbean's newest ships. I leave tomorrow. I'll be spending my nights playing piano in the sunset lounge and my days on the beaches in Mykonos. I can't wait. So, you see, no conflict. Okay, just to clarify, though, you have the room reserved for four hours but I'm only contracted for two, so you tell me, what do you want to start with?"

He spoke as he strode over to the black baby grand set in the corner of the room, rested his satchel by one of the thick piano legs, and took a seat on the bench, placing a folder on the stand in front of him.

I dug the sheet music out of my bag and walked it over to him. "This is the new song they want the Marleys to perform at the final audition," I said, passing it over the piano. "Hey, if we're going to spend the next couple of hours together, we should probably at least know each other's first names. I'm Avery," I said, extending my hand.

"And I'm ready," he said, straight faced, not even lifting a finger from the piano. "Do you really want to be wasting time with pleasantries when you have a Broadway audition in two days?"

I pulled my arm back and crossed it over my chest. "No, I guess not."

"Okay then, let's get started."

As we approached "Ready's" two-hour finish mark, my voice was growing raw and the notes were not sounding nearly as strong as they had been last week. Not even close. With every clunker I hit, Ready's face puckered dramatically, showing no attempt at hiding his horror and even less restraint in calling me out. After a voice crack that practically knocked him off his piano bench, Ready slammed down the keyboard cover with a huff.

"I think that now would be a good time to call it. We could definitely both use a break." He packed up his music, shoved it into his bag faster than I thought humanly possible, and scurried from the room, certain to not return.

My rehearsals had been going so well until these last few days, our Europe trip igniting a kind of fire under my skin I hadn't felt in years. But now, with the audition looming so close, nerves were starting to take hold again. Notes I was hitting easily last week felt completely out of my range, my throat literally buckling under the pressure of this huge opportunity, and I couldn't help but fear that this upcoming audition would be a repeat of the past.

I sat back down beside my bag and grabbed my water bottle, taking such a huge gulp that it ran down the wrong pipe, causing me to suddenly cough and choke violently. Water sprayed out of my mouth and across the mirror in front of me, and the drips slid down like rain on a window.

Charlie peeked his head into the room and tiptoed past the doorframe. "Everything okay in here?" He spied me wiping water from my face and then the mirror with the inside of my sleeve.

"Yup, all good now." I cleared my throat, the slightest hint of a tickle still sitting underneath my raw vocal cords. "I really appreciate you coming to help me out. The first two hours have been brutal. I am hoping to God that the next two go better."

"Well then, we'll have to make sure they do." He offered me a hand, motioning for me to get off the ground. "Rise, it's time to do our warm-up exercises."

"Charlie, these are stupid," I whined.

He cocked his head to the side and stared back at me, insistent. "They are not stupid. They are necessary. Now, repeat after me. The lips, the teeth, the tip of the tongue."

I jokingly rolled my eyes and repeated, "The lips, the teeth, the tip of the tongue."

"Was that so hard? Okay, next let's shake out our bodies. Arms, head, torso, hips, shake, shake, shake. Root your feet and let yourself flop about like an electric eel."

My brain flashed back to the pulverized octopus body bouncing around our cutting board at Le Cordon Bleu in Paris. *Flop, flop, flop.* The tentacles springing off the surface with every whack of the mallet.

"Avery, why aren't you shaking your body like an electric eel?" Charlie chastised.

I followed his instruction and let my limbs go limp, waving them around like one of those huge blow-up dancing inflatables that get propped on top of car dealerships to attract buyers.

"Yes! Finally!" Charlie said. "Keep it going for another sixty seconds. This is going to help you shake out your pent-up energy and reset to neutral before you need to get into the mindspace of your character."

I shook my body with all my might for one more minute until I was practically breathless and sweating.

Charlie called out, "Okay, last exercise. The silent scream."

"No. Absolutely not. I look completely ridiculous when I do the silent scream."

He nodded his head with a wicked smile. "Oh, I know, consider it my payment. Now, let's go. All the emotion you have deep down inside you, let it out without making a single sound. Use the whole space, really feel it. Go."

"Ugh," I grunted, but still got down on my knees, took a breath to cue I was ready to begin, and then proceeded to writhe around on the floor making a face similar to that of the *Scream* mask and pulled my hands through my hair like a woman crazed.

"Perfect, stay just like that," he said, snapping a photo of me with his iPhone.

I sprang up from the ground like a puma. "You did not just take a picture of me!"

"Oh yeah, I plan to sell it for big bucks once you're a Broadway star," he joked. "Now, let's get to work."

For the remaining hour and a half, Charlie and I continued to break down my scenes, focusing on character choices and meaningful blocking. The practice was like muscle memory, the questions to ponder and the endless possibilities of how to unravel this character's motivations, goals, and emotional arc all flooding back to me in a wave of nostalgia.

We ran the scenes at least a dozen times, and when I was still defaulting to sneaking glances at the stashed pages tucked inside my sleeve, Charlie furrowed his brows. "Um . . . the audition is two days away. When were you planning on being off script?"

"I . . . I don't know. It's a security blanket, and every time I try to rehearse without it, I can't seem to get the lines to stick."

"That's because you're still just *saying* the words. But, you need to believe them, embody them. Then, it won't feel like acting."

"The audition song was a disaster. I practically ran the accompanist out of the room."

"Oh, so that's who I saw peeling down the hallway like the road-runner getting chased by the coyote," he joked.

"It's not funny. I was bad, Charlie. Like really bad. I'm not going to be ready."

"You're just getting in your own head, which is normal before this big of an audition. You need to stop overthinking it so much. You *were* Marley. I saw it and they saw it. Now you need to see it."

"What if I can't? It's happened to me before. I never told you what happened at the *Wicked* callback I had a few years ago. I completely choked. Well, technically I *mooed.*"

"Mooed?"

"Never mind. Let's just say I botched it big time. I couldn't take the pressure."

"Yeah, but think about who you were then and who you are now. Do you really think you're still that same girl?" he asked.

With all my old insecurities and self-doubt bubbling back up to the surface, as much as I wanted to tell him I wasn't, it was hard to be sure. "You know what, I think I'm ready to call it a day."

"Sure, whatever you want. Feel like grabbing a drink or something? There's a pretty cool spot right downstairs," he said.

"Thanks, but I can't tonight. Gabe's been trying to ease my stress these past few weeks by plying me with carbs and butter. I really appreciate all of your help with getting me ready, though, mentally and physically, for this whole thing. I don't think I could have done it without you. So, definitely a rain check on the drinks—my treat."

"Absolutely. We'll have a proper champagne toast when you get the part."

"How can you always be so sure?"

"Because you're BrAvery Lawrence," he answered without missing a beat.

"One saucy rendition of 'Big Spender' more than a decade ago does not a brave person make," I joked, eyeing him playfully.

"You know, it wasn't the song that earned you that nickname." Charlie turned me around so we were both facing the smudged mirror. He leaned in close to my ear, his face so close to mine, and whispered, "If you could only see what everyone else sees," and squeezed the top of my shoulder before heading out.

I stayed in the studio for another hour until a janitor said he needed to clean the room for the night. I glanced down at my watch. It was after 8:00 p.m., well past when I told Gabe I'd be over to his apartment. I fished my phone from my bag and saw I had three missed calls from him and two texts. I dialed him back as quickly as I could.

"Oh good, you're not dead," he joked, picking up the call before it even had a chance to fully ring.

"I'm so sorry. Rehearsal didn't go well . . . again, and I stuck around the studio a little longer than I planned on."

"Don't worry about it. I set some dinner aside for you. What time do you think you'll be here? I can throw it in the oven."

"I know I said I'd come by tonight, but would you be upset if I just head back to Bushwick? With the audition right around the corner, I could use a good night's sleep."

"Oh, Ave, any chance I could persuade you to come here instead? I have something I want to talk to you about and besides, I've been missing you. If you have to go home, I understand, *buuuuut* if you can come by even for a little bit . . ."

I sighed, knowing I couldn't resist the invitation. He'd been so patient and so understanding of my ups and downs over the past few weeks since we got back from our trip, and truth be told, I missed him too.

"Aww . . . you've been missing me?" I asked sweetly.

"More than you know," he replied.

"Oh, damn you and your charm!" I teased. "I'm on my way."

I hurried out of the building, hopped on the E Train to Tribeca, and jogged up the block toward Gabe's apartment. It was hard to believe that less than four months ago, I showed up at his front door not even knowing he'd be on the other side. None of it made sense then. And while I still couldn't explain the how, with each day that passed and our relationship blossoming, the *why* was becoming more and more clear.

Like the ghosts in *A Christmas Carol* who revealed the past and present so that Scrooge could reconcile his future, the phone booth had given me the opportunity to reconstruct my own. I'd reunited with the man I loved, reignited the career I always wanted, and as long as I had Gabe and Manhattan, my future looked pretty damn bright.

Chapter Thirty-Six

I buzzed into Gabe's building, and he had the door flung open before I even passed the lobby. He rushed into the hallway and scooped me up into a big hug, his arms tight around me, and lifted me right off my feet. Kissing me playfully with quick smooches to my cheek, he pulled back, setting me down, and said, "Damn, I've missed you."

"Oh good, I was worried you greeted all of your visitors like that. I guess absence really does make the heart grow fonder. If I'd known I was in for that kind of a reception, I would have stayed away even longer."

"Oh, honey, you ain't seen nuthin' yet." He waggled his eyebrows mischievously, a sexy grin sweeping over his face, and pulled me by the hands into the apartment. "Sit. Relax. Let me pour us a glass of wine. I grabbed a few bottles of that pinot noir that you loved from the Finger Lakes." His voice disappeared as he turned and made his way to the kitchen.

"What are you up to? What am I missing?" I called out to him as I surveyed the immaculate living room for clues. *Did he have a vanilla-scented candle lit?!*

He came back into the room carrying two glasses. "Can't a fella just woo his lady?"

"No, please woo away, but this feels a little too good to be woo. I mean, true. C'mon, what's going on?"

Gabe chuckled at my misspeak and handed me a glass. "Cheers, to us." He lifted his and clinked it to mine. I continued to eye him suspiciously as I took a sip, his face distorted through the bulb of the bottom. He scooched a bit closer to me on the couch, took my wine, and set it down beside his before taking my hands into his own.

I could feel his fingers trembling, and I looked up at him, alarmed. "Are you all right? Why are you shaking? What's going on?"

"I give speeches in rooms to hundreds of people. I don't know why I'm so nervous right now. I mean, I do, but I thought somehow I'd be a lot smoother," he muttered.

I looked around, confused. "Are you talking to me?"

"Yes, no, I mean . . ." He breathed out and stood up, drawing a small box from his pocket as he bent down to one knee.

"Oh my God, what are you doing?"

"I kinda thought it'd be obvious," he joked as he popped open the velvet box to reveal a beautiful teardrop diamond ring surrounded by a sparkling halo of smaller stones. "Every day since you knocked on my door on Christmas, I've thanked my lucky stars we were given a second chance. Avery, I want to spend the rest of my life with you by my side. You are the source of my happiness, the center of my world, and the whole of my heart. Will you marry me?"

I wasn't aware I had stopped breathing until I heard my pulse booming in my ears. As my vision turned hazy and my head filled with ringing, I surveyed the moment: there were no confetti cannons, no kicklines of Broadway dancers, no Sutton-*freakin'*-Foster. In fact, it was the exact opposite of Adam's proposal. Simple. Intimate. Impromptu. It was perfectly Gabe.

My hands were clasped over my mouth, and I struggled to put my words and thoughts together. "Are you sure . . . like really sure? It's only been a few months."

And while I knew we had a much longer history than that, it all still felt a little too fast. Maybe I was missing something? What was the big hurry?

He came up off his knee, took his place next to me on the couch, and lifted a hand to my cheek. "*Seven years* and a few months. We've let so much time go by. I don't want to lose another second."

He pulled me in for a kiss, and any doubt in my mind that he was serious disappeared off the radar. I relaxed into his body, my chest rising and falling with his, and wrapped my arms around his neck, deepening the pressure of the kiss with my fingers in his hair. Soon I was breathless and dizzy from delirium, and he took the opportunity to pull the ring from the box and slide it onto my finger.

I looked down at my hand, the reality of the moment really sinking in. "Gabe, it's beautiful, but ring or not, you don't have to worry about losing me. I'm not going anywhere. We're exactly where we're meant to be. I, of course, want to marry you, but this is all a lot right now with the audition on the horizon, and what if I actually get this thing? God, I can't even imagine trying to plan a wedding if I get cast. This is my dream and it's finally within reach. I need to focus on this final push to Tuesday, and then we can talk about the future. There's no need to rush things."

Gabe fell silent as his brows knit together. "No, actually, there kinda is. I've been offered my dream job: chief of staff for the secretary of Housing and Urban Development."

"What? When did that happen? That's amazing. I'm so proud of you." I threw my arms around his neck. "But what does having a new job have to do with us getting married? I get that you'll be busy, and if you're worried about not being able to take time for a honeymoon, we can put that off. I understand."

He drew back, allowing my arms to slip from around him, and looked me in the eyes. "Avery, the job's in DC."

"DC? Washington, DC? No, what? I don't understand."

"What don't you understand? I want you to come with me . . . to DC. Come and marry me and we can live happily ever after the way we were always meant to."

I dropped my head into my hands, feeling a wave of nausea wash over me. "DC? No. No. That's not how this is supposed to happen. That's not how this goes." I backed away from him, hands raised and waving with emphatic gestures. We were supposed to . . . I don't know, but not this. No version of what I'd imagined our future life together would be had me moving to Washington, DC, in a few months.

"How *what* was supposed to happen? How what goes?" He stepped toward me, taking me by the wrists, lowering them down, and rubbing his thumb over my knuckles. Just the feeling of him taking me by the arms and caressing my skin calmed me down, and I took a few deep breaths as I watched his lips. "Avery, you're not making any sense."

My eyes lifted to his, tears brimming at my lashes, threatening to spill. "What about my audition? What did you expect me to do if I got the part? How did you expect me to choose?"

"I love you, Avery. You love me. The phone booth and Christmas and Paris and Charles Dickens—it was all for this moment. The universe conspired to bring us back together and look at where we are. You have to see it?"

I did see it, but now it all looked completely different. *What the hell had just happened?*

"Look, I'm tired, and confused, and overwhelmed. And the last thing I want to do is hurt you." I leaned over and kissed him hard. "I do love you, Gabe. This isn't about that." I twisted the ring off my finger, closed my fist around it, and handed it back to him. "I'm not saying no. And please believe there is a part of me that is screaming yes at the top of my lungs. But that other part just needs a little more time to think this all through. At least until after the audition's over."

He slipped the ring back into the box and snapped the lid shut. Though he was putting on a good show, the hurt reflected in his expression was undeniable and it struck me like a knife under my ribs. "I guess, take whatever time you need. I'll give you your space. I'm not going anywhere."

I raised my eyebrows and my lips drew into a line. "But actually, you are."

"No, I'm asking you to come along with me. Won't you? Please, Avery?" he pleaded.

Does he even realize what he's asking?

I grabbed my coat and whispered, "The audition. I should go," before kissing him once more and walking out of the apartment.

I barely slung the jacket over my shoulders as I pushed open the glass front door of the building into the night air with only one clear destination in mind—the one and only place I knew would have the answers I so desperately needed.

Chapter Thirty-Seven

I raced around the streets of Tribeca, trying to remember where the phone booth had been. I looked up the falafel place in the West Village where Lyla and I had ended up after visiting with Miss Tilly, and started ambling around from there. But the streets looked different basked in the city lights of New York at night, the darkness threading through the alleyways and narrow streets making me disoriented. I searched for anything recognizable, but it all seemed to have shifted once the sun fell behind the skyline.

I retraced my steps and practically spun myself in circles until I was weary, mentally and physically exhausted from the wallop of the past twenty-four hours. I was just about ready to abort the mission and come back the next morning, but I knew I'd *never* sleep. The phone booth had taken me to the past, pointed me to the present, and now I desperately needed it to tell me what I should do with my future, how to choose between the two things I loved most.

I looked around again, racking my brain for some mental cue or faint memory I could lean on for direction. And all of a sudden, across the block I spotted Benny's Bagels and Bialys—I remembered the name because I thought to myself how much I loved the alliteration of it. *I have to be close now.*

I used Benny's as a compass and turned down one more street, everything growing more and more familiar as I went. Excited at the sense of finally being on the right track, I picked up my pace and made it to the end of the block in record time, and um . . . there . . . was still . . . no phone booth.

I paused, completely mystified, and scanned the vicinity, certain it couldn't be far, when across the street, I saw it—not the phone booth, but the *absence* of the phone booth, marked by the sad string of Christmas lights that once adorned its top that now lay in a pile on the sidewalk, a crusty tangle of cords, abandoned on the cracked concrete. I raced over to get a closer look. In the glow of the streetlamp above, a few exposed bolts and thick metal cords glittered next to the colorful plastic bulbs, the only indication that there had ever been a structure there at all.

"No, no, no," I started to stammer, my mouth clearly understanding more quickly than my brain. The saliva evaporated from my tongue, and I could barely squeak out another utterance of denial.

I turned around, wildly searching for someone, *anyone*, to ask about the missing phone booth. Seconds later, I spotted an older man in a tweed newsboy cap watering bouquets of fresh flowers outside the bodega on the corner.

"Sir? 'Scuse me, sir?" I frantically waved my hands in his direction.

He set down his watering can and turned to me. "You okay, miss?"

"The phone booth that was here? Right here," I said, pointing to the large divot in the sidewalk, the still-exposed metal wires looking particularly unsafe. "The one with the sad string of Christmas lights. What happened to it?"

He shook his head as he approached. "The city came and carted that thing away a few days ago. Damn shame too. It was the last phone booth in Manhattan. You know, I've owned this bodega since 1972, and I can't tell you the number of people who came in needing change for that phone and ended up buying a pack of smokes or a candy bar. That phone booth's brought me a heck of a lot of business over the years."

"What do you mean they carted it away? Who did?! Where'd it go?"

He shrugged his shoulders. "The worker mentioned something about it going to a museum. Funny to think a phone booth would be considered a significant archaeological relic, but I guess, eventually all technology outlives its usefulness, right?"

"No. Not right. That phone booth was *extremely* useful. Necessary even," I said, gesturing my hands in the direction of the empty space where the booth once stood.

"Oh, did you need to make a call?" He reached deep into his pocket. "You can borrow my phone. Here," he said, offering it to me, until he noticed I had been clutching my own phone tightly in my grip. He eyed me, clearly confused by our entire exchange.

Just as he went to retract his jutted hand, I noticed the faint glimmer of something peeking out from inside his jacket. Was it a silver-bell pin? Was he another ghost or harbinger leading me to my fate? That had to be the explanation I was looking for. I motioned to his lapel. "What's that?"

He looked down. "What's what?"

"There, under your coat?"

He pulled his jacket to one side, revealing a shiny badge, the name Lou engraved on the silver plate. "My name tag?" he asked.

"Sorry, I thought it was . . . something else."

Growing impatient with my short attention span and seemingly disconnected line of questioning, he asked, "Hey, lady, do you need a phone or not?"

Lou had no idea how loaded a question that actually was. "You know, I'm not sure," I answered.

He grunted, shrugged, and turned his attention to laying a plastic tarp over the bouquets to protect the delicate flowers from the cooler overnight temperatures. Once finished, he said, "If you change your mind, I'll just be inside the store," and swung open the door, a jingle ringing brightly in the space between us.

I did a full turn in my spot, surveying the entirety of the street one more time, desperate for it to all be some kind of mistake. But no, the phone booth was gone. Really gone. The only evidence of it ever being here at all was the string of Christmas lights in a coiled mess on the ground. I picked them up and draped them over my shoulders like a scarf. I must've looked crazy, but I didn't care. I closed my eyes and rubbed the colorful bulbs like Aladdin with his genie lamp, hoping for something, anything to happen. Still nothing.

My chest tightened as hot tears flooded my eyes. How the hell was I supposed to make my decision now? I needed the phone booth's magic to reveal the final piece of its master plan for me. Dizzy at the culmination of my impending audition, Gabe's proposal, and the general uncertainty of my future, my vision warbled like strobe lights and I backed myself up until my legs hit a set of concrete stairs. Plopping myself down on the stoop, I drew in long, deep breaths to slow my heart and wiped away the tears that were now falling freely down my cheeks.

I glanced back to the exposed wires where the booth once stood and could have sworn I saw the small flicker of a spark. Maybe that was a sign? My mind shot to Gabe, and the electricity I felt between us every time his lips were on mine. Finding a love like ours was as rare as getting struck by lightning . . . and we were lucky enough to get struck twice.

Gabe was my proverbial fork in the road, and we'd been given a chance to make different choices this time around. To live the life we were always supposed to. This was *always* about finding my way back to him. Wasn't it? Or was the answer so painfully obvious that maybe I didn't need the phone booth to tell me what to do?

But if that were true, then why did I come looking for it in the first place?

Chapter Thirty-Eight

I made it back to Bushwick a little after 11:00 p.m., and the girls were all squashed on the couch watching the British version of *Love Island* in the living room.

"Oh my God, Gemma, you can do better than that player, Colin," Lyla yelled at the screen and continued to hand-feed her turtle, Sir Hank the Second, who was propped in her lap, one piece of popcorn at a time. "Can't you see how much Angus loves you? Swap, dammit. Right, Hank?! She should *swwaaaaappppp*!"

"You shut your mouth! Colin is so freakin' hot. I would take a bullet for that man. She should definitely *not* swap!" Sevyn rebutted with an almost comical level of intensity.

Oak, without missing a beat, rolled her eyes and said, "Well, clearly you aren't the greatest judge of character, Mrs. Tinder Swindler." Oak continued as she filed her nails at a violent pace, "She'll swap if she knows what's good for her. Colin and his abs have her completely fooled. She has absolutely no idea he's been snogging Natalie this whole time."

Sevyn grunted and tossed a handful of popcorn at the screen. "Stupid cow."

Oak looked up at me from her fingers that were practically smoking from the friction of the file and said, "Do *not* tell Ass we started the new season without her!"

"Since Ass travels so much for work, we binge a lot of shows without her and then play dumb when she gets home." Lyla extended her finger to point to every person in the room. "We all took the Netflix roommate oath and now that you're a bona fide roommate, you have to take it too. Repeat after me, 'I solemnly swear to fake all my reactions as if I were experiencing the show for the first time and never unintentionally reveal a spoiler.'"

I held up my right hand and stifled a giggle with the other. "I solemnly swear to fake all my reactions as if I were experiencing the show for the first time and never unintentionally reveal a spoiler."

"Good. Now *please*, someone take that thing away from Oak, she's gonna sand her fingers down to nubs if she keeps stress filing!" Lyla shouted from the farthest spot on the couch as I made my way into the room.

Oak gestured with the file to the box of wine tipped delicately over the kitchen sink. "Av, grab a glass and come sit and watch *Love Island* with us. It's our very finest cardbordeaux."

Sevyn added, "You're gonna need more than just one glass to keep up with all this drama. Gemma's about to make the biggest mistake . . ."

"OF . . . HER . . . LIFE!" the three of them hollered through bursts of laughter, as if they'd been practicing it all night. (Which I was certain they had.)

I poured myself a mugful of the red blend and settled onto the couch with them. I tucked my legs underneath me and gestured to the TV. "So, what's happening here? I've never seen this show."

Lyla rested Hank on the coffee table, grabbed the remote to hit the pause button, and turned to me, her face serious and focused. "Okay, on day one, the contestants couple up based on first impressions, but then later, they have the option to re-couple. Tonight's a big night. Gemma needs to decide if she is going to stay with that wanker Colin, who's been cheating on her with Natalie, or swap for Angus, who's been pining for her since they got to the island."

"The choice is so stupidly obvious," Sevyn said.

I reeled around on her and snapped far more harshly than I'd intended, "Is it? Maybe she doesn't know what to do. Maybe she's conflicted even though the choice does seem stupidly obvious. Maybe she doesn't want to choose, why can't she just have both?"

Oak, confused by my question, tried to explain. "Well, 'cause she's paired up with Colin. And you know, what's that expression, 'One in the hand beats two in the bush.'"

Sevyn, without missing a beat, chimed in, "True . . . unless she wants two in her bush!"

Oak paused her stress-filing to grab one of the decorative pillows and chuck it at Sevyn. "That's not what that means!"

Over the sound of Sevyn snorting through her fits of laughter, Lyla rolled her eyes and said, "Ignore them. We pretty much lose our minds when we watch *Love Island*. And besides, she can't choose both, the show doesn't really work that way."

I responded under my breath, perhaps more to myself than to her, "Well, it'd be so much easier if it did."

Lyla narrowed her eyes and hit pause on the remote. "Avery, what's going on? Are you okay?"

Hesitating for a moment, I set my mug of wine down on the coffee table and blurted out, "Gabe proposed to me tonight."

"What?!" they all cried out in almost perfect unison.

Sevyn motioned to my left hand. "C'mon girl, let's see that bling-bling."

"No"—I shielded my hand, tucking it in the other, and rubbing my knuckles anxiously—"I didn't take the bling-bling."

"You didn't take the bling-bling?!" Sevyn said, her eyes practically bulging out of her head.

Lyla parroted back with a justifiable amount of sass. "She didn't take the bling-bling!"

Oak scooted to the edge of the couch. "Why? Why didn't you take the bling? I mean, the ring?" She sucked air through her teeth and grimaced. "Was it heinous?"

"No. God, no. It was beautiful." Channeling the swept-off-my-feet exuberance of a lovestruck teenager, I threw myself back into the deflated couch cushions, recalling the feeling of the ring on my finger and the hopeful look in Gabe's expression when he popped the question.

"So then what happened?" Lyla asked, reaching for Hank, who was slowly but surely making his way across the coffee table, and setting him back in her lap.

"He proposed and then dropped the bombshell that he's moving to Washington, DC, for his dream job. He wants me to go with him." I looked up and into their enthralled faces, eyes wide and mouths dropped even wider. "I should have just said yes, right? Gabe, *my* Gabe, wants to marry me and make a life with me. Why didn't I just say yes?"

"Well, why didn't you?" Sevyn asked, as if the answer was as obvious as the question.

"I don't know. Everything about it seems . . . right. And yet, there's something that just feels off. Maybe it hasn't been long enough yet?"

"Haven't you known the guy for like almost a decade?" Oak asked. "Maybe I'm wrong, but I figured when you know you like, *know*. And if you don't know after this much time, maybe that's all you need to know . . ."

"No, it's not like that. I do love him and I do see a future with him. I just . . ." I grabbed a handful of popcorn from the bowl in Sevyn's lap and shoved it in my mouth, chewing animatedly to buy myself a moment to sort out my thoughts. But try as I might, I couldn't make sense of any of it. I swallowed and said, "The phone booth brought me to him. It led me to his damn door. If I'm not meant to end up with him, whether it's in DC or Timbuktu, then I don't know what any of this was for!"

Oak crooked a brow and leaned toward me. "Yeah, but didn't the booth also lead you to your audition for *Marley Is Dead*? So I think there may be a hole in your theory."

I spat out, "*Orrrr*, maybe it was just showing me how grueling and uncertain my life as a performer would be. Weeks of prep for a role I may not even get, and then I start again at square one, back at the bottom, singing for tips at Mimi's. Maybe all of this was meant to tell me that a life with Gabe would be the best option in the end. A sure thing. Happiness wrapped up in a big red bow. It has to be that. It's the only thing that makes any sense."

Lyla, thoughtfully observing the exchange, chimed in and said, "I think you're onto something there. Can I be brutally honest with you?" Lyla continued without waiting for my response. "You might get the role of Marley on Tuesday, but it's even more likely you won't. This industry can be a cruel and unforgiving slog, believe me, I know. I'm right there in the trenches with you singing for my supper. It's rejection after rejection. But you . . . you have a real shot at happiness with Gabe. I guess what I'm saying is that it's okay to get off the ride, Avery. Nobody will think any less of you if you decide to get off."

"No! I got off the ride once, and I don't want to do it again. This audition is a once-in-a-lifetime opportunity. How am I supposed to walk away now? Don't I have to at least know how the story ends?"

Lyla scrunched up her face. "Let's be real, hon, don't you already know how it ends? You say yes, soar off into the sunset with your Prince Charming, and never look back."

"I can't do it. I would spend the rest of my life looking back," I managed past the tears tightening in my throat.

Lyla set Hank down on the floor and crossed her arms in front of her chest, a smile erupting across her smug face. "Then I think you know what you need to do."

I blinked hard. "Lyla Jeffries, did you just use some reverse-psychology Yoda mind trick on me?"

"Tricked you, I did and honest, you were." She grinned devilishly, imitating the old green guru from *Star Wars*. "Seriously, though, deep down, you already know what you want."

"But Gabe's such a good guy. He's everything Adam wasn't. He's genuine and cares so much about making the world a better place."

"Just because someone's good doesn't mean they're good for you. I'm not saying you don't love Gabe, and I can't give you an explanation for why he came back into your life." She shrugged. "But *you* get to decide what your future looks like, not the booth."

Sevyn shifted her feet off the couch and set the bowl of popcorn down on the end table. "I mean, so long as we're dishing out some honesty, I'm not really feeling your new haircut."

My hand shot to my head, surprised by the turn of conversation. "I—I didn't get a new haircut."

"Oh, well, um . . . I'm gonna get a refill on the cardbordeaux and grab some more snackies." Sevyn hollered over her shoulder mid-scurry to the kitchen, "I'm restarting the show in five. Take a bathroom break if you need it!"

Lyla turned to me. "Ignore her. Your hair looks great. The audition's in less than forty-eight hours. Go get a good night's rest, and we'll do one last run-through tomorrow at Mimi's."

I shook my head. "I don't know if I'm ready. I botched the song at rehearsal today, and I'm still struggling to remember my lines."

"You're ready. You've prepared as much as any human possibly could. So now you need to stop thinking about it, and in the immortal words of Princess Elsa, it's time to let it go." Her eyes widened and she popped her index finger in the air to signal a flash of insight. "Ohhh, maybe I'll perform that song tomorrow at the diner. It always kills with the matinee crowd, especially if I can convince Charlie to turn on the snow machine. He hates cleaning up the mess."

I smiled. "Thanks, and I really appreciate the pep talk. I think I will turn in. I'll catch the rest of the episode tomorrow. I'm invested now in what choice Gemma makes," I said as I climbed off the couch and grabbed the empty popcorn bowl from the end table to take to the kitchen.

"Angus, if she knows what's good for her," Oak called out from the couch.

"Night, girls," I said, chugging the rest of what was in my mug, the heavy red wine drying my tongue and sliding all the way down my throat with a warm heat. I put the cup in the sink and offered a wave as I padded down the hall.

I closed the door to my bedroom and slunk down on the bed. My thoughts drifted to Marisol, who always seemed to have a sixth sense when it came to my audition insecurities. Even when I said that things were going fine, somehow she always knew what was really bubbling underneath the surface. That's when she would step in and help me see the world through her fearless eyes.

We started a tradition that every time I would get too critical about my ability or performance or get too in my head about a part, we would make a date and jump on the subway out to Coney Island and forget real life for at least a little while.

It'd been almost a decade since the last time I visited the old-timey amusement park, home to the notoriously rickety wooden coaster the Cyclone. Despite Marisol's words of encouragement on all our trips, I'd never been brave enough to *actually* ride the ride. But the faint smell of Nathan's hot dogs, the haunting melody of tinny carnival music, and the taste of the ocean's salty breeze were calling to me. Maybe it was exactly the type of distraction I needed to overcome the mounting self-doubt and get out of my head.

Chapter Thirty-Nine

From the moment we met Christmas Day my freshman year at NYU when Gabe took me home to meet his family, Marisol and I became fast friends. Like her brother, she was confident and sometimes brash. She told it like it was and never made apologies, honest and loyal almost to a fault. I admired her confidence and fearlessness and used to hope that some small fraction of her self-assuredness would rub off on me, if even only by osmosis.

Back then, she was a junior at The New School studying filmmaking and, much to her brother's chagrin, believed art was as important a calling as politics or policy making. I remember one time she and Gabe got into a particularly heated argument, which she ended by flashing a tattoo of a Tolstoy quote she'd recently gotten across her back that read, "Art is not a pleasure, a solace, or an amusement; art is a great matter." I don't know what shocked him more, the sentiment or the size of the tat.

The last time we took a trip to Coney Island together had been a few days before my ill-fated *Wicked* audition. Marisol stood waiting for me outside Gabe's and my apartment, wearing her iconic shit-kicking boots paired with a cute pleated miniskirt and a vintage rocker T-shirt.

"Hey!" she greeted me. "No offense, but it looks like you haven't slept in a week."

"More like two," I replied with a small shrug and a side smile. "I can't believe I've even made it this far. The other auditioners have agents and long résumés. I'm completely out of my league."

"If you want to run with the big dogs, you can't piss like a pup. You're a freakin' bullmastiff, you just aren't seeing it. You will, though. All right, Coney Island, here we come!" she said, linking her arm into mine and leading me down the steps into the subway station.

An hour later, we emerged in not only another borough but a whole other world, the briny air floating off the nearby Atlantic Ocean coating the insides of our mouths and nostrils.

"What do you think? Boardwalk first, then that frog slappy game I always kick your ass in, and then we ride the Cyclone?" Marisol asked.

I raised my right eyebrow. "Yeah, we'll see."

"C'mon, live a little, Lawrence," she said, guiding me toward the bright-yellow awning of Nathan's Famous Hot Dogs, the iconic Coney Island landmark.

Marisol marched up to the counter and ordered us each two hot dogs with the works, two Cokes, and a basket of fries to share. "Go find us a spot outside, I got this," she said.

I reached into my pocket for a twenty. "You sure?"

She shooed me from the counter. "Put that away. Your money's no good here."

I stepped outside and found us a table on the boardwalk. The gentle wind coming off the ocean made it feel about ten degrees cooler than in the city, a welcomed change considering how unseasonably warm it was for May. Coney Island was packed to the brim with people enjoying the summerlike temperatures. Fishing enthusiasts dangled poles over the edge of the railing while kids dipped their toes in the waves, screeching at the tops of their lungs when the cold water climbed up their shins. I turned my face into the sun and soaked in the rays. After spending the last week in a rehearsal studio getting ready for the *Wicked* audition, the fresh air and sea breeze felt amazing.

Marisol approached, one hand holding the tray, the other shielding it from any rogue seagulls eyeing our meal. She set down the food and took a seat on the other side of the picnic table bench, swiping a fry off the top of the pile and popping it into her mouth as she sat down.

"Okay, we got hot dogs, kraut, relish, a little mustard, and a little ketchup. And I couldn't help myself, I grabbed two knishes for good measure. I mean, is it even a trip to Nathan's if we don't get knishes?!"

My mouth watered at the mention of the potato-filled, deep-fried snack. I reached for one and ripped open the crispy crust to allow the steam to pour out. I squeezed a glob of deli mustard from a packet onto the logo-emblazoned wax paper, plunked the corner of the knish into the condiment, and took a healthy bite. Swallowing it down with an ice-cold gulp of Coke, the sweet bubbly drink contrasted the salty food, creating the most perfect combination—like every other time.

"This was a good idea. I don't think I've eaten an actual meal all week," I said.

"Nerves?" she asked between chewing.

"Nerves . . . terror . . . dread. The audition is the best opportunity I've got. I can't blow it. I've worked too hard."

"You're putting way too much stock in this one moment. You were an actress before this audition, and you'll be one after. Don't they say the road to success is paved in rejection?" Before I could give it another thought, Marisol slapped her hands on the table and changed the topic. "So, what do you think?" she asked. "Should we sit here and digest or live dangerously and go ride the Cyclone?"

"I think I need to digest," I said, hoping to put off riding the coaster for as long as I could.

"Wimp. Fine, let's hit the arcade, and then we can go scream our heads off on that old death trap."

We let the Nathan's settle in our stomachs while we played a few rounds of Whac-A-Mole followed by Skee-Ball and then ring toss. Marisol won a huge green stuffed animal she promptly named

Elphabear, which she offered to me for good luck. I was having such a good time I'd almost forgotten about the audition and nerves.

Marisol checked her watch. "The Cyclone closes in a half hour. It's now or never."

"I'm good. We had Nathan's, I kicked your ass in Whac-A-Mole, you got me out of my head for a while. All in all, I'd consider it a pretty successful day. Best friend mission accomplished." I nudged her before wrapping an arm around her shoulders. "But seriously, I am feeling a lot less stressed about everything, so thank you. You always know just what I need."

"Exactly, which is why I am insisting, no, demanding that we ride the Cyclone before we get out of here."

"I hate roller coasters."

"This is not a roller coaster. I mean, yes, it's a roller coaster, but really it's more of a spiritual experience."

"Next time, I'll ride. I promise."

She cocked her head and eyed me skeptically. "You say that every time. Lawrence, have I ever steered you wrong?"

I thought about all the great advice she always gave, the millions of times she told me exactly what I needed to hear even though I didn't want to listen, and the countless moments she'd been there for me like few others had. "Ugh, okay, let's do it before I change my mind."

Marisol took my change of heart as her cue to pull me toward the ticket booth and buy us each a ride. At the end of the day, with the park nearly closing, there was practically no wait, which left me no time to try to bail at the last minute. We handed our tickets to the barker and squeezed into the seat, a measly bar pressing down on our lap as its only safety measure.

"This?! This thing is what's holding us in?!" I cried.

"Only like three people a year die on this coaster, so your odds are pretty decent," Marisol joked as she took my hands from where they were clutching the handle for dear life, and raised them in the air along with her own, the safety check not even completed yet.

"Oh my God, I don't know about this, Marisol. I think I need to get off."

"You can't get off now! Just breathe and enjoy the ride!"

My peripheral vision was starting to narrow, and the world was getting dark around me as panic set in. "No, seriously, I have to get off. Please let me off." I used my hands that were still raised in the air with Marisol's to wave furiously to the young man operating the ride.

"The guy is all the way at the front. Just relax, I promise you, it'll be over before you even know it."

"Sir! Sir!" I started screaming, my arms flailing to the point of looking like I was trying to fly away. "I need you to let me out. I need to get off the ride. Like right now!" Sweat was pouring off my forehead, and my hands, which had moved to gripping the bar, were now contorted into two birdlike claws I couldn't unclench.

Marisol, seeing the color drain from my face and the sheer terror in my eyes, said, "Okay, okay. Let's get some help. Sir! Sir!" she screamed along with me.

A different teenager in a red Cyclone shirt finally looked in our direction and raised a hand in the air to signal to the operator to halt the ride.

"She needs to get off, please ask them to lift the bar," Marisol instructed, my hands still as rigid as the rest of my body.

The safety latch popped open, and the kid swung the metal bar up to allow us out. Marisol waited for me to get up, but I was still frozen, stuck in the seat.

"C'mon Avery, you're okay. I got you." Marisol tucked her hands under my armpits and hoisted me up, the worker extending his hands to steady me, and I climbed out with the help of Marisol's guidance.

We exited the ride and I immediately plopped down on a wooden planter, beads of perspiration still pouring down my cheeks and back.

"I'm so sorry. I really didn't mean to push. I swear, I thought you really had it this time. But, I mean, on a positive note, *that's* the farthest you've made it like ever! Like the ride almost actually started this time," she joked and leaned into me playfully.

"Silver lining."

"Silver lining," she repeated. "Well, either way, you'll get that white whale someday, Ahab. I just hope that you still had a good time even though you may have PTSD forever."

I looped my arm through hers and gave it a hard squeeze. "Of course I did. It was just what I needed, like always."

Seven years had passed, almost a decade of heartbreaks and missteps later, and now I stood in front of the Cyclone by myself, wishing like hell that Marisol was beside me coaxing me back onto the ride. But she wasn't. This time I'd need to do it alone, with only the memory of Marisol's encouragement to push me to take the leap I'd always been too scared to take on my own. With a trembling hand, I pulled a ten-dollar bill from my pocket and shoved it into a ticket machine that had certainly been a new addition since the last time I'd been there. The contraption spit out a voucher for the ride, along with my change, and I snagged it before I could talk myself out of riding.

I handed the young kid my ticket and climbed into the seat, sliding all the way to the side as if to let someone in next to me, but the spot remained empty. It was like stepping back into a memory, the smell of the salty air and the worn red leather snapping me right back to that day with Marisol almost ten years ago. I could practically feel the weight of her body up against mine, smushed into the tight roller coaster car.

Instinctively, I white-knuckled the handlebar as it locked into place, and my chest tightened as the familiar sensation of crippling fear started to trace its way through my veins. But I wouldn't get off the ride. Not this time. Come hell or high water, I was going to see this thing through.

As soon as the car started to inch up the track, I sucked in a deep breath, the air inflating my diaphragm and pushing my stomach against the safety crossbar. I closed my eyes and could hear my heartbeat competing with the coaster climbing up the first monster hill. Awash with a mix of dizziness and exhilaration, I focused on the past several months, each ratcheting up of the coaster marking a shift in memory—*click*, Adam getting arrested; *click*, reuniting with Gabe; *click*, going back to Mimi's; *click*, moving to Bushwick; *click*, meeting my new roommates; *click*, crushing the *Marley* audition; *click*, Gabe proposing; *click*, and now hanging in the balance was my uncertain future. *Click, click, click.* I couldn't see beyond the crest of the top, which was rapidly approaching. Though not seeing the track scared the crap out of me, I recalled Marisol's constant advice to just have faith—leap and the net will appear, right?

And as we climbed to the top and the wheels began to tip over the peak, I slowly opened my eyes to take in the view, the tracks still invisible underneath me. This was it. Releasing my grip from the crossbar, I outstretched my arms as high as they could reach to throw my hands into the air, let out a long, loud, cathartic *"MOOOOOOOOO,"* and finally . . . let go.

Chapter Forty

"The lips, the teeth, the tip of the tongue. The lips, the teeth, the tip of the tongue," I repeated over and over to my reflection in the dressing room mirror after already having done the crazy electric eel exercises. Charlie was right. The techniques helped, if for no other reason than to distract me from the nervous energy burbling up from deep in my gut.

Joanna, the casting assistant, rapped lightly on the open door. "About ten more minutes, then we'll take you in. How do you feel? You good to go?"

I smiled warmly through my nerves, eyes bright and feeling prepared mentally and physically. "As ready as I'll ever be," I responded.

"Try not to be nervous," she said. "Trust me, we want you to succeed as much as you do. I'll come back to get you in a few."

"Thank you," I replied, and turned back to the mirror. "The lips, the teeth, the tip of the tongue. The lips, the teeth, the tip of the tongue."

My phone buzzed from inside my bag. I bent down to get it and saw a message on the screen from Gabe:

Gabe Cell: I loved her against reason, against promise, against peace, against hope, against happiness, against all discouragement that could be.

Me: A Tale of Two Cities?

Gabe Cell: Great Expectations.

Me: Ugh, Reginald would be so disappointed in me.

Gabe Cell: No, you'll have his heart forever. The same way you have mine. Break a leg today. Love you.

My thumb hovered over the keypad ready to text back the words I felt so strongly, but Joanna knocked again, interrupting my concentration.

"Three minutes," she called.

"Okay, thanks," I responded, and quickly shot off the text before I turned the phone to silent and tucked it back in my bag:

Me: Love you too.

I chugged the rest of my water, smoothed the top of my bun, and applied one last coat of lip gloss. Then, for good measure, I let out the most dramatic and exaggerated silent scream of my life straight into the mirror, chuckled at how ridiculous I surely looked, and with renewed vigor, walked toward the wings to wait for my name to be called.

"Ms. Lawrence, we're ready for you," said a voice from the audience, and I stepped onto the stage and into the spotlight, the glare practically blinding me. I couldn't tell if there were five people in the audience or fifty, but it didn't matter—in my head it was opening night, and I was performing to a packed house. In the pit sat a small-scale orchestra cued up with their instruments at the ready and their music perched in place.

The opening notes of the song began to play and I dug deep, channeling the me who sat in that roller coaster car enjoying that incredible view, the me with her arms in the air wild and free, and I gave that audition every effin thing I had. I hit every note, every nuance, every beat like I'd been born to do it. The director and producers were clapping thunderously, and I knew without a doubt that this part was mine for the taking.

"That was wonderful, Avery," the director called out from his seat over the din of excited chatter from the room full of executives and the production team. "We have a new scene we'd like you to perform with an actor who'll read in for Scrooge. Joanna has the pages for you, if you want to grab them and take a few minutes to look over before we call you back in."

Joanna came rushing out from the wings with a packet of papers. "So you are going to want to look at pages 28 to 31. It's a scene between Marley and Scrooge. She's desperately in love with him but has come to realize everything she sacrificed to be with him—family, friends, her own ambitions. She pleads with him to be a different kind of man, but as you know, he's incapable. He'll be her downfall, but she follows him down the garden path anyway. The scene is followed by the song, 'These Chains I Wear,' Marley's 'I Want' song. Here's the music. Do you have any questions?"

My heart was in my throat, and even though I knew this was all a good sign and part of the process, the on-the-spot stuff was where I always doubted myself most. "Um . . . how long do I have to prep?"

"Well, the actor is supposed to be here around one thirty, so what is that . . ." She peeked at her watch. "About fifteen to twenty minutes or so?"

"All right, thanks. I'll just head to the dressing room."

"Oh, we have a small rehearsal space downstairs if you'd rather use that. Or the lobby. Or you can go outside. Wherever you'd feel most comfortable. Just come back up to the stage at like 1:25."

I opened up the script on the floor of the rehearsal room and turned to page 28, my eyes zeroing in on Marley's dialogue. I scanned the sentences for key words and phrases, trying to get a sense of the overall tone. From what I could tell, it was a pivotal moment in the show, Marley confronting Scrooge about the man he's revealed himself to be.

I turned to the sheet music and sight-read it the best I could, spot-checking myself on a small keyboard plugged in by the far wall. Charlie had played the track a couple of times for me on YouTube, so it wasn't totally foreign, but it was still a tough number to learn mostly on the fly. I tapped out a few trickier measures on the plastic keys and sang the notes back, mirroring their rhythm and tone until they lodged in my memory.

Fifteen minutes flew by in a flash, and before I knew it, I had to be back onstage. Though I'd looked through the pages quickly, I'd spent most of the time on the song, hoping that the acting bit would come naturally once I was up against a partner. I hurried back upstairs and into the auditorium.

Joanna spotted me. "Perfect timing. The actor's onstage. When you're ready, you can step out and begin the scene."

I glanced down at the script, committing the first line to memory: "Past, Present, and Future, the Spirits Three, they are alive with a message bound within me." Stepping onto the stage, I recited the words again out loud and waited for the actor to reply.

"Marley," he croaked through a raspy voice of utter surprise, leaping off the couch where he'd been seated watching television. He pantomimed flicking off the TV with a remote and turned back to me.

I took two steps closer to him. "Still alone, I see?"

"Nobody could fill the hole you left in my heart," Scrooge said.

"What heart?" I replied coldly, the line like sniper fire straight to the core.

Then, instead of seeing the actor reading across from me, I saw Adam's intense face, his greedy eyes, his serpentine smile.

The actor's posture softened, his shoulders slumping forward. "You know I had one once. You occupied every square inch of it."

"Until I didn't. Until your other pursuits pushed me out," I cried.

"You always knew who I was, Marley. Who I've always been. I never hid it from you."

And suddenly, it was as if I was speaking to Gabe, the actor's forlorn face now morphing into the same face I'd known since I was a freshman new to the big city. The Gabe who had lofty dreams of making the world a better place. The emotion rising in my chest made it difficult for the words to come out in anything more than a strangled whisper.

"I lost myself because of you. And now I wear the chain I forged in life," I replied. "I made it link by link, and yard by yard." I held up the imaginary chain, tears pricking my eyes, begging him to see the links for what they were—the sacrifices I'd made for him, which paved my way to never creating a life of my own. "I girded this of my own free will and of my own free will, I wore it . . . I *still* wear it. I am forever tethered to the mistakes of my past—both the ones I made and those I didn't because I was afraid . . . of losing you. Of failing on my own. Of not being good enough. So instead, I became nothing. I have no one."

The actor advanced toward me, his body pressing up against mine, and traced his fingers down my cheek.

I topped his hand with my own and whispered, "Don't you understand? I am the ghost of my former self, Ebenezer, a thin veil, a shadow of who I should have been."

"Don't blame me for your shortcomings, Marley. You were the one who didn't choose, who didn't have enough backbone to stand up for yourself. You allowed others to make your decisions for you." The actor shouted louder and louder with each emphasized point, backing me across the space with his accusations.

Suddenly then, minus the aggression, the words and sentiment reminded me of Marisol, of exactly what she was trying to explain to me when we'd had our fight about Adam. What she'd been trying to tell me since we met, this whole time. This. Whole. Damn. Time.

At the same moment of my remarkable epiphany, the pit swelled with the sonorous echoes of orchestral bells. Silver bells?! Ringing out like the truth, like the clanking of metal on metal—the bells breaking apart the links of my very heavy chain.

And finally, it all became astonishingly clear—the phone booth hadn't taken me back to reconcile my past with Gabe like I'd thought, but instead to mend something entirely different.

Chapter Forty-One

When the audition ended, the team thanked me for my time and let me know they'd be making their final casting decisions by the end of the month. For as great as the first half went, I was equally unsure of how my impromptu scene measured up to their expectations. But either way, I did what I had set out to do. No regrets. I laid it all out there, and the rest was out of my hands. I expelled a deep breath and stepped out of the building feeling lighter than I had in ages. Though still riddled with uncertainty, I felt somewhat freer now that the audition was behind me. Sometimes you don't realize the weight of what you've been carrying until you finally lay it down.

I slid on my trench coat and yanked my hair out of my tight bun. The warm April rain had petered out, leaving a cloudy but dry afternoon. I pulled out my phone to call Gabe and let him know the audition was over, but when I got to his name, I scrolled past it until I landed on Marisol's. It'd been almost six years since we last spoke. I didn't even know if this was still her phone number.

Before I could second-guess myself or talk myself out of it, I clicked on the message icon and typed out:

Me: I did it. I finally rode the Cyclone.

Not expecting a response, I started to shove my phone back into my coat pocket but stopped when I saw the three flashing dots indicating

Marisol was in the midst of answering. A small gasp caught in my throat, and I held my breath awaiting her reply.

. . .

Marisol Cell: And how was it?

Me: Fan-freakin-tastic.

Marisol Cell: Yasss, Queen! Yes!

Me: I know we have a lot of ground to make up, and I have a lot of sorrys to dole out, but long story short, I miss you.

. . .

The three dots flashed for what felt like forever, and then finally her message appeared.

Marisol Cell: I miss you too.

Me: Can we meet up and chat? Wherever, whenever. You name the place and time, and I'm there.

Marisol Cell: As luck would have it, I'm actually in the city today seeing a matinee with my son. Could you meet me in Times Square around 5?

Me: Want to meet at Mimi's?

Marisol Cell: Sounds perfect. See you then.

I tucked my phone back in my pocket, not realizing how hard I'd been smiling. My cheeks ached, and I was surprised to feel tears wetting my lashes. Her son? After so much radio silence, I would finally get a chance to set a few things right with Marisol, and it was more than overdue.

After making a few stops along the way, I arrived at Mimi's around 4:00 p.m. Charlie was onstage filling in for Kai, playing Shrek to Lyla's Princess Fiona. They were just finishing up a raucous rendition of "Big Bright Beautiful World" when I walked inside.

I was smiling and whooping heartily at their bows, and they in turn leaped offstage at the sight of me to ask a million questions about how the audition went. My heart swelled with their exuberant enthusiasm and obvious pride as they ushered me toward the dressing room.

"So, did you slay it like I knew you would?" Lyla asked.

"I definitely . . . for sure . . . I gave it . . . yeah, I slayed it!" I answered, unable to hide under meekness or modesty anymore. I was freakin' proud of myself, and it was okay to be excited about how much I was finally putting into pursuing my dreams.

Charlie swooped me up in his arms and swung me around in the air.

"Hey there, watch those green hands, mister. I know better than anyone how hard it is to get that makeup off," I joked, my arms around his neck squeezing him tightly as we spun.

"Sorry," he said, putting me down. "I'm just really proud of you."

"I don't know if I got the role, but I sure as hell gave it my damnedest."

"I knew you would," he said with a wink, "but, what are you doing here? You're not working tonight. Shouldn't you be out celebrating or something?"

"I'm meeting someone here. An old friend. Marisol, actually."

Charlie's brows curved into a firm arch. "Well then, let me clear off the VIP table for you two."

"We have a VIP table?"

"For Very Important Performers and you, my friend, certainly qualify."

"Thanks, Charlie."

He held up his fingers. "I should go wash this all off before I greenify anything else."

"Good idea."

I settled down at the VIP table, otherwise known as the table farthest from the bathrooms and closest to the stage, and watched the front door for Marisol. At exactly 5:02, a woman with pin-straight dark hair in a black blazer and leather pants walked into the diner holding the hand of a young boy with brown wavy hair who looked a lot like Gabe. Our eyes met as a smile broke out across her face, immediately putting me at ease. She crossed the diner as I stood up to greet her and, without even so much as a moment's hesitation, pulled me in for a big hug.

"I'm mad as hell at you and we obviously have a lot to discuss, but damn, it's good to see you," Marisol said into my hair, her grip on me tightening with each passing second.

Her shampoo smelled exactly the same. Clean and fresh, notes of gardenia woven through its scent. My throat constricted, tight with tears of joy, and I held on, relishing in her embrace and waiting for her to be the first one to let go.

"This is my son, Oliver," she said, pushing forward the four- or five-year-old boy.

I leaned down to make his acquaintance. "Nice to meet you. I'm Avery, an old friend of your mom's." I stood back up and turned to Marisol. "Wow, he looks just like Gabe."

"The Salgado genes run strong, nary a trace of my Irish Catholic husband, much to his chagrin. And if you can believe it, this Puerto Rican chica's now walking around with the last name Fitzgerald. Who woulda thunk it, right?"

"Son . . . husband . . ." I shook my head. It all seemed so unbelievable. "So much has changed."

"And not so much," she said, motioning to the booth. We took seats on opposite sides of the table, and Oliver slid in next to his mom.

Charlie swung by to set down some waters. "Can I get you ladies anything?"

"I'm fine," Marisol said, "but he might like something." She motioned for Oliver to take a look at the menu.

"We have some awesome options. My favorite is the My Fair Lady Fingers Pudding," Charlie said.

Oliver scrunched up his nose and looked to his mom for some backup.

Charlie, reading Oliver's not-so-subtle expression, offered, "Not a pudding fan? How 'bout you come check out the dessert case by the counter and pick out something you like better." Charlie collected the menus from the table and looked over at Marisol. "Is that okay?"

Marisol nodded and Oliver hurried off, leaving the two of us on our own for a few minutes.

"Was that . . . ?" she asked, pointing a finger toward Charlie as he walked away.

"Yeah, Charlie. He manages the place now."

She nodded and took a sip of her water. "Ever since Gabe told me you were working here again, I've thought about stopping by at least a dozen times."

"So, Gabe told you about us? I was hoping he would. I'm so sorry about your mom, by the way. I . . . I was really blown over when Gabe told me." I reached across the table, put my hand on hers, and gave it a squeeze.

"Thank you. It's been hard. Harder than I imagined, but Gabe has really tried to be there for me . . . as best as he can. You know Gabe," she said with a shrug and a lift of her brows. "And, he didn't really tell me about you two, actually. I kind of worked it out myself. Out of nowhere he suddenly was bringing up your name all the time. Then when he mentioned he was seeing someone and that it was getting pretty serious, I asked him point-blank if it was you. I'll admit I was surprised at first. I'd just assumed all these years later you and Adam had everything tied up in a nice big red bow. But then Gabe filled me in on all that too."

"You were right about Adam. Everything you suspected—about me, about him—it was all true."

"I'm sorry to hear it. I'm not sure you believe me, but I always just wanted you to be happy."

"I know that. Now. I was too self-absorbed, though, to see it then."

"You weren't self-absorbed. If anything, I think it was the opposite. You were *too* absorbed in everybody else—namely Gabe and then Adam—to put yourself first. It was impossible to watch, especially when you were . . . well, *are* . . . so freakin' talented. You worked so damn hard in undergrad and you were so passionate about making it back then. I hated that Gabe wasn't the cheerleader in your life like he should've been. But even more than that, I hated that you didn't stand up for yourself and fight harder for your dreams. As for Adam, I guess I hoped you'd choose *you* for once, but you just weren't ready. Maybe I shouldn't have pushed so hard . . ."

I grabbed her hand again, but this time I did not let go. I looked straight at her, locking in on her big brown eyes. "I wasn't ready. But you didn't push too hard. You were the only one—including myself— who put me first, who saw the me I wanted to be, and who fought for that girl when no one else did. *You* were my cheerleader and very best friend. And I am so sorry that I lost sight of it all."

Marisol stayed silent for a moment, tears brimming in the corners of her eyes, until she nodded and squeezed my hand in response. The gesture said more than words ever could.

While we were laying it all out, I continued, "Did you know that Gabe proposed to me a few nights ago?"

"He what?" Marisol exclaimed, her brows weaving together in confusion. "The last time we spoke he told me he thought he was going to be offered a job in DC."

"He was offered the job and he accepted it. He's asked me to go with him."

Marisol slumped back against the cushion of the booth as if stunned with a sudden blow. "He did?" She sat quietly for a moment, her eyes working out the scenario in her head. "Do you know what you're going to do?"

I stared at Marisol, never having imagined we'd have this moment of reconciliation. If the phone booth had taken me to Marisol's door instead of Gabe's on Christmas Day, I would have slammed it closed and walked away. I wasn't ready to face her then because I couldn't see who I'd been, let alone who I had become. But now, everything was different. We were different. The past had somehow collided with the present, opening up a million possibilities for the future. *This . . . this* had been the point all along. Just as I had suspected, it had never been about Gabe at all.

"You know, I actually do think I know what I'm going to do," I answered.

Her mouth curved into a smile. "Good."

Charlie brought Oliver back to the table, the corners of his lips still smudged with sticky-sweet whipped cream. "He settled on a Chocolate Sundae in the Park with George. On the house."

I mouthed a "thank-you" to him for the ice cream and for helping entertain Oliver while Marisol and I took a much-needed moment to catch up.

"You have a very polite young man here. He's welcome to come and hang with me and raid the dessert case any time," Charlie said, offering Oliver a high five. He responded by enthusiastically slapping his small hand up to meet Charlie's.

"Thank you. I'm sure this will rank higher in his day than the show we just saw. Okay, bud, we better get going or we'll miss our train. Put your jacket on, please," Marisol instructed Oliver, sounding so mom-like. It was a surprising yet delightful shift from the girl I'd known back in college. As he wrestled himself into his coat, we stood from the table and Marisol reached out to pull me into one last hug, holding me tightly as I returned the embrace.

I pressed a soft kiss to her cheek as she withdrew. "I'll call you. Maybe we can meet for dinner next week."

"That'd be great." She smiled and clasped Oliver's hand in her own. "Hey, love you," she called over her shoulder as she led him toward the exit and out the door.

"Love you too," I called back after her, the silver chimes on the door tolling like bells as she left.

Chapter Forty-Two

A few hours later, I found myself back in Tribeca at Gabe's apartment, my thoughts flashing back to Christmas Day. I remembered standing in this exact spot, mascara running down my cheeks, shivering under Adam's Princeton hoodie, not knowing who would be on the other side of that door. Then, seeing Gabe's face, I'd felt as if the nightmare I'd been living had maybe transformed into a wonderful dream.

I used to think that my life had two possibilities, two paths, Gabe or Adam. A or B. But over these last few months I'd come to understand I was wrong. There were other letters of the alphabet, other avenues, other outcomes, and I was the one who would get to choose.

I knocked lightly on Gabe's door and moments later he opened it, a broad, welcoming smile on his face, and motioned for me to come inside. He took my coat, hung it on the back of a chair, and said, "I've been trying to call you, but your phone keeps going to voice mail. Have you been in the audition this whole time?"

I slung my bag off my shoulder and rested it by the door. "No, I finished up a few hours ago."

His eyes went round. "A few hours ago? Where've you been all afternoon?"

"Actually, I met up with Marisol."

His face contorted in shock. "Marisol? How? Why?"

Unsure of how to answer his questions, I remained quiet for a moment. He raised his brows as an indication that he was waiting, and instead, I said, "Did you know I was afraid of roller coasters?"

He seemed utterly confused by the change of topic. "Roller coasters? I don't think so. I guess, we've never ridden one together, but I didn't know you were afraid of them."

"Can we sit down?" I asked.

He nodded and led me over to the couch.

I continued, "I am afraid of roller coasters. Terrified, actually. Marisol tried to get me to ride the Cyclone for years, but I've always chickened out at the last minute. Do you know where I went yesterday? Before my audition?"

He shrugged. "I don't know? I assumed you were rehearsing somewhere. I was trying to give you your space like you asked."

"I wasn't rehearsing. I went to Coney Island, and I rode the Cyclone for the first time ever. And do you know what? It really wasn't so bad. It was actually kind of great."

He searched my eyes for meaning. "I'm sorry, but I'm not following you."

"I can't marry you, Gabe." The words fell out in one breath before I could even consider their weight.

Gabe reeled back, his eyes scanning my face for more. "Wait, did you get the role?" he asked, trying to put the pieces together.

"No, I won't hear anything for a few more weeks."

"Then I don't understand. What are you saying?"

I cast my eyes to the ground to avoid the hurt now flooding his expression. "I can't marry you because we shouldn't get married. I think deep down you know it too. We're trying to make this thing fit because we want to believe that the universe has it all worked out for us. But that just isn't true."

He cupped my chin, gently nudging it in his direction, forcing me to meet his gaze. "No, you're wrong. We've been given the gift of a second chance, and we get to make it work this time," he said, urgency filling his voice.

I stood up and walked over to the window, taking in the expanse of buildings out over the horizon. "Except we were so caught up in the here and now, we never bothered confronting all the reasons that didn't work the last time. You haven't done anything wrong. And neither have I. You are who you are, and I love who you are. You're an incredible human being, and I don't want to ask you to change all the things that make you *you* . . . for me. And I know you wouldn't want that either. That's the thing—the thing people don't talk about enough. How it's possible to love someone and want everything good for that person, but despite that, also know it still isn't meant to be." I turned to face him. "I want you to go to DC and do all the amazing things I know you'll do there. But I can't go with you."

"You don't have to come to Washington with me right now." He advanced toward me, but I backed away, afraid that if he stepped in too close or grazed against my skin just the right way, I'd completely lose my nerve. He relented and swiped a hand over his chin while he thought. "We can do long distance for a while, you know, until you're ready to move to DC. Lots of people do."

For a while. Deep down, though—he'd never admit it, and maybe he wasn't even aware—he still saw my dreams as secondary to his own, much like Adam had. Maybe I'd even given them both that impression over the years. But it wasn't how I felt now. Not anymore. It wasn't Gabe who was "The One That Got Away," it was me. *I* was the one who had gotten away, and I wouldn't let that happen again, even if it broke my heart and his to be the one who had to say it.

I held up my hands to create a barrier between us. "It isn't about the distance and isn't about not wanting to go. It's about wanting to *stay*. You once told me I could light up Manhattan if I just let myself. And I want to try, *need* to try. You know it too, Gabe, we want . . . we just want different things."

He gently lowered my arms and stepped in close, his body hovering over mine and his eyes pleading with me to just give in. "I want you," he whispered, his hands coming up to rest on my cheeks and then tracing their way to the sensitive skin on my neck.

I thought my heart was going to shatter into a million pieces right there, but it stayed surprisingly resolute. I pulled back and rested my palm on his chest. "No, you want the me that would pack up her whole life right now, give everything else up, and follow you without a second thought or single ounce of regret. But I'd be filled with it. It would poison us. Maybe not at first, but over time."

"But I love you. And you love me." He shook his head, moistened his lips, and looked into my eyes. "You jump, I jump, right?"

"No, Gabe. Not this time. I can't jump. I do love you. If that was all this was about, my answer would be easy. But don't you see, in so many ways we're right back to where we were seven years ago when we sat in that café, our passions pushing us to different places. Places I know deep down we both want to go, and should go, without anything or anyone holding us back."

"Holding us back . . . ," Gabe repeated in a whisper with a disbelieving nod, as if the words were too heavy to say with more force.

He stayed silent for a moment, not firing back a rebuttal, his default, which was all the confirmation I needed to know that though this was painful beyond measure, somewhere in his gut, he agreed.

Gabe sighed, releasing both the breath in his lungs and the weight of the truth, something that, up until now, he'd been reluctant to acknowledge. "So what happens to us?" he asked.

My eyes brimmed with hot tears, and I swallowed past the tight knot in my throat. "We go our separate ways, wish each other well, and cheer one another on from the sidelines, the way we should have been doing all along. Just think, we finally replaced that question mark with a period, and maybe now we can close this door and really move forward."

He pulled me into his broad chest. "For what it's worth, I'll never be sorry you came knocking on mine." His thick lashes hooded a heavy gaze, his expression wistful and full of reflection.

Without even thinking, I recited aloud the words that had become almost like a prayer to me. "'No space of regret can make amends for one life's opportunity misused.'"

"It wasn't misused. And I have no regrets. Not a single one," he said, and pressed his lips to the top of my head.

"No, me either." I inched up on my toes, pushed my fingers through his wavy hair, and kissed Gabe goodbye for the very last time.

Chapter Forty-Three

I slid my time card into the clock and waited for the familiar punch before grabbing the set list off the wall and heading to the dressing room. I glanced down. *Ugh, not again.* I appreciated Sir Andrew Lloyd Webber as much as the next gal, but if I had to pour myself into a spandex unitard for the *Cats* megamix one more time, I was gonna give Charlie a "Memory" he wouldn't soon forget.

As I started to open my makeup case on my dresser, a loud bang made me practically jump out of my skin. "Jesus Christ!" I shouted, and reeled around to find Charlie dressed in a long white robe and Birkenstock sandals and holding a shepherd's staff.

Charlie yanked off his full beard and mustache combo, the sound of the sticky spirit gum pulling from his skin almost painful. "Superstar, in the flesh." He gestured and took an exaggerated bow in place.

"I didn't know Jesus was such a bull in a china shop."

"Yeah, new staff." He waved it around gingerly, careful to not whack the doorframe again. "Haven't broken it in yet."

I smirked and turned back to the mirror to get ready for my shift.

Charlie set down the large wooden rod, kicked off his leather sandals, and sat on the edge of my vanity stool while I set tubes of green paint out on the counter.

"An Elphaba day? Is rent due?" he joked.

I took a sponge and began to pat the verdant creamy base across my forehead. "Nope."

"I thought you were doing an *Evita* set and some Mama Rose today?" He stood up. "So should I tell Mack to cue up 'The Wizard and I' instead?"

I swiveled around in my seat to face Charlie. "I was actually thinking I might give 'Defying Gravity' a shot."

Charlie looked at me quizzically. "BrAvery Lawrence, did you find out about *Marley Is Dead*?!"

I shook my head. "Nope, not yet. Haven't heard a thing."

He cocked his head to the side, confused by my song request. "So then what's with the change of heart and goofy smile?"

"Because it doesn't matter. If I don't get this part, then I'll go after the next one and then the one after that. I know what I want and I'm not backing down. And I'm certainly not going to let a little high E above middle C stand in my way."

He started to walk out of the dressing room. "'Defying Gravity' it is . . . *after* the *Cats* megamix," he yelled back.

"Charlie!" I cried in defiance.

He peeked his head back into the doorframe. "What can I say, you look so damn good in that unitard, Lawrence."

I smiled inwardly at his admission and couldn't help but call after him, "I knew it!"

When my shift had ended and Charlie and I were finishing up our closing side work, he nabbed me by the elbow and asked me to stay for a few minutes longer, unless I had somewhere to be. I assured him I didn't. So, he directed me to take a seat on the diner's small stage and said he'd be back in a moment with a special surprise. I tucked my coat and bag in a booth and climbed onto the platform, sitting cross-legged in the center as instructed.

He approached holding a pie dish and cupping a protective hand around one lit candle, its flame threatening to extinguish with each brisk step he took in my direction. Under his arm, he tucked two small plates, a few utensils, and a handful of napkins. I rose to help him, grabbing for the items that threatened to slip from under his elbow, and with an impressive bit of athletic dexterity and balance, Charlie hopped up onstage, the pie never in danger of wobbling free from his grasp.

He handed me the plates and forks and then carefully took a seat across from me on the floor, placing the pie dish between us, the flame still glinting brightly in the dim light of the closed diner.

"I asked the chefs to whip up something special for you. I wanted to make it myself, but that is something maybe best left to the professionals, especially if we were hoping for something relatively edible," he joked.

I scooched in closer and peered at him over the candlelight and smiled. The thoughtfulness of the gesture was all I really needed. If it was delicious too, that would just be . . . well, icing on the cake, for lack of a better phrase. "So, what is this exactly?"

"This is a pie I created in your honor. I'm calling it The Impossible (Chocolate) Dream Pie. For my impossible dreamer and the badass who has been brave enough to go after what she wants . . . no, deserves. So, make a wish!" He pushed the tin in my direction and waited for me to close my eyes and blow out the candle, but as I did, he suddenly sprang up off the ground and cried, "Wait! One more thing and it'll be perfect!" He hopped down off the stage and over to the panel of switches on the wall to flip on the snow machine.

As silvery white flakes floated down over the stage, I bent forward, resting my hands on the floor. Leaning into the candle, I closed my eyes, and for a minute, I struggled to come up with what to wish for because finally, for the first time in a long time, maybe ever, I had everything I could ever want.

But just in case, I blew out the flame anyway.

Epilogue

December twenty-fifth, exactly a year to the day from when my life had imploded back on the Upper East Side, the white lights of the stage were blinding me from most of the theater's house, but I could still make out just about every single person in the front rows. Everyone was on their feet screaming for me during the final bow on the opening night of *Marley Is Dead*, which was making its Broadway debut on Christmas Day. Marisol, Charlie, Gabe, my parents, Lyla, Sevyn, Oak, Kai, friends, *everyone*. Their hoots and hollers seemed to never end, and I bowed again and again, the entire audience on its feet singing their praises for Broadway's newest "triumph" according to the *Times*... and pretty much every other publication in the city.

I soaked it all in—the heat of the spotlight warming my face, the roar of the crowd echoing in my ears, the beads of sweat trailing down my back under the heavy folds of my woolen costume, the clammy palms of my castmates during the curtain call, and the pinched tightness of my cheeks from smiling so damn hard. I felt lighter than air, certain I was going to float right off the stage and up into the catwalk overhead.

From above the thunderous ovation, I could hear a faint chanting of "BrAvery! BrAvery!" from Charlie, who was pumping his fist in the air like he was trying to lobby for everyone to join him. And then Gabe, who had come home for the holidays to see Marisol, front row center for opening night. By the look of delight on his face as pure pride washed over him, I could see he finally understood why I didn't say yes.

The applause faded out as we backed behind the falling curtain. I had told my friends to meet me at the cast party at Sardi's and grab a drink or two without me, that I'd be there as soon as I could. I headed back to my dressing room, the aroma of fresh flowers elevating my mood even higher. A gorgeous oversize frosted poinsettia from my costar, Aaron Tveit, who'd nabbed the role of Scrooge. The show was a bona fide hit. Whatever came, I'd done it. I'd accomplished my dream, and the fact I was able to help my parents get theirs in the form of an RV they'd be driving to Destin in the morning was just icing on the cake.

Smaller posies and vases filled the space, tokens from fellow cast members, fans, celebrities, and other well-wishers. I just about died when delivered to my dressing room were gifts from both Lin-Manuel Miranda *and* Sutton-*freakin'*-Foster! I had an absolute fit, screaming and jigging about, clearly fangirling so hard! My (almost) six hundred thousand TikTok followers got such a kick out of the whole thing (thank you, Lyla and @AntiquesJoeShow for the reposts!).

I plopped myself down in front of my vanity and took it all in. The tangle of Christmas lights I'd taken as a token of the phone booth were strung from the top of the mirror, still broken and unlit, but an essential reminder of all that it took to get me here. Next to Elphabear hung pictures of special moments that paved my road to *Marley*, photos of celebrity visits, and newspaper clippings of the rave reviews that had been pouring in throughout the workshop and previews. One of my favorites was a large cast photo—big smiles, center stage, arms slung around one another, me laughing in the middle. I swear I've never looked so happy.

I made my way to the stage door, bracing myself for what lay beyond it. As soon as it swung open, I was met by a wall of sound, fans screaming my name, sticking pens and notebooks in my direction as the security team kept them at bay. My heart swelled, graciously, and I took about fifteen minutes to sign as many autographs and take as many selfies with them as I could. I thanked them all for coming and encouraged them to come back soon. I wiggled through the crowd, scrawling out a last few signatures as I went, and finally gained a clear passage to make my way to Sardi's.

As soon as I arrived, I was greeted with a whole new round of cheers—the sound just as loud by a crowd a fraction of the size. My closest family and friends welcomed me with a glass of champagne as they raised theirs high. Twinkling strings of soft-white lights paired with oversize glittery snowflakes elegantly strung from the ceiling with thick satin ribbons at different lengths created a supremely festive atmosphere for the cast party. The restaurant even had its own tree set right inside its entrance; a tall New York City–themed spruce glittered with baubles and trinkets that represented notable city landmarks, with most of the Broadway shows having ornaments of their own. Instead of a star at the top, obviously a large Yankees tree topper.

I circled around the room greeting everyone—friends, family, castmates—and spotted my roommates taking full advantage of the open bar.

"Oh my God, Avery, you were fantastic," Lyla gushed.

"Unbelievable," Oak echoed.

"You were good," Sevyn deadpanned as Lyla shot her a nasty look. "What? I don't love live theater. People just like breaking into song like that? It's unnatural."

Before I could respond, I was bum-rushed by a short girl with bright-red hair. "Avery, you were magical and the show was magical. I was completely blown away. A tour de force. Seriously."

"Wow, thank you so much . . . I'm sorry, and you *aaarrre?*" I managed, still squeezed tight in her arms.

She pulled away. "Oh, em, gee, that's right?! We've never met. I'm Ass!"

"You're Ass?" I turned to Lyla and Oak for confirmation. "That's Ass?"

"That's Ass," they said in perfect unison.

I erupted in a burst of laughter and couldn't keep myself from shouting, "TO ASS!" as I raised my glass in the air. My roommates, Ass included, joined me in the toast and took a sip of their drinks.

Charlie came up behind me, and I stepped away from the girls to speak with him. "Wait, whose Ass are we toasting to?"

"I'll fill you in later."

"You better."

I laughed. "Anyway, thank you for the support and your unwavering friendship. It has meant more than you could know." I kissed him softly on the cheek and squeezed his arm. "I hope you'll still let me drop by Mimi's to give a little cameo performance every once in a while?"

"My God, if people got wind that you'd be there, we'd be mobbed! Just let me know when you're coming so that I can properly staff," he joked. "But seriously, Dorothy, you know that Mimi's will always be here with open arms to welcome you back."

"Well, you know what they say? There's no place like home." I winked, hoping he'd see that I too was mirroring our conversation from when I'd first been hired back at the diner.

I refilled my glass from a bottle resting in an ice bucket that had been decorated to look like the bottom half of Santa's red suit. "Excuse me—hey—up here!" I directed everyone's attention to the front as I climbed up on a chair, backlit by the luminous tree that sparkled behind me. "Before we all get carried away celebrating, I just wanted to say thank you—all of you—from the bottom of my heart. Just when I thought my life had hit the very, very bottom, somehow, someway, each and every one of you helped me crawl out of that hole and then start to climb, higher than I ever thought possible. This whole time you have supported me and loved me, and I am so damn grateful I could burst."

Tears of unadulterated happiness were leaking freely from my eyes. Hardly able to control the wave of emotions racing through me, I wiped at my cheeks with the back of my hand. I straightened my posture, sniffed hard, and cleared my throat. "I'm so excited about my future with *Marley Is Dead*, and with Manhattan, and mostly, with all of you. So, I guess there's only one thing left to say." I raised my glass high in the air. "In the wise words of Charles Dickens, 'God bless us every one!'"

Clink.

AUTHORS' NOTE

On May 23, 2022, the last phone booth in New York City was removed from its post on Seventh Avenue and West Fiftieth Street, just south of Times Square, and moved to the Museum of the City of New York.

ACKNOWLEDGMENTS

To Maria Gomez, for your unabashed enthusiasm and for making us part of the Montlake family. We shared a vision for this book and knew as soon as we met that this partnership was a match made in heaven. We couldn't be more ecstatic to have you in our corner.

Thank you to Angela James, our encouraging developmental editor, who saw all the potential in this story and pushed us to make sure it was on the page. Our agent, Jill Marsal, whose feedback and advice helped make this book what it became, thank you for steering us in the right direction and having faith in this tenacious duo.

From Beth:

Thank you to my sister, Leslie Merlin, for showing me what it is to keep pushing toward your dreams. My mother, Diane Zamansky, my very first "editor" who would routinely return my letters from camp with corrections and revisions, red-marked for spelling and grammar mistakes. You taught me how to write and gave me my love of the written word. I will forever be grateful. And my father, Arthur Zamansky, who wouldn't have read a single page but would have been prouder than anyone. Alice Ahmadieh, my mother-in-law and friend, your support means the world to me. Thank you Alyson Schwartz (my touchstone) and my crews both near (Raleigh) and far (NYC/London) who keep me grounded, laughing, and sane. I am lucky to have such wonderful people in my life. A million thank-yous to Danielle Modafferi for pulling me from the slush pile and becoming not only my "ride or die" writing partner, but one of my very best friends. Always, for Mashaal Ahmadieh, you are my archetype for every leading man. Without your unwavering belief, guidance, and love, none of this would have been possible. Finally, thank you to my beautiful Hadley Alexandra, far and away my greatest accomplishment.

From Danielle:

Once upon a time, I wrote a novel and then promptly swore I would *never do it again*. Instead, in 2016, I took my newly earned MFA in Writing Popular Fiction and my decade-plus of classroom experience as an English teacher and decided to become an indie publisher as a way to coach other authors on how to craft their best books. And it was through this experience that I met Beth, the first author I signed to my press. Together, we wrote and developed The Campfire Series (*One S'more Summer, S'more to Lose, Love You S'more,* and *Tell Me S'more*), and later *Breakup Boot Camp*. With each subsequent project, our creativity and collaboration soared! From day one, we just kinda stumbled into a process of cowriting quite naturally, and from that moment, we both agreed that we'd rather make a go of it together than on our own . . . and damn, I'm so glad that we have.

Long story short, Beth is the yin to my yang. Where I tend to overwrite flowery description and gushy emotional stuff, Beth is more straightforward and better with clarity and scene structure. (Case in point, check out the correlative length of our respective acknowledgments! lol!) We just complement one another so well, and only together have we finally reached the summit of accomplishing this lifelong goal.

Meeting Beth has proven to me that the world truly works in mysterious ways, and I am so grateful to her and for her every single day. Beth, my dear, "Because I knew you, I have been changed for good." Also, a special thank-you to her wonderful family (Hi, Mash and Haddie Bug!) for all of the support and man-hours you have put in to help Beth dedicate time to writing with me. I know how much of a team effort it is, and I am really grateful to you all for sharing her with me.

To my Firefly Hill Press family for their continued love and support. I love what we have built together and hope to continue to support your writing careers and books well into the future. And so much love to the hivemind at Seton Hill University Writing Popular Fiction (especially my June 2011 class)—I am so lucky to learn from and continue to be inspired by all the writers in my life.

To all of my students—both past and future. Thank you for teaching me to not take life too seriously, to enjoy each moment (even the hard ones), and to appreciate that learning is a lifelong process. Thank you for teaching me as much as I hope to have taught you.

To my crazy-amazing family and the friends who love me just as fiercely—I am just so lucky to have you all in my corner. To my soul sisters: Ariel Raia, Stephanie Call Dunn, Erin Bales, Ashley DeMain, and Samara Westmoreland-Touchton—near or far (usually far!), I love you all to the moon and back. To Shelley Raley, my angel above. To all my intelligent and courageous nieces and nephews: Annalisa, Sara, Logan, Colton, and Connor—Tati *looooves* you! To my incredible sisters, Laura and Karli, thank you for always being there for me, whether I was in need of a laugh or a cry or a swift kick in the pants. You ladies fill my life with so much happiness, and I am forever grateful to have forged such a special and unique relationship with each of you.

To my parents, Thomas and Patricia Modafferi, I could never adequately put into words what I owe you, what you've given me, and all the ways you've inspired me. Being a creative free spirit has been a bit of an adventure to put it mildly, but the only reason I feel emboldened to explore the world so fearlessly is because of you and your unending support. Thank you for encouraging me to be *me*. "Love, your baby girl."

From Both:

And last but certainly not least, to everyone who has shared this book with loved ones, bought this book for others, recommended this book because it brought you joy, TikToked about this book, or otherwise supported us and our dream of bringing this thing to life: thank you from the bottom of our hearts. Follow us on social media and come say hello: @merlinandmod.

ABOUT THE AUTHORS

 Beth Merlin earned her BA from George Washington University and her juris doctor from New York Law School. A native New Yorker, Beth loves anything Broadway, romantic comedies, and a good maxi dress. When she isn't writing, you can find her spending time with her husband, daughter, and two cavapoos, Sophie and Scarlett, at home or at their favorite vacation spot, Kiawah Island, South Carolina.

 Danielle Modafferi, a high school English teacher and pun enthusiast, earned her MFA in Writing Popular Fiction from Seton Hill University in 2014 and, shortly after, founded Firefly Hill Press in 2016. By day, she helps her students discover the magic of language, but by night, she's a writer and publisher on a mission to unleash her creativity and help others do the same. If there is ever time left in the day, Danielle loves working on a good upcycling or art project, traveling to faraway (and some not-so-faraway) places, and snuggling with her two yorkipoos, Jackson and Liam, who are also incidentally her biggest fans.